Fated

Book One of the Faery Chronicles

Helen Sutton

Copyright © 2016 Helen Sutton

All rights reserved in all media. No part of this book may be used or reproduced without written permission, except in the case of brief quotations embodied in critical articles.
The moral right of Helen Sutton as the author of this work has been asserted by her in accordance with the Copyright, Designs and Patents act of 1988.
This is a work of fiction. All names, characters, locales and incidents are products of the author's imagination and any resemblance to people, places, or events is coincidental or fictionalised.

ISBN: 1533158088
ISBN-13: 978-1533158086

Cover art by Jaimie Manlove at www. riposte.rocks
Graphic Design/Cover layout by Mx Flick
(https://www.facebook.com/mxflick/)

Fated

◀Chapter One▶

It began when I met the madman. When he left me alone in Faery. Perhaps even earlier.

Yes.

I think it began - *really* began - when I blew my bus fare on a burger and walked home on a bright and brittle October evening. One of those crisp, clear days when you can almost see sun and frost warring on the edges of evergreen leaves.

I love days like that.

Blake, my stepdad, dropped me off at work that morning, but couldn't pick me up. Hence the whole burger-stuffing-piggy-show being a bad idea.

What can I say? I'm a healthy seventeen year old girl. I get hungry.

The roads and streets of Marham were perched around

the edge of Marham Gorge; a lovely wooded cleft in the landscape. Going by road took me round till I almost doubled back on myself. Cutting through the Gorge and strolling through the woods took twenty minutes off the walk. Seemed a no-brainer on such a beautiful day. The sun had barely begun to slip below the horizon as I wound my way down the craggy path and into Marham Woods, bright leaves crackling underfoot.

I took the main route to cut through, light mist damping my face. It was bitterly cold in the shade, making me stamp my feet down and blow on my fingers more than once.

Anyone sensible would've had gloves.

The little bridge crossing the stream was only just ahead of me when I paused, startled. A rustling, swaying noise came from the woods. It sounded as though someone - or something - was coming through. At speed.

Just kids, I thought, tramping a little further down the path. The noise grew louder and closer; coming straight towards me. And then I heard it.

A low, rumbling growl.

A very dog-like growl.

I froze for a horrified second, blood pounding in my temples. Dogs have always scared me, and this sounded *big*.

I began to run towards the bridge. Turned the bend as the growling came closer. My head went down and my arms pumped as I tried to put distance between myself and the beast.

Fated

A black shape streaked towards me. It was *huge*.

I ran faster, sprinting for the bridge as though it could save me. My feet hit the wood of the narrow structure just as I felt the air move behind me with the passage of the biggest dog I've ever seen.

That would be why I ran headlong into the guy crossing from the other side.

I must have been so focussed on my dog phobia I hadn't seen him coming.

With an *oomph* he grabbed my shoulders to avoid being sent flying. I gasped with surprise and embarrassment.

'Sorry. Didn't see you there' I said, looking up at the victim of my headlong flight.

And stared.

Spiked, prematurely silver hair. Barely twenty. A totally normal looking guy. Except he *wasn't*. There was something off. Something about him didn't feel right. It was almost as though my eyes wanted to slide off his face.

'Don't apologise, sweetheart. You've been marked.' He sounded slightly foreign.

Sure enough, there was a smear of mud on my jacket. He must've slipped on the steep path - because he held up his scrawny hands with a rueful grin, and I saw that one hand and arm were covered in the stuff. That grin held my attention. It was all wrong. Nice, even teeth, but for a second they seemed pointed. Red-stained razors.

The damn dog had me seeing things.

I smiled sketchily and jogged slowly up the path. Wasn't in the mood to hang around.

Further on, I turned to look back. The stream glittered so brightly in the fading sun it dazzled. It almost managed to distract me from the sight of the stranger - still in the centre of the bridge. He must've been scared of dogs too, I thought, when I realised where he was looking. On the furthest bank, a little way along from the bridge, stood a black dog bigger than the guy himself. It appeared to be some kind of shaggy, muscular hound. Completely black and wolf-like. The weird thing was that while the young guy was intently gazing at the dog - the beast had its muzzle raised in *my* direction. Watching me and not him. Eyes caught the failing sun and flashed a strange red colour.

Chilled to the bone, I turned and ran home.

***

My name is Briana Cadman, Bree to friends and family. During term time I'm a student at the local college. In the break I was making a bit of extra cash stacking shelves at my local supermarket. I'd have said no, but my boss can be rough on employees that stand up to him. I needed the money.

Oh, the glamour.

Not that *I'd* have known glamour if it kicked me and stole my lunch money.

Not then.

A tactful friend once told me I was 'striking looking'. It's kind of hard to define what that means. I think it probably means 'I'm being kind'. My eyes are my best feature. They're green and gold streaked; a little slanted and quite large. I spend *way* too much on eye make-up. My hair is brown. I've never been able to dye it. For some reason even bleaches won't take. I wear it long as the wretched stuff grows too fast to keep a style.

Mum was home when I fell through the door, which was a pleasant surprise. You never quite know when she'll be around. She works in an old folk's home and the hours can be erratic. That's my Mum. Trying to look after everyone.

'Have you been running?' She looked up from a pan of browning mince.

'Thought I could do with the exercise, Mum' I planted a kiss on her cheek, sneakily palming a handful of grated parmesan.

She slapped my hand with the spatula, laughing. 'I don't see you as an exercise queen somehow, Bree. How's *that* going to work with the whole getting up at noon thing?'

I grinned. 'You got me. There was a dog. A big one.'

'Now *that* I believe.'

Upstairs, I threw myself onto my bed. Now I was in my sanctuary, I felt my heart rate slow. My breathing became steadier, more regular. With my iPod on full blast, I could float into a world of music and let the fear drift away as my nerves unclenched.

The Clash. Classic.

The warm smell of Bolognese sauce permeated my room making my stomach rumble in happy anticipation. I was thoroughly content. Sometimes home is absolutely the best place to be. Familiar and safe.

Of course, I was already far from safe, but I didn't know that.

The moment was perfect.

***

The next few days were uneventful. I managed to stay off the burgers and out of the gorge, enjoying the warmth of the bus ride home. All the dogs I saw were so normal, I almost *liked* them.

My best friend Chloe and I hung out a few times, and I sat and held her bag for her as she had highlights run through her hair. Chloe thought you couldn't be too blonde.

I'd have loved to be more like Chloe.

Pretty, tiny, and catnip to boys, she'd been on my side since the first day of school. I was lucky to have her. There was an assertiveness in her I lacked.

She once hit a boy she *really* liked.

For calling me names.

Greater love hath no friend and all that.

Chloe was in a primping and preening mood ready for a Halloween party our friend Jack was holding. She'd talked about nothing else all week. Was determined to drag me protesting along in her wake.

'Fancy dress, too? This just gets worse. No. I'm *definitely* not going now,' I groaned. 'I don't have a costume, anyway'

'Wrong again, girlfriend. Auntie Chloe has already taken care of it. Bree Cadman,' she smirked. 'You *shall* go to the ball!'

I caved in. Then and there.

There are times you know resistance is futile. Chloe had spoken. I knew I wouldn't win. I rarely did.

There was no *way* this was going to go well.

That's how - the next night - I found myself standing next to Chloe in front of her bedroom mirror. Gazing in disbelief at our combined reflection.

'This proves it. You're wrong in the head. What on earth made you think of *this*?' I asked.

'Good, isn't it?' she mused. 'We're one pair of sexy chicks, girlfriend.'

I kind of had to agree with her. 'Slappers' would've been another word. I think the pantomime posters in the high street had been messing with her head. Because there we stood - looking like something from Babes in the Wood. There were even jaunty little caps. With feathers. In matching colours. Robin Hood and Will Scarlet. Apparently Jack was going as Friar Tuck.

I'd never felt such an *utter* berk.

Chloe opened a can of cider and her whimsical streak surfaced. She insisted we cut through the Gorge to get to Jack's house. That way we'd be able to get some '...epic pictures of Robin in the greenwood. Come *on* - you know you want to...'

It's hard to argue with that kind of logic.

I gave it a go, though.

Failed.

I knew the dog had to be long gone. Had kept an eye on local news stories; expecting to hear some kid had been bitten in the gorge.

All the same - as it grew closer to leaving time - my stomach began to tie itself in knots. A heavy feeling at the thought of leaving the house had me pacing the room. Panic I didn't entirely understand. Desperate, I grabbed Chloe's can and downed it. The warmth of the alcohol brought something thankfully close to courage. I took hold of my bag and gave Chloe a hard look. Took a deep breath of air scented with her perfume. Violets and green grass.

'Let's *do* this. Come on.'

Without waiting, I made for the door, hearing her laughter behind me.

***

There were no lights in the Gorge, so Chloe'd brought a small maglite in her bag. I'm *never* that prepared. For *anything*. Bright as it was, the beam seemed increasingly puny as we ventured further down the path.

Into the dark woodland.

The air was so quiet even our breathing was weirdly loud. The mist seemed denser by torchlight. Glowing. It got thicker the further we went.

My neck hair stood to attention as we got closer to the bridge. Prickling unease across my shoulders and palms. Eerie as the Gorge had always been at night, there was a peculiar feeling in the air. Too still.

As though the world had taken a breath.

Was holding it.

Our voices hushed; conversation stuttering and dying away. The still darkness swallowed up the sounds we made. Even the trees seemed to be listening, leaning in to hear.

The whole world was as off kilter as the foreign guy.

As we crossed the bridge I started to feel exposed. Certain we were being watched. The cider-induced courage melted away. My pulse quickened, loud in my head. Strange, sweet smells curling through the air.

Chloe made me pose on the bridge for a few photos, and I took some of her. Our attempts to fool around and joke fell *horribly* flat. She shivered, brushing her blonde curls back over a slim shoulder.

'Let's just get to Jack's, Bree,' she said, unusually subdued. 'I'm cold. And it's scary here in the dark.'

I had to agree.

We walked fast - had barely turned the corner - when I heard something that made my breathing speed, my heart lurch. The sound of breaking branches. The rustle of undergrowth.

The terrible – *rumbling* - growl.

I grabbed my friend's hand. 'Chloe, *run*.'

We pelted up the path, stumbling in our haste to get away.

'What *is* that?' panted Chloe.

'Dog. *Big* dog.'

The noise grew closer. The black hound bore down on us, snarling as it came. Swerving, I pulled Chloe down a rabbit run, no longer caring about direction. The massive beast followed. I saw the movement of the smaller trees as it hurtled through them. Crashed its way towards us.

We *ran*.

It could only have been minutes. To my burning lungs, it was a slow forever. Acid tipped breath bursting from my chest. Chloe raced ahead, the long path rising before us. The wooded gorge bottom fell away more steeply the further we climbed.

A loud snarl sounded behind us. I swear I could feel breath on my heels.

That's when it happened.

I fell.

Stumbled on a tree root and rolled. Down the slope; bouncing and bruising as I went. Arms and legs a painful tangle. Landed in a winded heap. Chloe hadn't noticed, was still running. I was going to call out to her when I realised the creature was picking its way down the slope.

After *me*.

And its eyes *were* red.

If I called out to my friend, it would draw attention to her. As it was, she stood some chance of getting away.

Of finding help - when she realised I wasn't behind her.

I hauled myself painfully to my feet and ran back into the wood. I'd no light, so the way was darker and harder.

The silence more oppressive.

As I ran, I rebounded off trees; whipped in the face by branches and nastier, wetter things. My chest was gripped by a tight band. Mouth full of the smell of wet leaves and rotting undergrowth. Sparkles danced in front of my eyes. My legs ached with the effort. Every time I fell, I expected to feel teeth. The thought alone got me on my feet.

Kept me moving.

I thought the beast must've been playing with me - as it seemed sometimes to veer at me from the left, sometimes from the right. Once or twice it was so close behind I could feel its panting breath. I darted this way and that. Terrified tears running down my face. Trying to put some distance between us.

And then I realised. I wasn't being chased.

I was being *herded*.

Horrified, I found new strength to haul myself faster - more recklessly - through the endless trees. The eerie cry of a horn shattered the unearthly silence; a weird high pitched keening in its wake. I staggered grimly onward. My breath too loud and burning my chest.

Something brushed my cheek.

A line of searing fire.

I'd barely drawn breath to gasp when the huge beast erupted from the woodland. Barrelled me through a rocky gap I'd never seen before.

Helen Sutton

Into a cave. One I knew couldn't be there.

And *that's* when I met the madman.

◄Chapter Two►

I landed awkwardly on uneven stone. Expected to feel teeth sinking into my flesh. Waited, cringing.

Instead, the beast made a huffling noise, and I felt shaggy fur brush my leg as it passed me. Raising my head, I carefully pushed myself into a sitting position.

An involuntary groan surprised me as the movement caused pain in places I hadn't known I'd hurt. My body ached enough to be one big bruise - and my face was still alight.

Something sticky on my cheek. Raising my hand to my face, I found it slick with blood. Shivering with cold and adrenaline slump, I scrubbed my hand across my tights and the stony floor.

Trying to scrape the nastiness away.

The beast crossed to the other side of the large cavern. I examined my surroundings by the dim greenish light, sucking in deep breaths. To one side was a natural ledge heaped with furs and rough blankets. I could see – and smell - herbs drying, hanging from a tall frame set near a central hearth. Logs stood in for seats. The trickling sound of a spring gurgled nearby. Faint, fresh scent of water cutting through the dust and the bittersweet herbs.

The dog lowered its massive head, drinking noisily.

It was even bigger than I'd thought.

Seriously, that thing must have been the size of a small pony. It sank to its haunches and regarded me with a steady stare. Too exhausted - and hurting too badly - to attempt escape, I was helpless to do anything but stare back. Tears stung my eyes, blurring the cavern.

Sudden movement at the entrance.

Another large, dark shape looming towards me.

Whimpering, I dashed the tears away; smearing more blood across my face. Some touched my lips. I hung my head. Shuddered at the nasty coppery taste.

Dirty bare feet, large and pale, stopped before me. Looking up, I found a grimy hand extended to take mine. Pulled myself up.

Fell. Again.

Flames danced fiercely across my cheek. The world span at dizzying speed. My captor bent and I was lifted in a pair of arms clad in not much more than dirt and fur. Through tangled elf locks of filthy long black hair, I caught a glimpse of oddly flashing silver.

And was placed gently on the sleeping platform.

Furs were pulled tight around me, to counteract the juddering shivers I couldn't control. I focussed on that silver, curious. The man's iris was a silver disc. Pupil-less. His gaze vague and disturbing.

'You're blind,' I said.

Then the fire and the pain and the spinning became too much. I sank gratefully into darkness.

***

After that everything came in feverish, nightmare snatches. A haze of impressions. My face burnt fiercely. Although something cool was applied in a thick paste, I *screamed* as fire raged through my veins and my body scorched. I remember my shoulders being lifted and liquids dripped down my throat. The taste was foul but they brought welcome sleep - and a break from pain.

Something hot, slick and slimy ran across my cheek and I recoiled. Cried until more of the paste was applied.

I couldn't have told you how long I lay there.

It felt like *centuries*.

Sometimes a strange voice cut through the potion torpor. Wavering in tone, it laughed a lot. *Not* a pleasant laugh. There was no sanity in it. I was afraid of that voice. The things it said were odd and unsettling.

'Burn brightly, always burning. It won't be the same until you breathe on the springs. The three can wash away

what was given. I've seen it. Too much. The darkness to come. Too much ... my failure ... my flame ... .'

Nonsensical rants ending in fits of visceral sobbing. The voice faded, moved to another part of the cave. All I heard for hours was anguish. Sorrowing cries.

It was joined by another.

Never at the same time. Equally unnerving, *this* voice spoke to me gently as my dressings were changed and those foul brews dribbled into my mouth. Rich and mellifluous as honey - soothing as spring sunshine - it assured me all would be well. That I'd be taken care of.

I began to listen out for *that* voice.

'We're almost at the crisis' it said, a long, cool hand on my forehead. 'You'll stand or fall by this, tonight. Fight now.'

I *wanted* to fight.

Wanted to please the voice that flowed like molten chocolate, sending shivers of pleasure across my skin.

'I want to lick your voice,' I said solemnly.

My only answer was a rich, amused chuckle. The world went away again as the fire burned higher and hotter.

Realisation dawned slowly. The blind man was both the harshly laughing madman *and* the honey toned physician.

There was no-one else.

I should've been afraid - but I wasn't. Not even of the dog, which had taken to curling up close to the sleeping platform. Occasionally I'd feel hot breath on my nose as it peered into my achingly swollen face. I realised the caveman talked to the dog, too. A lot.

Calling it Cooshy.

When my cheek finally burst, I knew the slimy thing I'd been feeling was the dog's tongue. I felt it again, lacing my face with agony as it licked away the foul smelling matter. The pain eased.

I realised silver-eyes was sitting on the edge of the sleeping platform, face hidden beneath those wild, sooty elf-locks. He could've been any age from twenty to fifty.

On impulse, I reached out and pushed some of the matted hair aside.

'You got a face under there?' I asked.

'*Don't*,' he said, ducking his head.

All I caught was a flash of black brows and grubby cheekbones as he tried to pull away. I snatched at his chin and made him face me. Cool skin, smooth and youthful beneath my fingers.

'You've been helping me.'

'Yes. I think you'll live, now.' A little wry - but there it was.

That lovely chocolaty voice.

Even knowing it came from a guy dressed like Fred Flintstone couldn't prevent the hair dancing at the nape of my neck.

I pulled myself upright with some difficulty. Examined his face. Thought maybe he'd be beautiful - under the dirt and the madness. I used to think beautiful was kind of a silly word to apply to guys.

But I know now that the Fae are very beautiful.

And that beautiful does *not* mean safe.

Or good.

My heart broke for this strange, mad creature as I recalled the desperate sobs I'd heard. Whatever had turned him into this must've been traumatic beyond belief. Compassion squeezed my ribs. Stole my air.

I leaned carefully forward and pressed gentle lips to his begrimed cheek.

'That's for looking after me,' I said, caught in a sudden scent of cinnamon, green growing things and wild open spaces.

His scent.

It called to something untamed and joyful inside me and I caught at his hand, desperate to smell more - to get closer...

With a roar, he hurled himself backward - hands clasped to his eyes - and tumbled from the platform to land sprawling on the gritty floor. He curled into a ball and the eerie laughter began again.

'You poor sod,' I whispered, watching as the great dog herded him to a smaller pile of furs by the fire and settled patiently at his side. Exhausted still, my chest aching queerly, I slid back down and let sleep take me.

***

I half awoke some time later to the sound of talking.

'I understand your objections, Cooshy - but a gift like this should be repaid'

Honey-voice again. Alive with a strange joy.

Pausing, he continued 'Maybe gift *is* the wrong word. They don't all take it well, I know, so far down the bloodline. But with *her* blood? I'd imagine it won't be easy for her. But surely she's the right to at least *see* them when they come for her again? And they *will*.'

A longer pause this time; impression of swift movement.

'Enough.' Curtly. 'It's my gift to give - and *my* decision to make, Hound.'

The madman's shadow dimmed the light. He sat next to me and brushed my hair gently away from my face. Opening my eyes, I saw his were no longer silver. They had pupils now.

Inky black - against fierce gold irises, like a hawk's.

The colour *glowed* in his filthy face.

'Oh, wow,' I was captured by the glittering eyes and that spicy, outdoorsy smell. 'You know, Cooshy's a stupid name for a dog that big. Sounds too cute. No offense.'

I heard a huffing behind him and the dog loomed into view. The madman turned to look intently at the hound, and something strange passed between them. My rescuer's lips twitched.

'Then we'll rename him in your honour. Call him Guest. That way I'll have two.'

The dog harrumphed as though he disapproved. I had to smile.

'I'm Bree.'

'Hello, Bree,' said the madman. 'You can call me Leiloken.'

He sounded like the strange guy on the bridge. The intonation slightly off. A blurred sound, like English wasn't his first language.

'Hey Guest.' I held out a shaky hand.

The hound sniffed it, running a deliberate tongue across the inside of my wrist. I giggled.

'I think I actually like that dog.'

I *was* still woozy.

Leiloken gave a quiet laugh and leaned back over me. He ran a finger across the centre of my brow and then - to my immense surprise - laid his forehead against mine. Cool as rain on grass; a soothing tingle against my hot head. I was cocooned by that wonderful scent.

Delicious.

'I want you to sleep again.' His voice a faint murmur. 'When you wake things will seem a little - *different*. Try to forgive me.'

He kissed my forehead softly and was gone. My contentment faded with every inch of distance. I was asleep before I knew it.

When I came to myself the dog was standing over me.

'Hi, Guest.'

You're awake at last. I must get that poultice off now the swelling's gone. We'll see how well you're healing.

The words dropped into my mind from nowhere, as that shaggy head tilted to one side. Crimson eyes burned into mine.

'Bloody *hell*! A talking dog.' My jaw sagged.

Not a dog. A Cu Sidhe. A Hound of the Sidhe.

I could hear the difference in the way the dog said it. Coo Shee. Two separate words - leaving me wondering how I could ever have misunderstood it as Cooshy. I knew sidhe was an old word for fairy.

Guest was a fairy hound.

I was having a conversation with a massive, talking, red-eyed fairy hound.

I was as mad as Leiloken.

*You'll find everything seems altogether different now, Bree. My master -rather unwisely, in my view - has given you what he **persists** in seeing as a gift.*

'Meaning?'

I was glad I was mad.

Otherwise, this would be weird.

He's opened your inner eye, girl. You'll see the Wild Hunt coming for you next time. I must've looked confused, because the Cu Sidhe continued. *Here. Sit up and see.*

Holding onto his head, I sat up.

The cavern had changed beyond recognition.

The greenish light I'd been seeing came from tiny winged beings, so bright I could make out nothing but the barest suggestion of their shape. Thumb sized - dozens of them. Tiny, rapid voices rose in shrill song. It was unintelligible, but my heart sang too, with the beauty of it. The spring babbled musically; water shining with an dazzling radiance. My breath caught in my throat.

'What *are* they?' I breathed.

Light sprites. Elementals. Raw manifestations of the glamour - the magic - of Faery. Not sentient, but alive.

Of course they were. Silly me.

'Well, I guess I'm not in Kansas any more, Toto,' I said. To the giant dog beside me.

I don't understand

I grinned. 'Never mind. It probably doesn't translate.'

Hmm. Let's get this poultice off and see how you're healing. My master's hunting, so there'll be food for you soon.

A wave of nausea flooded me at the thought of those grimy hands doing things to a dead animal. To prepare it. For me to eat.

Yummy.

I *don't* think.

Guest's tongue got to work removing the goop plastered to my now swelling-free face. *There's clothing here for you, little Bree - and my master will be a while yet. Would you like to bathe in the spring while I guard the cave mouth? I've noticed women **like** to bathe. A disgusting habit.*

Fated

I stroked his ears with an unsteady hand, unable to resist petting him. The fur was soft and rough at the same time. He felt like an expensive teddy.

'That's kind, Guest. You're a very thoughtful dog.'

I giggled, realising how ridiculous that sounded. The fluttering trills of the winged creatures lifted higher and louder in accompaniment.

My master thought of it. I take no credit. He's very concerned for your comfort.

'Whatever. I'm glad you offered. I probably *stink*.' I looked ruefully at my torn and filthy clothing. My hands were almost as dirty as Leiloken's.

Yes said Guest gravely.

I glared at him until he loped out of the cavemouth.

My legs were new and trembly as I made my way gingerly to the spring. One arm clutched the pile of garments and the other was outstretched for balance. Beyond blissful to scrub away the thick dirt with a sweet smelling oil I found beside the water. It seemed to work pretty well as a shampoo substitute, too.

The scent reminded me of my peculiar host.

I found that comforting, though I couldn't have said *why*. Was gentle with the injured side of my head, wincing as my fingers found a tender spot. The wound extended into my hairline. Bristles under my hand made it clear a patch of hair had been cut away.

I must've looked a total scarecrow.

The garments I pulled on were clean, but worn thin with use and time. Soft pants went on first followed by a long sleeved, thong-fastening shirt. I'd to roll the bottom of the pants up a *long* way. A thicker, laced waistcoat-type thing finished the outfit; falling almost to my knees. Shabby remnants of gold braiding in tatters at sleeves and hem.

The faded black material was beautifully soft against my skin. Soft as a whisper and smoother than silk. Tugging it down and wrapping my Will Scarlet belt around my waist, I noticed a darker patch on the chest. Tried not to look at it too closely.

Or speculate what it could be.

There were worn half boots by the bed in some kind of buttery soft leather, but they were *huge* on me. I kept my own footwear.

What doesn't go with Vans, right?

Clean and dressed, I settled myself by the fire. Basked in the warmth and the scent of my drying hair. Perched on a log with the flames warming my face, I dozed as I waited for the dog and his master to return.

Guest loped in first. I raised my head to smile and he stopped dead.

Stared at my face.

His ears flattened for a moment before he turned and bounded back through the entrance. A low growl lingered behind him.

'Was it something I said?' My sarcasm caused a startled fluttering from the tiny light sprites above me.

The beast was soon back, and he stopped to crouch on his haunches before me.

By the Lady of all, it's an uncanny resemblance, I heard as he lowered his head to sniff my hair. *This may be uncomfortable for you, little Bree - but he **has** to see this. We knew you must be of **that** bloodline, but even so...* He sighed. *I only hope he doesn't react **too** badly. Be brave.*

'See what?' I demanded.

It went unanswered as Leiloken's shape blocked the entrance.

He strode over, seeming to grow with each step. I hadn't appreciated till then just how tall he was. I mean *tall*. He loomed over me. Moved with swift grace to crouch where the dog had been a moment before. Lifted his eyes to my face.

And stilled.

Frozen.

What little colour he had beneath the dirt drained away, leaving his face ghostly and greyish. His eyes grew wide, mouth slacking open. Concerned, I leaned towards him. He recoiled. Ragged breath sounded harshly in my ears.

With visible effort, he placed a hand on the side of my face.

Those fierce eyes bored into mine.

I ought to have been afraid, but sensed no menace from him. Time stopped for long seconds as his hand shook against my cheek. My breath stilled. I stared, unable to break away from that hypnotic golden gaze. He ran one thumb gently over my lips and I found myself leaning slightly into his palm.

A loud cry of woe - shockingly sudden - burst from him.

He hurled himself away, panting loudly.

Didn't stop until his back hit the opposite wall. Slid slowly down it as those dreadful sobs tore from his chest. Sorrow on sorrow. The dog growled ominously and bounded after him. I watched in horror as Leiloken banged his fists into the rough cave wall. Again and again.

Not stopping.

Even when the blood *ran* from his hands.

'He's *hurting* himself. Isn't there anything I can do?' I asked Guest, appalled.

You've done enough. The Cu Sidhe's mental voice was soft. *I'm sorry, little one. There's no good you can do here. Leave me to care for him.*

There was such sadness in his voice that something tore inside me. Left me feeling raw. I stumbled back to the sleeping platform and cried myself quietly to sleep.

To the sound of that dreadful sobbing.

***

My last awakening in that cavern was unpleasant. Upper arms gripped almost painfully in two large hands, I felt myself being lifted off the platform. That outdoorsy green scent curled around me.

I looked into Leiloken's face. And was certain I saw no sanity in his eyes. Something fierce and intense burned there now.

My veins ran with ice.

I feared him for the first time.

Looking around, I was dismayed to see Guest curled up by the fire. His snores a rumbled counterpoint to the words of the madman.

'You have to go, bright flame. Go away. Go far. Go *now.*' He dragged me towards the cave entrance.

'What have I done? Why?' I said loudly, digging my heels in as hard as possible.

Hoping to rouse the Cu Sidhe.

Leiloken span towards me as we reached the cave mouth, eyes settling anywhere but on my face.

'You have to go. *They* must see you. You're too bright. Too bright - and I'll burn again.' He gave a choked laugh. 'Tell them my sorrow. Tell them the dark times are coming. Again. Tell them I'm lost and you're found. Tell them of the three springs. Remember...'

He pulled me closer to him, bending a little. Finally looking at me so that we were eye to glittering eye. Noses almost meeting and my feet barely touching the floor.

'The brightest flames don't live the longest, and tears of compassion can put them out forever. Dim your flame, bright one. Don't choose what I see. Choose a longer span.'

With that last bit of nonsense he pulled me closer still. I felt his breath on my lips as brilliant, glowing eyes roamed my face. He looked almost hungry.

For a long, still moment, I thought he was going to kiss me.

I'd have *let* him - with that weird lush smell wrapping itself around me.

Instead, he gave a sharp cry and threw me away from him. I fell through the cave mouth and into the waiting mist, the sound of his voice echoing crazily behind me.

Dazed and confused, I pulled myself to my feet and did the sensible thing.

Began to run.

◀Chapter Three▶

My frantic feet crackled through leaves. I ran blindly into the fog weaving between the trees. I'd been running for some minutes when I realised something was wrong. These weren't the trees of Marham Wood, but something older.

And *bigger*.

I stopped. Put my hand to my side as the stitch bit deep. Looking around, I realised I was in a strange woodland. Ancient. The trees were huge, some with trunks my arms wouldn't reach halfway round.

Not that I felt like tree hugging.

The floor was thickly littered with fallen branches and scrubby shrubs, making the going hard. None of the trees were like anything I'd ever seen. They grew immensely tall - some with trunks spiralling where they reached this way and that, grasping for sunlight. Others grew in pairs, leaning in towards each other with branches thickly intertwined. Bark strange, unlikely colours.

Some grey, almost black. Here and there a deep emerald green, or sullenly glowing crimson. Leaves ranged from the acid yellows of fresh spring to the burning reds of autumn. With every shade of green - some almost blue - in between.

Everything glowed with a weird radiance.

Sweet, soft smell of leaf mulch and churned earth. Of rain on leaves and musky autumn winds. Something indefinable - some aroma - in the air making me think of the odd fog in the Gorge.

I could hear the high giggling of tiny light-sprites flittering in bee-like swarms. Couldn't see sky. The canopy of branches and leaves overhead was too thick. What light did filter down was muted, stained with colour from the foliage. It could've been any time, day or night.

I couldn't tell.

Something *swished* through the undergrowth close by. An impression of movement. Soft sound of small voices murmuring, and it was gone - moving away into the forest. Similar movements pattered through the higher branches above me, leaves rustling in their wake.

A small creature looking like nothing so much as a gnarled garden gnome erupted from the bushes nearby, and sped into the undergrowth.

I heard frantic panting as he passed.

Fated

Turning in a full circle, no path presented itself. I slid down against the trunk of the nearest tree, bark rough against my back. Lost, alone, and still weak from the fever. My bag was gone, and I'd no idea where I was - or what had happened to me.

Everyone would think I'd run away.

Or been murdered.

I could've been ill and unaware for days. Even weeks. I'd no idea how long I'd been with the madman. Was probably nothing but a statistic by now. A face splashed across the local news.

The police weren't going to find me *here.*

Pierced through with a terrible loneliness, I sat with my arms round my knees and cried. Wanted my Mum. My home. My bedroom. To curl up under my own duvet and sleep for a week. To be a child again, safe and cosseted.

I think I *knew* I'd never be safe again.

My heart dropped heavily in my chest and I sobbed for the emptiness inside. Not only homesick, but achingly longing for something that was gone.

Something beautiful.

Something I couldn't describe.

I couldn't have told you what it was I wept for so wretchedly. But I *knew* the loss of it was something I'd mourn forever. It was as if I cried for hours.

I may have done.

The tears ebbed and passed. I became aware of a massive,

black shape next to me. Panting breath loud in my ear. Soft fur pressed against my arm and side. I leaned my head against Guest and wrapped my arms round his shaggy neck in relief.

Are you feeling better now, little Bree? The huge Cu Sidhe rubbed his muzzle against the side of my face.

I almost flinched thinking of those long teeth.

'Yeah. I think so.' I felt myself relax. Listened to his steady breathing and felt that powerful heart thudding inside his chest. 'Why are *you* here? You're not going to make me go back? Are you?'

I trembled slightly. Thought of the ghastly look on Leiloken's face as he'd flung me out into ... wherever we were.

No, little one. You can't go back there. Guest's mental voice sounded serious. *It would not be - wise - for you to be around my master now.*

'You think?' My sarcasm was acidic. 'Guest, your master's a full on nutjob. The man's completely *mental*. You'll never see me anywhere *near* that freak again. Not *ever*. No offense.'

In sorrowful tones the Hound replied.

*No. It's true he's not who he once was. He was **glorious**, little human. One of the most dazzling at either court. If you could have seen him then...*

He gave a deep sigh and shook his head.

I know you've great compassion in you. Don't judge him too harshly. He's a poor, broken thing now. A shadowed shell. The substance nothing but a faint flicker.

*When he's more – **himself** - you can see traces of who he was. But those episodes are all too few. He's being eaten away by a cursed madness, steeped in guilt. And grief. I expect one day there'll be nothing left of him but the raving shell. In the meantime, I serve him still.*

He is my master.

Guest spoke simply and with great canine dignity.

'You love him' I said, understanding this strange beast a little better.

*Oh, yes. I love him. Many of us did. We'd have followed him into the underworld and stormed the City of the **Dead** - had he asked it of us. So many bright warriors, and of all that Host only **I** remain.*

'What happened to them?'

A brief, fierce snarl. *They **died.***

'Why've you followed me, Guest?' I asked. 'I'm beyond glad you did. But why aren't you with your master?'

A fair question, little Bree, and I'll do my best to answer it. We'll talk as we travel, though. We shouldn't tarry here long. There are things in these forests that regard humans as playthings. Or dinner. Sometimes both.

That great snout nudged me to my feet and we moved deeper into the bizarre forest.

'You were going to tell me why you're here. What's happened to me? Why am *I* here? Nothing makes any sense - and I don't know what to think.' I blew out and glanced up into the dense branches interlocking above. 'I don't even know where I *am*.'

The Cu Sidhe rumbled low in his chest before giving a doggy huff.

So many questions, little human. I'll do my best to answer what I may.

Leiloken's cavern exists in the Elsewhere, the void between worlds. We rescued you when it touched the realm of men. Now it's touching Faery - the realm your people once called the Otherworld. And so - here you are.

I've not left my master in the thousand years and more since madness took him. But when he flung you into the depths of Celidon Forest, I had to follow. When he's himself he rarely countenances cruelty, so I'm here to take you somewhere we'll find help. We can get you home - if we find the right people. But it won't be simple.

We wove our way through the massive trunks. That dreadful feeling of loss crept across me once or twice. I found if I kept my hand on Guest's springy fur, it ebbed to a bearable level. Still there, but muted.

An echo.

*When you came to us, it was because I was trying to keep you away from the Huntsman who Marked you in your woods. My master was **very** anxious that I help you.*

'I remember' I said. 'The boy on the bridge. He said he'd marked me. There was something really hinky about him, too.'

Hinky? The dog sounded perplexed. *What is hinky?*

'There was something off about him.' I shrugged. 'His face - all of him, really. It was like I couldn't focus on him. Or I could see him two different ways at once. He was wrong, somehow.'

He was glamoured to look human to you. It's interesting it made you uneasy. We knew you carried Fae blood. The fact you could sense the wrongness - even before you were given the ability to see through it - would suggest it runs strongly in you.

Guest sounded thoughtful.

*It may be why he chose **you** for the Hunt. It would add spice for them to know they'd be dining on something with Fae blood.*

'They wanted to *eat* me?' A horrified squeak.

*Oh, most **certainly**, little Bree.*

*They'd have found your tender meat very sweet indeed. Humans are playthings to some fae. Food to others. They're too afraid of reprisals now to eat one of the noble Fae, but that doesn't mean they've lost the taste for Fae flesh. You'd be a **very** acceptable substitute.*

The Wild Hunt mark and hunt one human every Samhain. They never stop once they've chosen. They'd have hunted you for sport - and devoured you for pleasure.

I began to shake.

I'd come so close to death, and hadn't known. If it hadn't been for Leiloken...

You do well to be afraid, child. They nearly had you.

*I **had** to take you through the doorway to save your life. The next arrow would've pierced your head, not grazed your cheek. You're a rare kind of human, Bree. Many wouldn't have survived the venom of the elf-shot. Your Fae blood saved you.*

*Even with my **master's** aid a true human wouldn't have survived the venom on that arrow. As for my master....*

A sorrowful, doggy sigh.

Let's say, that in tending to you he was more himself - for longer - than I've seen him for centuries.

He whimpered softly.

'I suppose this is where I thank you for saving my life.' I said.

Still afraid of what so nearly happened to me.

NO!

The Cu Sidhe's voice reverberated around my head as a growl escaped his muzzle.

*You **never** thank the fae, child. Insult one of the noble Fae like that, and it'd be fatal.*

I could hear the capital letter differentiating the two drop heavily into place in my mind. Noble Fae and fae.

Clearly some fae were more equal than others. Nice.

I've issues with that.

To express gratitude is to acknowledge a debt to be repaid. To thank is to acknowledge that debt - and dismiss it with no intention of repayment.

*It's the **height** of rudeness and ingratitude. You humans have some nasty habits. That's among the worst. To do that **here** will kill you more quickly than you can imagine. The Fae are swift to anger - and long to hold a grudge. Try to avoid it.*

'Ok, then. I'm grateful to you, Guest. I owe you.'

He bowed his head formally.

Now, I think it's time I found us somewhere to rest tonight. If we're where I believe we are, there's someone nearby who'll give us shelter.

'Another debt?' I raised my eyebrows, arms folded.

He gave an amused huff. *Just so. Settle yourself here and don't move. I'll try to find her, if I still can. I'll not leave you for long, little Bree.*

With that, Guest turned and loped off.

I did as he suggested and settled myself in a comfortable nook created by the gnarled tree roots at the base of a crimson tree. Curled up so comfortably, my eyelids grew heavy. Waking, I heard the noise of quiet sobbing. Was surprised to find it was me. Tears streaked my cheeks again, and that wordless sense of longing *flooded* me.

Looking back, I cried more in those first few days in Faery than I had in my whole life. I'd never been one of those girls who cry over films and minor crises. I'd never obsessed over the guys at college. Or had my heart broken. Those things weren't on my radar. Chloe says it's because I have no feelings.

Wrong. I'm just not girlie.

I *hate* that wet stuff.

Yet here I was in tears again. And with no idea why.

I heard a high, fast panting. The gnome-like creature I'd noticed earlier tore past me. Couldn't have been more than two feet tall. I stood to watch him go, but he came to a stop just beyond me.

His eyes met mine.

And he stared as openly at me as I did him.

I guessed he'd probably never seen a real human before. I'd sure as *spit* never seen a one of whatever-he-was. He'd a broad face, wrinkled with age, and a long nose. His beard hung almost to his knees. Tatty jacket in a muted yellow. Ragged brown trousers met dear little red boots. I wanted to pick him up and cuddle him.

He was just that cute.

I smiled gently, moving towards him with my hand extended oh-so-slowly.

'Hey there, little fella.'

He blinked - eyelids meeting sideways like a frog's - and gave a grimace that may have been a grin. He was certainly showing some *very* pointed teeth.

Maybe *not* so cuddlesome.

Snarling, five more small creatures burst from the undergrowth. Leapt for the gnome guy. They beat and kicked him, cudgelling him with horrid, spiny clubs. He was driven to the ground. Curled into a defensive ball.

They were unlike the first creature. Sharp beaky faces.

Eyes dark slits of glowing excitement. Wide jagged slashes passed for mouths - a double row of shark-like teeth bared wide. Snarling and jabbering. Angular, twig-like bodies moved with a jerky rapidity.

One sank its teeth into the bearded fae's arm. Another tried to gain purchase on a chubby little leg. The gnome-like creature squealed shrilly. The one biting his arm came up with a chunk of flesh in its mouth. Blood oozed between those horrid teeth.

I yelled in outrage. Picked up a stick.

And charged them.

Tried to chase them off. The one biting him noticed me first. Hissed a fierce warning. Four other heads turned in my direction and the jabbering grew louder.

They *went* for me.

I laid about me desperately. Bony hands tore at my clothing. My stick dealt a few good cracks. I wanted those claw-like hands off me. As the stick rebounded off the head of the one trying to *sniff* me in some weird way, it looked up at my face. Stopped.

And snarled angrily.

The nasty bullies let go of me as I raised my stick. Ready to administer a sound thrashing before letting them touch me - or the gnome - again. But they were changing.

They began to moan and swell - and *grow*.

Inflating like grotesque balloons, bodies bloated and misshapen. Their glowing eye slits grew huge. Mouths oozed blood; pale tongues flapping. Those hideously stretched arms reached for me. Their owners were towering above me now. I knew I couldn't hold them off for long.

If at all.

I'd give it a *damn* good go, though.

Screaming defiance, I swung wildly at the nearest creature. Was horrified when the stick rebounded off skin turned diamond hard.

I was going to die.

And be eaten.

And there was nothing at all I could do about it.

As I lowered my head in resignation, a terrible roar sounded behind me. A monstrous black form flew over my head. Landed, with a terrifying snarl, on four huge paws.

Guest snapped ferociously at the first creature, catching it by the leg. Sank his teeth in and shook it like a rag.

The creature sailed through the air, shrinking as it fell.

The Cu Sidhe's eyes blazed scarlet as it turned on the other creatures and growled threateningly. But they were already deflating. Backing away, they'd soon been swallowed up by the forest as though they'd never existed.

I sagged with relief.

Guest was still growling when he swung his head around to look at me.

*I told you to stay put, **not** start a fight! Foolish human, those Spriggan would have eaten you slowly while you* *screamed. What possessed you to **attack** them?*

'I was trying to get them off the little fella.' I waved my hand in the direction of the weird garden gnome.

The little fae lay where they where they'd left him, bent bonelessly over a tree root. Looked barely conscious, breath ragged and eyes glazed. His arm was bleeding freely, and I was sure I could see his face turning grey. I went to him and crouched. Laid a concerned hand on his knobbly forehead.

'Can we help him, Guest?' I looked up into the Hound's huge face.

Why?

Serious red eyes under shaggy brows.

'Because he'll *die* if we don't. He's going to bleed to death - if we don't do *something*.'

I grabbed the bottom of my shirt. Tried to tear some away. The material may've been soft, but I couldn't get it to give. Even with my teeth. I held the hem out to my canine companion.

'*Please*, Guest'

He sniffed rather judgementally, but sank his teeth into the black material. Between us we'd soon torn away a strip sufficient for my needs.

'I'm not going to hurt you.' I made my voice gentle.

The little guy was so far gone I doubt if he heard me. I tied the strip of cloth around his upper arm as tightly as I could.

'That should stop the bleeding' I told the Hound 'but he *really* needs that arm seeing to. Before it's infected.'

Guest let out a long, reluctant sigh.

I've secured us lodgings for the night at the cost of a future favour. Am I to take it you wish me to add to my debt, by asking our host to help this Portune also?

'Oh.' I was taken aback. Looked at the little fella - the Portune - again. My resolve stiffened. 'Yes. Please.'

Very well. I see compassion's got the better of you. Bring him with us, if you must.

He turned back in the direction he'd sprung from.

Lifting the Portune carefully, I followed him.

***

The Portune was no bigger than a toddler, but he'd grown heavy by the time I stumbled to a halt.

Guest stopped before a small knoll jutting from the forest floor. He put his snout to the ground. Gave a weird high whine. The hair on the back of my neck and arms stood on end. I *wasn't* reassured by the sight of a glowing doorway fading into existence in the side of the mound. The Cu Sidhe looked briefly in my direction.

Follow

He stepped through the doorway. Heaving myself forward with one last effort, I followed him into the hillside. I expected the inside to be damp and earthen.

I was wrong.

What met my eyes was a homely room constructed of one overarching piece of wood. It looked smooth, as though carved - but I later discovered the trees helped to create these spaces. Sent their roots to surround them.

It was a living home.

The room was roughly circular. Low, broad wooden chairs were heaped with cushions. Mossy green curtains lined the space around one side. What *really* caught my attention was the cooking pot visible at the rear of the room. A glowing stone beneath the leather cauldron appeared to be acting as a source of heat. Something was bubbling away. And it smelled *wonderful*. My stomach rumbled in appreciation. Nearby was a table that appeared for all the world to be growing from the floor. Mushroom-like stools sprouted around it.

All taken in with the quickest of looks as our round little hostess sprang nimbly from a chair. Broad smile splitting the wrinkles on her nut brown face.

I couldn't help but *stare*.

She stood level with my chest and wore a long skirt and jacket in shades of rust and brown. So coarse looking, I wondered if they'd been made of wood bark. Her bare feet flashed beneath her skirts as she moved, displaying seriously gnarly toenails.

Conker coloured hair curled thickly close to her head, and the smoke from her long clay pipe wreathed around it before dissolving into the air. Sharply curling elongated ears peeped from her curls. Snub nose covered with a dusting of reddish freckles. She chuckled warmly as she saw me weighing her up.

The little woman stood taller as I examined her, stepping back to lift her chin and look me firmly in the eye.

It was those eyes that set my fears to rest. That made my knotted stomach unclench. They were the rich brown of loam. Twin pools of bottomless kindness.

I let out a breath I hadn't realised I was holding.

'Yes,' she said, in a voice as warm and brown as her eyes. 'You're safe now, human Fae girl. For a little while, at least. You must be tired. I'll let you rest now, and afterwards you can eat and regain a little strength.'

I smiled, feeling a bit mothered. And rather liking it.

'You're very kind, and I'm grateful.' I was careful, remembering what Guest said about thanking the fae. 'I *totally* want to rest and eat - *really* I do - but please...'

I paused to look down at the unconscious Portune I still held. 'Is there any way you could help *him*? First?'

She gave a little cry and something wordless passed between her and the Cu Sidhe.

'Daughter of men and Fae,' she said kindly. 'There's nothing to stop me doing *both*. Put him on this chair. Why, you must be exhausted carrying his weight.'

'He's not heavy.'

I placed him on the chair she'd indicated. Yawned widely. At that moment I wanted nothing more than sleep. As the little woman fetched water and bandages made of what looked like cobwebs, Guest nosed one of the heavy curtains aside - and I spied a small alcove with a wide bed in it.

Threw myself on it, fully clothed.

That short chick must take in a lot of tall travellers, I thought blissfully, stretching my aching body across the gossamer soft sheets. Was aware of the Hound tugging a mossy blanket across me. As the warmth enveloped me I fell into a deep sleep.

And knew no more.

◀Chapter Four▶

I dreamed terrible things. *Not* a night I ever want to repeat.

Awoke trembling with the dawn to feel the steadying hand of my little hostess on my arm. A feeling of warm relief flooded me at her touch. I leaned into it, smiling.

She jerked back suddenly and I mewed in disappointment.

Frowning slightly, she seated herself on the side of my bed and held out her arms. I hugged her fiercely, revelling in the feeling of comfort she brought me. She stroked my hair and kissed the top of my head gently.

'There's food here for you.' She indicated the bowl. 'It's from the human realm. No Faery ingredients. You'll be safe eating it.'

I barely stopped myself thanking her. Just nodded and picked up the simple wooden bowl and spoon. The appetising scent of a rich, herby stew assailed my nostrils and I inhaled appreciatively.

'It smells good. You're very kind.'

'It *is* good, human girl. Luydla's known for her cooking.' That brown face crinkled into a smile again. 'You eat now. As for *me* - I need a word with that no-good Hound out there.'

She slipped from the bed and strode through the curtains.

Snapped *'Barghest!'* in a sharp voice.

Very different from the tone she'd taken with me. Hungrily spooning up the tasty stew, I grinned to myself at the idea of the little woman ticking off the huge Cu Sidhe.

Dumb mutt and his master obviously should've been feeding me more.

Just saying.

It was strange how well those curtains muffled sound. No matter how hard I strained my ears, I picked up only fragments of the conversation carried on beyond them. My hostess sounded sharply cross, and I could only guess at Guest's answers most of the time.

What kind of curtain muffles a mental voice, anyway?

'...murmur murmur...clearly Fae-struck, you stupid Hound...murmur murmur...trying to kill her?'

*Rumble rumble... should I have done? My options were limited, Brownie........rumble rumble......rumble rumble ... such a **profound** effect on him... rumble rumble... far more so than I've ever seen...*

A sharply snapped question too rapid to follow.

No. In truth, I don't believe it's coincidence either. But what....rumble rumble...Tir na n'Og.

'Murmur murmur... murmur....to the courts will *take* too long... murmur... dangerous... murmur murmur...you've both been gone so long... murmur.'

What else can I.... rumble rumble... my master... whine...dire predictions...rumble...an old enemy.

'But....murmur murmur before you *reach* Tir na n'Og...murmur murmur...only a day's ride away at the most!'

Rumble rumble...know?

'Murmur... of the younger Fae....murmur murmur ... kindly disposed...murmur...vouch for her...murmur.'

Settled, then.

I heard Luydla give a healthy snort as she approached my alcove. Pulling the curtain aside, she turned back and I saw her framed in the brighter light beyond as she spoke one last time to the Hound.

'Just be sure you're acting for the right reason, Cu Sidhe. Some things shouldn't be done - even for *him*. Your motives confuse me.'

With that she dropped the curtain and came over to where I greedily ran my finger around the bowl to catch the last dribbles of gravy. She exchanged the empty bowl for two others filled with water. One hot; one cold.

'Its Faery water, but I hardly think drinking a little will do much harm *now*' the Brownie told me ominously. '*He's* already done enough damage. This bowl here's for you to wash. You'll want to get the bloodstains out.'

Bloodstains?

I looked down at my hands and top. They *were* a little stained. My waistcoat – I found out later they called them jerkins - crinkled as I moved. The Portune must've lost more blood than I'd thought.

Nasty.

'Wait.' I held out a hand, as Luydla made to leave. 'How's the little fella? The Portune, I mean.'

Her smile was broad. 'Healed and gone, human Fae girl. Healed and gone. That was a good deed you did there. A life debt the Portune owe you, now. That'll help.'

With that she was gone.

I turned my attention to washing myself.

***

We'd an uneventful day or so after we left Luydla's home. As we left she'd pressed a small bundle of 'human food' into my hands and offered the services of herself - and her folk - should I ever find myself in true need.

'No favour exchanges,' she told me. 'Just a gift to be called in when you will.'

I looked uncertainly at Guest.

'I'm not sure what I should say,' I whispered.

He huffed with laughter. *You should say 'Accepted with*

gratitude'

So I did.

With a beaming smile for me - and a pointed look for the Cu Sidhe - she whirled and disappeared back into the hillside.

When night fell we curled up among the roots of a great grey tree. Guest said we were safe there because the lesser fae would know better than to mess with us under a Dryad's tree. I was disappointed not to see the Dryad. But no matter how hard I tried to stay awake, my eyelids drooped hopelessly. Guest sat up all night guarding me as I slept rolled against him. Fingers and face deeply buried in fur, and that spicy canine scent cocooning me.

Touching him was the only way to keep the grief and emptiness at bay. Never truly gone, it was quieter and less sharp all the while we were in contact. As we walked, I tried not to lose my grip on his shaggy fur.

As the second day faded, I was surprised to see the flicker of flames through the trees ahead. My companion stopped for a second. Took a few deep sniffs.

Ah, the Brownie woman spoke truly. It's one of the younger Fae up ahead.

He began to move again.

We'll *rest in this clearing too, I think. Try not to be afraid, little Bree. The Fae can seem rather – overpowering - to humans.*

'I'll do my best not to fall to the floor gibbering,' I said snarkily.

Good.

I crossed my eyes at him, pulling a face.

The mouth-watering smell of roasting meat reached my nostrils and I was obscurely cheered by it. Luydla'd cautioned me against eating Faery food, but the sheer normality of the smell lightened my heart. We stepped into the circle of firelight.

I *gasped*.

Sitting on a fallen tree beside the small fire was the most beautiful creature I've *ever* laid eyes on.

Shining hair - a deep blood copper red - fell away in a long curtain. Framed a lightly tanned face of almost impossible perfection. He wore green leather pants and a matching jerkin. Over his heart blazed a flaming golden hand holding a spear. He bent over a curving longbow. Wiping the wood with a soft rag, lean body swaying with the motion. On our approach he looked up - starting visibly as he took in the sight of my huge friend. He leapt to his feet, eyes widening. Gave a graceful half bow.

'Cu Sidhe,' His voice was light and joyful. 'You're welcome to join me.'

Guest inclined his head in return.

I'm grateful, my lord. We've come far and my companion's weary.

As they spoke I caught the faintest hint of a delicious citrusy scent, and began to edge my way around the fire.

Seeking the source.

'Rest, Hound. You and your friend are safe for tonight.' The Fae was tracking me with his eyes, a peculiar expression on his face.

Your words honour me, Lughan lordling. We accept gladly.

Damn, these fae were polite to one another.

I was tired - chilled to the bone - and only that wonderful warm odour was distracting me from my ever-present sorrow. Circling the fire, I realised the source of the scent was the green-clad archer. It grew stronger as I approached, and I couldn't stop a whimper of longing escaping me.

The Fae kept glittering green eyes on me as I edged towards him. A faint radiance illuminated his skin.

The Fae are *beautiful*.

And *he's* more beautiful than most.

All self control gone, I launched myself at him. Flung my arms and legs around his tall body and inhaled deeply.

He smelled of lemons and lightning. Of summer sunshine in bright meadows. A swirling note of woodsmoke in there, too. The blissful scent wound itself about me.

I wanted to roll in it like a puppy.

Buried my face in his neck, and moaned with pure pleasure.

'Lady's name!' He laughed; peeling my legs from around him and setting me on my feet. 'Do you greet *everyone* this way - or is there just something about me?'

He winked at me. Looked questioningly at the Hound.

She can't help herself, my lord. The girl is Fae-struck.

Even Guest sounded amused.

Damn mutt.

'Fae-struck?' The Fae lord took my shoulders, impish grin fading. He held me at arm's length for a better view. 'She's *human*. I hadn't realised, Cu Sidhe. She stands here in *those* colours - with *that* face...

'I'd never have known.'

*Yes. **That** face. My master initially made a similar mistake.* The Hound growled quietly.

Tired of the nonsensical conversation - and longing to get closer to that gorgeous creature - I struggled in his grasp.

'You're pretty.' I told him, fighting to get closer.

He wrapped an arm round my waist, pinning me to his side. I sighed in contentment. All the emptiness and sorrow fled, chased away by that wonderful sunshine smell. I looked up to see a warm smile dawning on his face.

'Stay close to me. I'll keep the despair at bay - for tonight at least.'

He helped me settle myself on the fallen tree, still clinging closely to his side. I laid my head drowsily on the strange Fae's shoulder. Rubbed my face happily against the soft material of his cloak.

He and Guest talked, but I wasn't listening.

Was too happy to be surrounded by that smell. To feel the warm touch of the Fae's hand. Little tingles of electricity ran through me at the brush of his skin.

'What's the name of your master, Cu Sidhe? Why's he left the girl in Faery - alone - when she's Fae-struck?' An odd tone in that pleasant voice.

*She's not alone, my lord. She has **me**. My master would've protected her himself, if he'd been able. **His** name's one that's not spoken - in this realm.*

A frown marred the Fae lord's perfect brow as he examined me more closely. His eyes fixed thoughtfully on the darker area on the breast of my surcoat.

'The emblem's been removed from this. It's clearly fae crafted, so not the girl's own.

'You say your master's name isn't spoken, Hound. And you bring a girl looking like - *her* - into Faery. Wearing the black and gold. You're setting into motion events which've scared the courts for hundreds of years. I know who your master is.

'And *I* won't speak his name aloud.

'You're the Barghest - most loyal of beasts and noblest of the Cu Sidhe. But it *scares* me. To think what you may be bringing on the courts.'

Guest rumbled and inclined his head in approval.

I acknowledge the name, Fae lord. I'm humbled I'm not forgotten. You couldn't have been born when we - shall we say left? - the realm.

'It's true I'm one of the younger Fae. But don't you *know* you're a legend among us? I grew *up* on tales of your master's doings. And hers. As children we played games acting it all out. They said you'd only return in the event of his death. Or a cure. By your speech, he's not dead. Is he cured?'

*Alas, no. Not **yet**. I've hopes of that human you're holding so tightly, though. He was **himself** with her. For so much of the time, I begin to believe it might be possible. She cured his blindness. I'd aid her for that alone - but there's more at stake here than you're aware of, lordling. Think of the prophecies...*

Poor Guest sounded so wistful, it took a moment for his words to pierce the contented fog.

'*I* cured him?' I sat bolt upright. Astonished. 'Seriously? How do you work *that* out, Guest? I didn't do anything.'

The huge Hound licked my hand briefly, making me giggle.

*You kissed him, little Bree. An innocent kiss freely given by one of your bloodline. That's all that lifting the curse of blindness ever hung upon and **you** - you did it unknowingly.*

'If she's of *that* bloodline, it *would* explain it. Why I didn't realise she was human. Why she looks so much like – *well*.' The Fae smiled. 'Barghest, I'll offer you any aid I can, if you're travelling to Tir na n'Og. There are ways of curing her there - if she survives them.'

Guest rumbled low in his chest.

*She **will**. I'll allow no harm to come to her while I live. If my master were himself, I know **he'd** say the same.*

'Loyal indeed, Cu Sidhe!' He laughed at Guest's vehemence. 'For that reason, please accept my help as freely given. I'll help you keep her alive until she can be cured.'

Accepted, my lord. You've my gratitude.

I yawned. Widely.

They might've been happy to talk all night, but I was bone weary. The only thing keeping me upright was the strong arm around me - and my fervent need to be close to the beautiful creature it belonged to.

He must've felt me drooping.

Slipping from the log, he pulled me with him to lie sheltered against it. I felt the warmth of the fire play across my face as he settled himself behind me. Curled his lean frame around mine.

I made a moany little happy sound, and pressed myself against him.

A low chuckle vibrated through his chest as his arm tightened around me. With the other hand he brushed the hair from my face. Ran his fingers gently along my scar line and into the bristly patch of shorn hair.

'You've had a hard time of it, I think.' He spoke softly, lips brushing my ear and making me shiver. 'Rest now. I *will* keep you safe.'

I turned my head to stare into those fascinating green eyes. Smiled sleepily.

'What's your name, pretty man?'

'I'm Finian Medyr of the Lughan, lady.'

I could feel his smile as he laid his head against mine.

'That's nice. I'm Bree.'

My eyelids were too heavy to keep open.

Guest placed one massive paw on my arm and huffed sleepily. Those great red eyes closed and his rumbling snore sawed the air. I snuggled myself back against Finian more firmly, trying to touch him with as much of me as I could. Waves of bliss flowed through me and I couldn't prevent little sounds of happiness. My arm reached back without my volition and I found myself trying to pull his leather jerkin out of my way.

I wanted - *needed* - to feel that glorious, glowing skin.

A little of his flat stomach became exposed. I tugged my own shirt up and out of the way at the back, pressed my own skin against that satin soft flesh. The beautiful anguish made me moan, the feeling of bliss intensifying to an almost unbearable pitch. After a few sharply drawn breaths, Finian took hold of my hips and gently moved me away. Like a possessed thing I tried to move back again.

Wanted to wrap myself in him completely.

He cleared his throat. Shakily.

'Bree, that wouldn't be wise.' His voice was coloured with laughter. 'I'm only flesh and blood. And some things are a little - shall we say *provocative*?'

I snorted at him, reluctantly abandoning the effort. Curled my fingers round his.

Safe between Finian and Guest, I closed my eyes and slept.

◄Chapter Five►

They were awake before me. I heard them talking softly in the chill morning air. Shivering, I sat up and gratefully reached for the steaming cup Finian held out.

'This'll warm you up a bit,' he told me.

I smiled my thanks before remembering my bizarre behaviour of the previous night. An appalled hand shot to my mouth. I stared in horror, cheeks flooding with heat. He laughed at my expression and draped his cloak around my shoulders.

I inhaled the delicious scent rising from its folds.

Tugged it tightly around myself.

'And this'll hold off the cold as we ride,' he grinned. 'As well as deal with the symptoms of being Fae-struck. It'll be permeated with my essence - which *should* hold it at bay for a while.'

'You know, that's the *third* time someone's called me Fae-struck.' I was irritable with embarrassment. 'What does it sodding *mean*, anyway?'

Finian lowered himself to the ground across from me. I squirmed - watching him keep his distance.

He was probably worried I'd jump him again.

'I'm sorry, Bree. I assumed the Barghest explained it to you.'

'*Ha!*' I snorted. 'Damn mutt never tells me *anything* I haven't nagged out of him.'

I shot the Hound a dirty look. Bringing on his huffling laugh again.

So I shot him an even *filthier* one.

Wisely, he remained silent as Finian began to explain.

'Humans who spend any length of time around us develop a kind of addiction,' he said gently, bending forward to hold my gaze. 'They crave the presence and touch of the noble Fae with a terrible intensity. When they're not around us they pine away. The touch of lesser fae *can* hold it at bay. But not for long. The despair - and desire for Fae contact - maddens them.

'Their bodies and minds are too fragile to handle it. They go mad. Not eating. Not caring for themselves. Eventually, they die. The effect's worse if they spend any time in Faery. It weaves a spell of its own. More subtle, but equally powerful.'

I was aghast.

'Is that what's happening to *me*? Am I going mad? Is that why I was so - well - you know?...' I finished lamely, my head in my hands

'No. *No*. We'll get you cured.' He shook his head, speaking quickly. Took my hand from my hair and held it between his own. 'We're taking you to Tir na n'Og. To the Seelie Court. There're Fae there who can help you. Healers. You've Fae blood in your veins. That means a cure's possible.'

I blinked, confused. 'What's a Seelie court?'

He raised his eyebrows - with another boyish grin - and looked slyly at Guest.

'Lady's name! The Hound really *didn't* tell you anything, did he? It must've been a long few days for you. Good thing you've me to entertain you, now.'

I had to laugh at his attempt to bow whilst cross legged. The Cu Sidhe lumbered to his feet.

Very amusing, my lord. **How** *I'm laughing on the inside.* His mental tone was dry. *May I suggest that -* ***if*** *you're done playing - we could actually set off to find that cure?*

Finian smiled, rising gracefully, and wandered a little way into the trees, returning with a gigantic white mare. I noticed the saddle and bridle were dyed to match his clothing.

I'll admit it.

I made the 'girl-sees-cute-animal' noise.

Tragic.

'She's huge, the beautiful beastie.' I stroked her velvet nose. 'How're you going to ride her, Fin? *You're* tall - but *she's* ridiculous!' The horse tossed her mane at me. 'No offense, girl. You're the gorgeousest horsie in the world but - *sheesh* - You're big.'

'*I'm* not riding her. *You* are.' Finian grinned.

'Are you *crazy*? I can't ride!'

He took me by the waist and boosted me into the saddle, swinging himself up behind me.

'We'll ride together, then.' He gave the reins a brisk slap. Touched the horse's sides with his heels. 'Coming, Barghest?'

I gasped with alarm as the animal began to move. Lurched a little. Fin tightened his arms around my waist and pulled me back to lean against him.

'I won't let you fall.'

*See that you don't. My master **wouldn't** be pleased.*

Guest fell into step beside us and we travelled on. The day grew warmer as we rode, making me loosen Finian's cloak.

A thought occurred.

'Finian?'

'Yes?'

'You said earlier your cloak could help me deal with being Fae-struck, didn't you?'

'That's right. It's been my preferred cloak for a number of years, so it's well and truly saturated with me.'

'Ugh.' I refused to dwell on *that* idea. 'So - I don't need to be touching you to feel ok? If I have your cloak on?'

'That's right.'

He reached around me to move a low, springy branch out of the way.

'Wouldn't that have worked just as well last night?'

'Yes.'

I looked around into his grinning face.

'So why the *hell* didn't you give me the cloak *then*? Instead of letting me drape myself all *over* you?'

My mortified ears began to burn and a hot rush crossed my cheekbones. He shrugged lightly, mischief in those glittering green eyes.

'I was cold'

I brought one arm behind me, flailing to slap any bits of laughing Fae that fell within reach. Got several. Face flaming, I faced firmly ahead - taking care to lean as far forward as I dared.

Stupid bloody elf-man was *not* making this any easier.

As we rode, Fin told me stories - and answered my questions about the courts. I forgot my embarrassment and listened, spellbound.

The fae fell broadly into two distinct groups, each aligned with one of the courts of Faery. The two held themselves apart from one another, with interbreeding strictly forbidden. I could see why, even then.

I *certainly* can now.

The Seelie Court - also known as the Summer Court - was home to creatures that liked the bright sun and weren't ill-disposed towards humanity. It was rare they'd bother a human in the mortal realm. Assuming they could get there in the first place - it hadn't been freely accessible for centuries. Seelie like the Will o'the Wisp would play tricks on humans. Lead them astray and enjoy their confusion. But the tricks were seldom harmful.

Not *intentionally*.

The king and queen of the Seelie ruled from a city called Tir na n'Og, which apparently meant 'land of the ever young'. Finian's eyes warmed as he spoke of his adopted home - where wonders were commonplace, and laughter and song always to be heard. He'd grown up on his father's estates, a half ignored youngest son.

In Tir na n'Og he'd been able to craft a place for himself, in service to the monarchs. There was deep affection in the way he described the elegance and grace of the court. My pulse quickened with curiosity to see it.

The other court - the Unseelie - was darker and *much* more dangerous.

The fae making up this court were a grisly bunch. Called themselves the Dark Host, or the Winter Court. And were *less* than friendly towards human girls like me. These were fae who'd torment and kill humans. For amusement. If Unseelie fae led you astray - as a Seelie wisp might - terrible things happened when you followed them.

Their Queen held court in a great black castle called Caer

Dubh up in the mountains. Her people loved the night and the dark places. I was glad we weren't going there.

A Fae-struck girl would be easy prey.

I *didn't* want to be prey.

Not an option.

***

As day faded into evening, we built a fire and settled for the night. Placing myself very deliberately away from Fin, I lay wrapped in his cloak with Guest shielding me from the wind. I ate the food Luydla'd given me. Finian prepared food for himself and the Hound.

He said we'd reach Tir na n'Og the next day. The forest had been thinning all afternoon. Great trunks of ancient trees gave way to younger, greener growth. To fresher, summery smells.

Once, I caught glimpse of a slender green girl swaying through the woodland at a distance, long mossy hair drifting out behind her as she passed on fleet feet.

I was overjoyed when Fin informed me I'd seen my first Dryad.

I've been entranced by the idea of those tree spirits ever since my Mum first read the Narnia books to me as a kid. With a sharp pang of homesickness, I wondered what she'd have made of her. My stomach curled into an acid ball of homesickness.

No, Bree.

Don't think about home.

Fated

It was almost noon when we crested a hill and I saw Tir na n'Og for the first time. Finian reined his mount in so I could take a long look.

It was *spectacular*.

Set in a valley, through which a wide river wound, I saw a high wall encircling a city that gleamed in the sun. Every building shone whitely, verdant gardens and bosky woods in between. In the centre rose the domes and turrets of a castle straight out of central casting. Brightly coloured pennants and flags snapped above palace, city and woodlands alike. The breeze they danced on carried faint snatches of music. My feet twitched with the desire to dance.

'*Ooh*,' I breathed. 'You never told me it was like *this*.'

I strongly suspect there's a lot he hasn't told us. It'd ease my mind were I more certain of our - **reception**.

'Beautiful, isn't it?' Fin ignored Guest's grumbling with a certain proprietary pride.

'What do you mean, Guest?' I asked. 'Should I be worried? Am I in danger?'

You've been in danger since the day I met you, little Bree. All of **Faery's** *perilous for humans. Stay close to Fin. Until we've been able to cure you.*

'Can't I just keep his cloak on?'

It was Fin who replied.

'You *could* - but being Fae-struck among crowds of us isn't safe.' He frowned, uncharacteristically serious. Held up a hand to forestall my brewing interruption. 'We're a joyful people, and an honourable one. But humans are *never* treated with the same honour we extend other Fae.

'Our games aren't to mortal tastes. We keep your people as pets. They're passed around between us when we tire of them, as it's impossible for them to return to your realm once they're Fae-struck. We enjoy tricking one another into handing them over. Or abducting them. Especially those with certain - er - *talents*, shall we say?

'It'd be dangerous for you to leave my side. Being Fae-struck, you'd be unable to stop yourself following one of the elder - more powerful - Fae. If they decided to take you. And they *would*, Bree. *You're* far too dainty a morsel to pass up.'

I glared at him, eyes narrowed and jaw set. Lifted my chin mutinously.

*He's right. The Seelie **are** gentler than the Unseelie. But they're still callous, when it comes to humans. You'd be well advised to stay with Finian and I - until you're cured. There're forces at play about which you've no idea. And I **haven't** left my master's side - after all this time - to fail now.*

Feeling a little ganged up on, I threw my hands up.

'*Fine.* Whatever.'

◄Chapter Six►

We passed unchallenged into Tir na n'Og.

I kept the hood of Fin's cloak pulled low over my face, only my hair visibly escaping. Guest trotted at our side, clearly familiar with his surroundings - and seemingly enjoying being back. He was baring those immense teeth in a kind of grin, tongue lolling from one side of his mouth. Held his tail high.

Exotic sights met my eyes on every side.

We passed tranquil gardens behind living fences. Bustling marketplaces swarmed with fae of every size, shape and description.

Here a gnarled looking dwarf stood fingering gossamer fine material, offered in every conceivable colour by a spindly green woman.

There a winged blue girl - no more than three feet tall -

stood shouting in a strange language and shaking her fingers in the face of a laughing old man with skin like mottled tree bark. He opened the cages that hung around him, releasing dozens of brightly plumaged birds into the air. The girl paid with what looked like a glass vial and a handful of iridescent dust before following them.

The aroma of deliciously spiced meats perfumed the air.

My stomach gurgled.

Loudly.

I looked apologetically at Fin, who didn't seem to have noticed. His face was set in firm, cold lines and he was holding an extended eye-meet with a Fae across the square. It was such a departure from his usual easygoing smile, I leaned forward to examine the other Fae from beneath my hood. I managed only the fastest look before Fin touched his heels to the horse's flanks. We trotted around a corner, and away.

That fast look made me uneasy.

An unsettling creature, with his proud, bony face and sneering expression. I'd a frightened impression of burning icy eyes and plaited blonde hair. What was *really* disturbing was there was something creepily *compelling* about him. Despite Fin's arms around me, I'd an unwilling desire to jump down and run to him.

I began to shake. Fin murmured reassuring nothings in my ear.

Damn.

They were right.

I'd go with anyone until I was cured - afraid of them or not.

Retreating further into my hood I leaned firmly against Fin. Turned my head to breathe in as much of his delicious sunshine smell as possible. Being intoxicated by Fin *was* embarrassing.

But it beat finding out what the consequences of falling under the sway of another Fae might be.

I was wrenchingly homesick. Unsafe.

Taking deeper breaths of Fin's mouth-watering scent in the hope of keeping myself under control, I was soon dizzy with a sense of profound well-being. I relaxed contentedly into his arms. Hummed with happiness. He laughed lightly; sending a shiver down my back and making my stomach flip. I knew it was because I was Fae-struck.

And ignored it.

Was still oblivious when we reached the shimmering castle.

Corridor after curving corridor - high and vaulted overhead - rolled away in all directions. From rooms beyond arched doorways floated laughter. And song.

I found myself standing before grand double doors, intricately carved from glowing golden wood. One hand laced itself in Guest's fur, and the other wrapped tightly around Fin's arm.

Are you ready, little Bree?

I swallowed.

Hard.

And nodded. 'I think so.'

*Go with Fin for now. He'll speak for you until it's time for **me** to make an entrance.*

'How long will that be?' Less brave at the thought of entering a room full of Fae without the Hound's comforting presence beside me.

He lolled out his tongue in the canine equivalent of a grin. Crimson eyes flashed with mischief.

*When it reaches a tipping point, little one. When it is **time!***

He turned on silent paws and retreated around a corner. Fin grinned at my crestfallen expression.

'I promised I'd keep you safe until you were cured, Bree. A little faith, please.'

He nodded at the silent Fae who stood sentinel in front of the doors and they each took a handle and swung them wide. Hand on mine, fingers interlacing my own for comfort, he walked me into the audience chamber of the Seelie rulers.

The space was *cavernously* vast.

Columns of carved white marble rose gracefully in a circle surrounding the domed roof. From their feet grew long swathes of mistletoe, honeysuckle and grape vines. They wove themselves around them, climbing to festoon the ceiling. Blossom and grapes grew overhead and emitted a wonderful scent.

Swathes of coloured light cut through stained windows

lining the central dome, puddling on the green etched marble floor.

Fae of all kinds stood around the great chamber. They ranged in size and shape so wildly that I gawped in astonishment at the fauns, flutter-winged sprites and other, weirder creatures.

The noble Fae were *dazzling*.

Bright eyes and beautiful faces - some merry and others cold as ice - melded into one whole. Skin tones varied in colour from deepest ebony to a white so pale it was almost blue. Their hair was long and wild. It ranged through every colour of the spectrum. Shone in the coloured light.

I could've stared for hours - but I saw what was in the chamber's centre.

And was *spellbound*.

A raised dais held two elaborate thrones, each formed of the twisting branches of thornless rose bushes. Golden roses bloomed among their leaves.

And there sat the most regal - and magnificent - Fae of them all.

The Seelie queen and king.

As wild and beautiful as their people, I could *feel* the weight of centuries in the gaze they turned on us.

Was glad of Fin's firm grip on my hand. Fought with every step not to try and break free. Not to run to the groups of fae and lose myself in touching them. Or worse, to throw myself at the Fae monarchs in utter adoration.

I had it *bad*.

Through the hood on my lowered head, I felt the penetrating glances of the fae. Heard their curious whispering as Fin brought us to a halt before the dais.

He bowed low.

Still clutching his arm, I curtsied.

Clumsily.

The queen leaned forward. Curling red ringlets shifted sinuously around her body as she moved, blazing bright against her cloth-of-gold gown.

'You've returned early, Finian. Has something happened?'

He cleared his throat. 'It *has*, my queen,' he said formally. 'In my care I have a lonely, Fae-struck girl...'

He was interrupted by some harsh toned comment from the throng behind. Unintelligible, but the ribald intent was unmistakeable.

A snarl of laughter followed.

The queen's hand fluttered in an imperious gesture for silence.

Fin continued, easy and unfazed. 'She was exposed to the influence of a *very* powerful Fae - without her consent. And was flung into Faery *without* his protection.'

'An all too common story.' The king shook his golden head sympathetically.

He *shone*.

These two were too much in my Fae-befuddled state.

I wanted to touch them. To stroke their long hair. Not caring where we were, I threw my arms around Fin and pressed my face against his chest. Inhaled deeply in an effort to regain control.

Heard the queen's pretty voice again. 'Finian, the Unseelie don't see things as we do. You're kind - but we can't rescue *all* their victims.'

'I know that, my queen.' Finian said. 'And the Fae that did this wasn't *exactly* Unseelie. He used to be one of *us*. Forgive me if I don't speak his name. I ask for Diern to do what he can to call her Fae blood. So she can go home. Partly because it was one of us - and partly...'

He paused.

The queen arched her coppery brows. 'Yes?'

'I'm sorry, Bree.' He whispered softly.

Then...

'And partly - for *this*.'

His voice rang out clearly as he spun me by the shoulders. Tore away the cloak.

Exposed my face to the assembled court.

A low susurration went round the room as fae murmured to one another. I gasped with horror as the desire seized me to spread myself in a thousand directions at once. To touch all the Fae. Roll in their aromas.

The king and queen shared a long look, before the queen stepped down to take my chin firmly in her warm grip.

'Look only at me, human child,' she said, not unkindly.

I looked into her exquisite face and began to drown in the limpid pools of her blue, blue eyes. All sound faded into a muted background roaring.

She studied me.

'I see your interest, Finian,' She sounded thoughtful. 'And I understand why she hasn't gone mad yet. With *that* blood she's well protected. But why do *you* wish to ask this of us? What concern is it of yours?'

*I asked it of him. It's **my** master who's responsible. Who wishes it.*

Guest's mental tones were loud as the great beast shouldered his way through the assembled Seelie and halted beside me.

The king blinked for several slow seconds.

Beamed at the Hound. 'Barghest, my friend! One comes with *her* face - clad in the remnants of black and gold - and *I* don't make the connection! I'm truly glad to see you. For your sake, we'll grant this request.'

Accepted with gratitude, my king.

I stood bemused, one hand seeking Guest's soft fur and sinking into it. He turned his head to lick it affectionately.

Queen Rhiannon and King Custenin, I'd like to present formally - at your convenience - the human girl Briana Cadman. Of the line of Morgen.

Another whisper crossed the room.

I hadn't a clue what was going on.

Could do nothing but stand there, gazing at that wonderful

queen. She released my chin and took my hand instead. Examined the patch on my clothing where a livery symbol must've been. Embarrassing to be wearing Leiloken's clothing. Clothing that hadn't been washed *once* since I put it on. Uncomfortably grimy and unkempt.

That wasn't what attracted Rhiannon's attention. She stiffened.

'Hound, who gave her these clothes?' The queen looked paler, a strange note in that fluting voice. 'Is your master dead, that they were *yours* to give?'

No, my queen. They were my master's gift to the girl, not mine.

'Oh. He still has moments where he's himself?' Softly asked.

*Yes. He was almost totally coherent for **weeks** while we nursed Briana through an infected elf-shot. It gave me - hope.*

'That must be the worst of it.' She sighed. 'To have moments where he's sane enough to know what he's become. If I started weeping for him - again - my tears would fill a lake.'

*Quite. In his better moments, he's as brilliant — as driven - as he ever was. You **know** if he were himself, he'd want the girl treated well.*

The King looked at me strangely.

'Yes. I rather expect he *would*. Let it be so. We'll acknowledge the girl, if she survives.' He raised his voice. 'Send for the healer Diern and ready the Turret Chambers.'

I heard his order repeated outside. Saw several lesser fae scurry away to obey. Some shook their heads and held angry conversations. Others looked puzzled. Or thoughtful.

Or *scared*.

I felt my arm grasped firmly by Fin, and was aware of the great Hound moving at my side as we were led from the hall. Stumbled through hallways and up winding stairs until we came to the Turret Chambers.

They were my sickroom for the next three days.

◀Chapter Seven▶

I awoke gradually, becoming aware of an arm draped over me and regular breathing on the back of my neck. Froze in confusion. Slowly opened my eyes. There lay Fin, blood copper hair fanning over the pillows, naked torso pressed to my back. Which was also naked - if you didn't count my bra.

I glanced down. We were both dressed apart from that.

Good.

I lay for a moment, waiting to remember.

Didn't.

What'd being Fae-struck made me *do*? And where was I? I sat up carefully, eased myself to the very edge of the mattress, and took stock of my surroundings.

I was on an immense bed, the base seemingly growing

from the floor. Branches tangled together above my head, forming a bower-like roof of white blossom. Midnight blue hangings of heavy, embroidered silk.

The room was octagonal with high arched windows.

One was ajar, letting in a shiver of cold air. The walls and furniture were silver wood with lush deep-piled rugs and wall-hangings shining with colour. Three elaborately carved silverwood doors, the knotwork gilded with gold leaf. They gleamed with precious stones inset in the wood.

I think the word my mind was grasping for was *opulent.*

A door opened, allowing a short, slim fae to ease her way through carrying a heavily loaded tray. There seemed to be an awful lot of food for two people.

A rumbling snore alerted me to the fact that Guest lay beside the bed.

I snorted.

That explained it. I've seen the mutt eat.

The fae girl looked up at the sound, round-eyed with interest. I stared back. Seemed only fair.

She was short, with pale green skin and pink hair to her waist. Blue eyes with no white or pupil. A pair of antennae peeked from among the curls on her forehead. The pointed peaks of her ears were very long and rose through her hair to stand tall at either side of her head.

I'd noticed that although noble Fae had a distinct upward point to the tips of their - otherwise normal - ears, the lesser fae had remarkably shaped ears of all kinds.

The ears alone would've marked her out as lesser fae - even if it hadn't been for the wings that sprouted from her shoulders. Shaped like butterfly wings and colours dazzling. A dusting of iridescent powder made them sparkle as they trembled in the faint breeze.

She was all the fairies of my childhood imaginings.

I smiled at her in utter delight.

Her answering smile was shy, and she ducked her head as she placed the tray on the table.

'There's food here for you, my lady. Would you care to bathe before you eat? Her majesty's provided clothing for you to use while you're with us, and there's a bathing chamber through there,' Her small hand indicated one of the other doors. 'I can attend you while you bathe, if you wish.'

'*Attend* me?' I asked.

What was wrong with my voice?

It didn't sound right. Was rich and strange. Had something happened to my throat? My hand rose to check, but no sore spot was obvious to my questing fingers.

'Yes, my lady. It *is* usual.'

I sighed. I *was* rather shaky. And the idea of passing out without anyone to stop me drowning *was* a little daunting.

'Fae not caring about privacy. Why didn't I see *that* one coming? Ok, then. And I'm Bree, not my lady. What's your name?'

'Dechtira, my lady. And I can't call you Bree. I'd be

punished for insolence.' She shuddered.

I let the little fae lead me to the bathing chamber. Felt silly getting undressed in front of her. She helped unclasp my bra and steadied my hand as I lowered myself into the pool.

Golden sandstone, with a dinky waterfall flowing from the chamber walls. I could've sworn - if I hadn't known better - we were in a grotto. Wavering ferns grew from patches of soil dotting the rock. I eased my body onto the broad ledge beneath the water. It was deeply soothing, with the pale greenish cast Faery water always has. I leaned against the side of the pool. Let my mind drift, as Dechtira's gentle hands began to massage my arms and fingers with sweetly scented oil.

Memory began to filter back.

I remembered the taste of some foul brew administered by a hunchbacked fae with a kind face. Saw myself sobbing, curled up on one of the rugs in the other chamber.

Vague images of Finian's concerned face leaning over me as he hoisted me into his arms. The feeling of Guest's fur pressed against my healing cheek as I dozed.

Dechtira's nimble fingers worked the oil through my hair and into a richly scented lather. It was *wonderful*. For someone who believed in equality, I could get used to it *way* too easily.

More memories, flitting past in fits and starts.

Half remembered nightmares. Scenes from the recent past.

Fated

My hands tearing at Fin's jerkin until he'd loosened it, laughing, and pulled it over his head to drop to the floor.

Tell me I *didn't*?

Saw myself ripping off my own top and pressing close to him. Guest's grumbling voice warning Fin not to let go of me. To remember I was Fae-struck.

Fin snapping he was perfectly aware of *that*.

Frowning, I realised I felt no pull from the fae washing me, or from Fin sprawled on that fancy bed.

Maybe they *had* cured me.

Result.

The thought made me smile. As did the realisation that - where Dechtira was touching the injured side of my face - there was no pain. I felt her fingers stroking through hair, not bristles. Strange.

More memories.

The hunchback again. Mumbled words in some strange language, as he touched me on the forehead and over the heart with a wooden staff.

My voice babbling about three streams and Guest's master.

Images of a wooden cup filled with a strange potion.

Guest gently nudging my hands away from my eyes as I tried to claw at them. Fin's serious expression as he bent to kiss me. The soft feel of his lips on mine. The intense pain tearing through me. My bones grinding and reforming. Flesh screaming with the effort of stretching along them.

Wait.

Go back.

Fin *kissed* me.

What had I done? How would I face him?

Hot humiliation spread across my face and neck. I heard Dechtira's tinkling laugh.

'Whatever you're thinking - stop it,' she said. 'I'd got you good and relaxed before you spoilt it.'

'Sorry to undo all your hard work' I rose from the water to wrap myself in the soft blanket she held out. 'I think I've some apologising to do. What's Fin going to *think* of me?'

'He'll think you were Fae-struck. Because you were. You're worrying for no reason, my lady. Lord Finian declared you friend in front of the whole court. He won't go back on it now.'

'*Very* reassuring.' Sarcasm. Again.

It was becoming my default setting.

She handed me armfuls of clothing. I examined it as she waved her hand over my hair, chanting in some complicated tongue. It had the unexpected effect of drying my hair, making it slip around my head in shining ropes as it styled itself.

That was kind of cool, actually.

'Dechtira, you're going to have to help me. I wouldn't even *begin* to know what to do with all this. I mean, separate sleeves?' I held one up, looking at it critically as it dangled from my hand. 'Who decided that *not* attaching them to your clothes was a good idea?'

She giggled at my confusion and began to dress me.

'Like *this*, my lady.'

***

Before long I was standing in front of the long glass in the main chamber, staring at my reflection in stupefaction.

The woman in the mirror wasn't *me*.

Before me stood a willowy Fae. Her face mine, but not. More beautiful than me. Features finer. Ageless. Her white skin shone. Dark hair intricately braided around the crown of her head, tumbling to her feet. Baring her tip tilted ears.

She wore an underdress in shimmering silver with the belled overskirt, tight bodice and wide sleeves midnight blue.

Striking colours.

The *most* striking thing about her was the silver-white streak that sprang from the right hand side of her head. Where *I'd* been scarred by elf shot. Her eyes were my own - large with wonder - and they glittered like the eyes of the Fae. I sought the healing scar on my cheek. Found the faintest of silvery lines. Raised my hand to touch it.

So did the Fae woman in the glass.

Wow.

It really *was* me.

So this was what Fin'd meant when he talked about calling my Fae blood.

I couldn't stop myself pumping my arm in triumph. 'Alr*iiiight!*'

Dechtira's silvery peal of laughter was joined by Guest's huffling snort as the Hound padded over. He examined me critically.

You're awake and aware of yourself again. That's good.

'*Good?* Guest, have you *seen* me? My own mother wouldn't recognise me. I feel like Cinder-frickin'-rella!' A wide grin split my face.

The mirror-woman copied me.

*Yes, I've seen you. The likeness to your ancestor's even **more** pronounced. We'll have to hope it doesn't cause too many problems.*

'Problems, schmoblems. I look *gorgeous*, mutt!'

'She's not wrong, Hound,' I could see reflection-Fin sitting up on the bed, shimmering hair a curtain round his lean torso and yawning face.

Hot warmth flooded my face as the mirror woman blushed.

'Fin, I think I need to apologise to you...'

'No apology necessary. It's been an interesting three days.' He grinned.

'Three *days?*'

Yes, little Bree. It's taken that long for your Fae blood to burn through your system and relieve you of your Fae-struck state. It's good you survived it.

'Well, *I'm* quite pleased,' I said.

Fin rose and walked towards me, making me jump. He stopped, uncertain.

I held my hands up, palms out. 'Please stay back. I remember - well - *some* of what I did. And I'm *really* embarrassed right now. I know you said I'm cured, but I'd be a whole lot happier if you stayed out of smelling distance.'

He laughed lightly and came closer, holding out an arm. 'Take a sniff. I promise I'm safe now.'

I glanced at the Cu Sidhe, who nodded. Placing my nose close to Fin's wrist, I inhaled suspiciously and smelled...

...nothing.

No desire to throw myself at him seized me.

'You don't smell any more!' I accused.

'I smell exactly as I always did, Lady Briana.' He smiled into my eyes. 'You just don't react the same way.'

I took a deeper sniff. The faint scent of sunshine was there, but muted. I felt nothing but a slight flipping in my stomach; the ghost of a shiver down my spine.

Beamed with relief.

You're cured, Bree. Your Fae side's stronger than your human, now. You'd survive the transition back to your own realm. Their majesties will offer to grant you a request - in recompense for my master's actions. You can ask to go *home. You're free. If you **want** to be?*

Go home? And leave Fin?

My stomach somersaulted again.

What was with the stomach thing? Why was I thinking of Fin first? Of his smile, his warmth - the feeling of his arms around me?

I sank into a chair with my head in my hands. Let out a heart-felt groan. All that effort to cure me - and I *still* fancied the pants off the stupid, grinning elf-man.

'Are you well, my lady?' Dechtira laid a small hand on my arm.

'Yeah, sure.' I raised my head. 'What do I do now?'

'You'll have an audience with their majesties,' the Pixie said. 'All three of you. They want to see you as soon as you're well enough.'

Audience with their majesties? Crush on an elf? It sounded like a sodding RPG game. What the hell had *happened* to my life?

'Oh. Good.' I said, staring straight ahead.

Then it all became too much - and I had to laugh.

Hysterically.

◀Chapter Eight▶

An audience with the Seelie monarchs was an audience before the whole Seelie Court.

Guest and Finian - strange in formal attire - escorted me to the great double doors before the audience chamber. They left me there to wait as they went in to take their places. I was to have a formal introduction to the Seelie Court.

Exciting and terrifying all at once.

I felt like the princess in a fairy tale.

That was spoilt within moments as the bony faced Fae I'd seen in the city eased himself through the doors. He executed a distant half bow, an expression of contempt marring his features.

'Lady Briana, I am Efnyssen of the Nysien. I've been commanded to escort you to their majesties' presence.'

He looked like he wanted to scrape me off the bottom of his shoe.

Git.

Swallowing down the heavy feeling in my stomach, I took his proffered arm.

We stepped through the golden doors.

The circular audience chamber was much as I remembered, although the fae gathered inside had aligned themselves on either side of the room, leaving a distinct aisle for Efnyssen and myself to walk down. We were maybe halfway when Guest and Finian stepped out from the throng close to the thrones. I let out a slow, relieved breath. Guest's voice rang out.

Your majesties, it's my honour to present the Lady Briana. A daughter of Morgen.'

All those eyes burned my skin. Gasps as the change in me was registered. The butterflies in my stomach grew to pigeons, and fluttered into overdrive. Efnyssen paused mid-step for a moment. Allowed the assembled fae to take a long look before we carried on. When we were close to the dais, he executed a florid bow and I attempted another curtsey. He melted back into the crowd.

The royal pair regarded me seriously.

'Lady Briana of Morgen's line, the Seelie Court recognises you,' said the king.

I had to stop myself thanking him.

'Your companions have explained the situation. It's the will of the Seelie Court that we grant you a boon. For what you've suffered at the hands of one once numbered among us.'

Eh?

I glanced quizzically at the Cu Sidhe.

*Their majesties are offering to grant you a request, Bree. You can ask for anything it's within their power to give. You **could** go home...*

I looked at Queen Rhiannon, who smiled and nodded encouragingly.

'The Barghest speaks truly, Lady Briana. We can return you to the mortal realm. You've a home and a family who miss you, no doubt?'

'Oh, yes.' I thought of Mum and Blake, worried sick about me.

It'd been weeks, according to Guest. I could be back in my own room, my own bed. I could spend time with my family. I hadn't realised how much I missed them until I thought about seeing them again.

Could almost taste Mum's cooking.

My eyes sought Fin's as he stood there, gorgeous in green and gold. His were shadowed, face very still. Finian looked away first.

I turned to Guest. 'When I leave, what will *you* do?'

I'll return to my master. For as long as he needs of me.

'You mean until he dies? Loses it completely and wastes away?'

I do.

There it was again.

That simple canine dignity piercing me to the heart.

The Cu Sidhe left his master to help me. He'd saved my life and taken on debts of honour to protect me. I felt *terrible* at the thought of leaving Faery, and never repaying his kindness. Never honouring my debt.

Being a rude human.

Suddenly, I knew what I *had* to do.

I raised my chin, turned back to the king and queen.

'I'm grateful for the request you're offering me the chance to make, and accept it with all my heart.' I spoke slowly and carefully. Afraid of getting it wrong and offending someone. 'But - your majesties - there's something more important than sending *me* home that I want to ask you for.'

The king leaned forward slightly, frowning. 'What would you ask of us, Lady Briana?'

'I want you to bring Leiloken home and cure him. Like you cured me.'

There. It was done.

An amazed ripple ran around the room and Guest gave a little yelp. The queen cleared her throat, glittering eyes wide and bluer than oceans.

'A boon was offered and a boon must be granted. This is your heartfelt request?'

'Yes, your majesty. If it's possible.'

Custenin frowned, sounded worried. 'It's *potentially* possible. But fraught with danger. For you - and for the realm. Will you accept all risk and responsibility for your choice? Do all you can to make this happen? And live with all that may come of it?'

'Yes.'

'Then your request's granted. We'll bring - *him* - home. And a cure will be found at all and any cost. Does this satisfy you? Have we a deal?'

'Yes, your majesty.'

Loud conversation swelled to fill the room as the fae split into smaller groups. Some seemed to be arguing among themselves. I felt an obscure surge of triumph.

Something oddly right.

Placed my mouth close to the Cu Sidhe's ear and whispered 'Life debt paid, my friend.'

He bowed his shaggy head.

*Accepted with gratitude, Lady Briana. Today you've **proved** your blood. Beyond all doubt.*

Curtseying again, I took Fin's arm as we were excused. He didn't look at me. Stared fixedly ahead at the walls or floor. *That* got old before we reached my chambers.

But I waited.

'*What?*' I demanded, whirling on him once the door was decently shut. 'Has my nose fallen off? Has my *face* turned green? Why won't you *look* at me?'

'Oh, Bree.' He sighed, shoulders sagging. 'I can't be around you right now. You dazzle me.'

A courteous half bow for me - a cold glare for Guest - and he was gone. Leaving me alone with the Hound, and Dechtira's overloaded supper trays. The great thing about my Fae blood being called was that I didn't have to be careful about eating Faery food any more.

I *hate* to waste good food.

We ate like hogs.

***

Being impulsive's always landed me in trouble.

It didn't dawn on me – *then* - that I'd blown my chance to go home. I only knew I'd been able to repay the huge Hound I couldn't help but love. And that staying in Faery...

Well. Staying in Faery meant not leaving Fin.

Was I really so shallow? Had I allowed my growing crush on the beautiful Fae lordling to overwhelm me *that* much?

Clearly, I had.

Picturing his laughing face brought a warm glow to my insides. I longed to be near him. Not because I was Fae-struck. Because what I felt demanded it. To drink in the perfection of his face, the graceful way he moved, the way it had felt to be pressed close to his chest...

Stop it, Bree.

This is *not* going to help.

I was left to my own devices for the next few days. Guest

closeted himself with the Seelie Librarian, seeking a cure for his master's madness in the archives. I wandered aimlessly around the castle. Marvelled at the strange and beautiful things I saw.

Without consciously meaning to, I sought Fin everywhere. He'd not shown himself again since I'd made my request. I came to the reluctant conclusion he was avoiding me. Every night I sank disappointed into my huge bed, agonised mind replaying every second of the time I'd spent with him.

Sad, Bree. Really sad.

Tragic.

On the fourth day I found myself in the wide octagonal hall at the base of my tower. The room was bare, save for a large portrait dominating one wall.

A portrait of *me*.

Me, but not. The Fae woman was dressed in the same midnight blue and silver Dechtira kept providing me with. She lacked my silver streak, but the likeness was eerie, if not exact. Her face was a touch longer than mine. Expression cold and haughty.

Even so, I could've used it as a mirror.

'Remarkable, isn't it?'

I turned to see Efnyssen padding across the room towards me. He didn't stop until he was uncomfortably close. Cold blue eyes bored into mine.

'And because of *this*,' he continued. 'Because you're so very like your ancestress, we've allowed you to put into motion the one thing that might doom us all. You stupid *human.*'

He spat the word like a curse.

'We've lived peacefully for centuries. We were *rid* of the madman and his insane warmongering - and *you* want to bring him back! *You*, of all people.'

'I - I don't know what you mean,' I stammered.

He stepped closer, narrowing the distance between us so I could feel him brushing against my bodice.

'*Don't* you?' he asked softly. 'Only one of Morgen's get could've cured his blindness. Just as only Morgen's blood can undo the curse of his madness. The time's coming when it's *you* who'll pay the price for this folly. It would've been easier all around if Finian'd had the grace to use you and pass you on. As he should've done.'

He ran one spindly finger over my breastbone, meaning all too clear.

'I'd have enjoyed you, little mortal. So young and tender and breakable. And you were Fae-struck, too. You wouldn't have denied me. Maybe it's not too late, after all. Your lordling's abandoned you. What do *you* have to offer to keep him around? Other than that long-dead face? You'll need a protector and I'm a power within this court. You could do worse than me.'

He held my shoulders and his mouth came down on mine.

Cruelly hard.

I gasped in pain. Tried to push him away. But he was taller - stronger - than I was. He shoved me hard; my back hitting the wall as he leaned his body into mine. I tried to bring my knee up.

Fast.

My stupid skirts got in the way.

He raised his head, laughing nastily. Mouth stained with the blood I felt trickling from my abused lips. With a look of enjoyment, he licked it away.

'So deliciously sweet, little human. I think you and I'll have *plenty* of time to get to know one another.'

'I wouldn't count on it.' A dagger appeared at Efnyssen's throat.

I slumped with relief as Fin's face appeared over his shoulder.

'Ah, the Lughan brat. Are you jealous, fire lordling? Afraid I'll use her up before *you're* finished with her? I thought you'd realised some time ago you can't stop me taking what I want.'

'Get out. Now.' Fin was incandescently angry. Eyes narrowed and brightly glowing; voice taught and crisp.

The knife pressed closer into flesh and a line of blood appeared at Efnyssen's throat.

'Very well, I'm leaving. For now.' Efnyssen raised his hand to push Fin's aside.

He turned in the doorway. Glared back at me.

'We're not done, *my lady.*'

He retreated in the face of Fin's implacable glare.

I stood frozen, breathless and fearful. Fin put his arms around me and gently drew me to him.

'I should never have left you alone, Bree. You attract *all* the wrong kinds of attention.'

I tried to laugh - it came out a choked sob. He brushed my hair with his lips and murmured softly in that language I couldn't follow. I slipped my arms around his waist and let the steady *thrum thrum* of his heart calm me. My own raced. I stared at the portrait, cheek crushed to his chest.

A small, golden nameplate read 'Morgen le Fey.'

No. Bloody. Way.

I read it again. And marvelled.

'The blood of Morgen,' I murmured. 'The blood of Morgen *le Fey*.'

'What?' Fin raised his head. Turned it to regard the painting. 'Oh. Yes. She was your ancestress.'

'So *that* asshat said. I thought she wasn't real. That she was just a story. My friend Chloe was into all that *years* ago. Does this mean the rest of it's true? There was an Arthur and a Merlin and a round table and everything? Wait while I tell her.'

He winced, glancing round, then laughed at my awestruck expression. 'To a degree. There was certainly an Artor and - his adviser - but I've never heard anything about a table, round or not. Most of the stories you'll have heard in the mortal realm are distortions of the truth. Faery guards it secrets well. The stories *you'll* know are scrambled - and largely untrue. Sometimes there *is* truth there of a kind, though.'

He gazed back at Morgen's portrait. 'I used to love the stories of Morgen and that time when I was younger. I'd stand here looking at her. Wondering what she was like. How she managed to do the things she did - to protect Faery. She must've been lonely at the end. When she cursed your madman to blindness and insanity. I used to imagine I could go back and comfort her.'

'Ohmigod, you had a crush on my Grandma!' My turn to laugh at the sheepish lordling.

He joined in. 'I suppose I did. I was *very* young...'

We laughed again. Suddenly conscious of my heart racing too fast against his chest, I pulled myself out of his embrace and turned to examine the painted face of my ancestress.

'She must've really *hated* Leiloken. To curse him like that,' I said.

'Hate him? No, Bree. She never hated him.' He frowned faintly, sympathy in the look he levelled at the portrait. 'She *loved* him. *Really* loved him - and always had. Fae don't fall in love that way very often.

'But *she* had to break him.

'He got the greatest war host Faery's ever seen massacred. In one pointless, ill-planned battle. His own nephew and brother-in-law were killed. My grandparents and great grandparents, too, and all because of *his* arrogance. Morgen was the only one who *could* stop him. The only one with that kind of power over him. She couldn't live with what she had to do.

'So she sacrificed herself doing it.

'She put her own soul - her *self* - into her mortal bloodline. For safekeeping. So that one day someone *could* save him. They were the most powerful and glamorous couple in Faery. A legend in their own lifetime. And she killed herself to curse him. It must have been unbearable for her.'

'She was very beautiful,' I mused.

'So's her descendant.'

My cheeks flamed with heat and I turned to see Fin flushing a similarly embarrassed red.

'That was inappropriate, Bree. I'm sorry. Let's get you back to your rooms. I'll feel happier knowing you're out of harm's way.'

He'd turned a bit formal again. Disappointed and relieved at once, I couldn't look at him as we climbed the stairs to my room. Wished I knew what to think. Was I reading more into his words than was actually there?

I'd have to be very careful or I'd end up *totally* embarrassing myself.

***

Guest was waiting for us, black muzzle broad in a canine grin.

I've news, little Bree.

'You found a cure?' I was delighted. To reunite the Hound with his master - safe and sane - was the best gift anyone could've given Guest.

*I believe so. I'm afraid I'll need **your** help to achieve it.*

Efnyssen's taunting words floated across my mind for a second. '*...only Morgen's blood can undo the curse of his madness...it's **you** who'll pay the price for this folly...*' I shook my head to rid myself of the uneasiness.

The sense that something significant was hurtling inexorably towards me.

Guest was my friend. I trusted the huge Cu Sidhe implicitly - was sure he'd never do anything to hurt me.

'What can I do?' I slumped into my favourite chair, padded and comfortable before the fire. Listened to the flames crack and pop.

I've found a prophecy in the library which talks about you. Shall I tell you what it says?

'Sure, Guest.' I eased off my shoes. Luxuriated in the feel of the thick rug between my toes. 'Fill me in.'

Very well. It says - 'From a town in Marenhame's forest, a girl shall be sent to remedy these matters by her healing art. Once she's consulted the Seers she'll dry up the noxious springs. Next, when she's restored her own strength by the invigorating drink, she'll carry the forest of Celidon in her right hand and in her left the buttressed forts of London.''

'That's pure nonsense.'

Another drooly, doggy grin.

*Yes, prophecies **can** be rather obscure. The passage before this refers to my master's madness. Which would imply that you - the girl from Marham - are the one who'll heal him. This was **meant** to be.*

'How do you know it's not just rubbish?'

*Because it was my master who said it. He always **was** the best Seer in Faery - sane or not. His sister wrote his prophecies down, and they're stored in the library.*

'Carrying forests? Doesn't sound too hard.' I rolled my eyes, smiling. 'Ok, mutt. Whatever. I'm in.'

Guest laid his head in my lap and I tangled my fingers in his rough-soft fur. Breathed in the smell of dog and woodsmoke and lingering food. Sighed contentedly. My friend was going to get his master back. Fin was around again - *and* he thought I was beautiful. He'd said so himself.

Altogether, I felt faintly smug.

Should've realised it wouldn't last.

◀Chapter Nine▶

If we were going by the prophecy, the first thing I needed to do was consult the Seer. Guest said it'd only take a couple of weeks to get to her underground home. We prepared ourselves for travel.

Dechtira provided me with fitted leather pants and a matching sleeveless jerkin to go over a soft shirt. All in midnight blue and silver. A heavy, soft, blue cloak served to keep the weather off.

Way more practical than the gowns I'd been wearing.

There were even boots. Which fit.

Fin elected himself my bodyguard. I was glad he was coming. The more I was with him, the more I wanted to be. It would've hurt me to my soul to be parted from him.

On the morning of our departure, Queen Rhiannon visited me in my chambers. Two stern faced guards bowed her through the door, withdrawing to wait outside.

'I've a gift for you,' she said, eyes a bright and eager blue and cheeks flushed. 'To show you go with my blessing. I want you to succeed, Briana. The man *you* call Leiloken was my hero as a young woman. I remember how magnificent he was - how brightly he shone. I want him that way again. This is for you.'

She handed me what could've been a silver tennis ball. Strange symbols were etched into the surface and tiny amethysts twinkled from their setting around its centre.

'It's beautiful, your majesty. I'm grateful.'

I was puzzled. Could hear the confusion in my voice.

She smiled and laid a hand on my arm. 'This is one of the last remaining Faery orbs. Maybe *the* last. There's a powerful glamour in them. This one can carry *anything* safely. And has healing properties.

'They said - once - that those who held the orbs held the destiny of all Faery in their hands. We lost the secret of making them aeons ago. I dreamed last night you'd need it, and I believe the goddess sent me the dream. It's yours. Take it, child. Bring him back to us.'

It was hard not to thank her. I curtsied. It was better this time.

'Accepted with gratitude.'

See?

I *can* be polite.

***

We set up camp in deep forest on the fourth night. Finian bent to retrieve his bow and quiver from beside his pack. Sparkling green eyes met mine.

'We'll eat well tonight, Bree.' He grinned with exuberance. 'There's good hunting in these forests. I can practically *guarantee* venison on the menu.'

I laughed at his enthusiasm, leaning back on my own pack and waving my hands in benediction.

'Go and play, silly boy' I dismissed him. 'And I'm holding you to the promise of steak for supper.'

'As my lady commands.' He bowed playfully and ghosted into the overhanging woods, fleet feet soon carrying him out of sight. My eyes lingered on him, pulled by some invisible force every step of the way. I was vaguely aware of Guest watching me, watching him.

*Don't grow **too** fond of him, little Bree. He's not meant for you, nor **you** for **him**. I can see he feels something for you. It may not be wise to encourage him. We used to have a saying...*

Heat scalded my face. I glared at the Hound, cutting him off sharply.

'None of your business, mutt.'

I'm trying to keep you from making a painful mistake. Both of you. I'm concerned. There are things you don't know.

'Yeah, well. When I'm desperate for your advice on my love life - I'll let you know.'

I'd not had time to fully process how I felt about Fin yet. Too new and too raw.

To hear Guest talking about it made me feel as comfortable as if the Hound had reached into my middle and yanked out a handful of guts. If my massive crush was that obvious to a *dog* - how much more obvious must it be to Fin himself? The thought made me squirm. I'd got Fin under my skin. A grain of sand rubbing me raw.

I didn't want to talk about it.

I get like that.

Thankfully, the conversation was cut short. A ragged group of bearded Portune approached us through the trees. They were in a grim state. Most were bandaged and limping. Some leaned on others for support. One was borne in a litter. They stopped a short distance from us, and the leader stepped forward. Bowed.

'May we share your fire? We're tired and injured. We'll owe you'

We ask for no debt. You're welcome here, small ones.

Guest inclined his head to the little guy.

'Our gratitude.'

The small men grouped themselves around the fire. Most slumped to the ground or leant against trees, sagging with tiredness and defeat. It was clear something dreadful had happened to them.

They were *exhausted*.

I did what I could to help clean and re-bandage damaged heads and limbs. Some of the injuries were horrific. Angry and weeping flesh caked in filth. The smell was beyond description. Putrid and wrong and sick-sweet with infection. I couldn't help cringing. But I gritted my teeth, and did my best for them.

The leader of the band came to sit beside me when I'd finished.

'Does the lady remember me?' he asked.

I realised now this was the Portune we'd taken to the Brownie after the Spriggan attack. Smiled to see him.

'Is your arm better now?'

'Oh yes. You saved me. I owe you a life debt and I'll not forget it.'

'You don't owe me anything. It was the right thing to do.'

'Many wouldn't see it so. Accept the pledge of Chief Aodhan of the Portune. Call on us when you need us and we'll be there.'

He didn't look like any chief *I* could've imagined. His hat was gone and his clothing tattered. None of the other little men looked any better.

'Accepted with gratitude, Chief Aodhan. I'm Bree. I mean, Briana of the line of Morgen.'

He looked at me for a moment with his head on one side.

'Lady's changed,' he said.

'Yes, they called my Fae blood. I was Fae-struck.'

'Lady looks like Morgen. Lady *feels* like Morgen. Portune were friends to the Water Lady. We'll be friends to Lady Bree, also.'

I smiled and gave him an impulsive hug in lieu of thanks.

He was just that cute.

***

Fin returned with venison, as promised. I was glad he'd done the messy business of gutting and skinning the animal somewhere else. I *was* going to eat it - but I *didn't* want the mental image of the dead deer ruining my appetite.

Especially after tending to the injured Portune.

Ugh.

It was thoughtful of him and I appreciated it. There was plenty for everyone and - after the Portune'd contributed vegetables - we dined on a more than passable meal.

Fin asked the Portune what'd happened to them. It was a gnarled little man with a dreadful slash across his face who answered. He spat into the fire.

'Evil things coming, Fae lord. Portune's lands and little gardens were attacked. Black, twisted giants with dark blades. They burned our homes and trampled our crops.' He snarled, angry. 'Many died trying to defend the village but there were too many of 'em. They took our children and wives for slaves and slaughtered half our men. We escaped. Fourteen of us of the hundred in our village. All the others taken or killed.'

'That's *terrible!*' I gasped.

Guest rumbled a low growl and Fin's face was set. Almost blank. Purely Fae, and alien in its sternness

'Something needs to be done about this,' said Fin.

*I agree. You Portune are the backbone of Faery. Your good crops and care for nature keep us fed - **and** form the base of our medicines. This can't be allowed.*

'Ha! And what can the two of you do? You don't understand. There are too many. Musta been at least sixty just for our little village. We're going to Tir na n'Og. Maybe the king will send help - maybe not.

'He's got to be warned either way. It doesn't end with Portune lands. Ulla and Purt, there,' He indicated the two with the worst injuries. 'They were injured when we tried to get through Celidon. Black things were there too. Burning and destroying. We lost three *that* day.'

'Surely the king'll send people to deal with it?' I asked.

'I hope so,' said Fin, paling. 'If they're burning Celidon, Dryads are dying, too. They only live as long as their tree.'

'Just so.' Aodhan jerked his bearded chin in a grim nod. Was still perched on a tree root beside me. 'Dryads are dying by the score. These creatures respect nothing. *Care* nothing for the bounties of nature. They burned the nursery trees where young acorns are fostered before they grow. Dryad babies burned to death before they'd even lived. That I should live to see *this*.'

I was horrified. Sick to the stomach.

'They killed the *babies*?'

'Baby acorns, baby Dryads. Dryads grow with their tree. They burned at least fifty I saw. I saved these, though.' He held up a small pouch, gently tipping out around a dozen acorns. They visibly pulsed and glowed with tightly furled energy.

I stroked one. It hummed under my hand, pulsing excitedly.

'They like you.' Aodhan smiled. 'Maybe acorns should go with you. Lady Bree can hide them away till we find a tree to foster them.'

'My father has citrus groves on his lands,' said Fin. 'You might be able to persuade the trees there to foster the acorns. Tell him what you've told me, and that I sent you.'

'That's kind. We'll accept and be grateful. Lady Bree will take acorns till Portune can come to Lughan lands? Will help Portune save the Dryads?'

'Of course I will.'

I didn't even have to think about it.

Aodhan scooped up the acorns and placed them tenderly back in the pouch. He offered it to me and I took it. As I went to put it in my belt pouch, the silver orb inside began to glow and - with a *blip* - the parcel of acorns melted into it.

It was the *weirdest* thing. The little guy patted my hand.

'Safest in there' he said. Winked once. Sideways.

I met Fin's eyes and he nodded reassuringly, with a soft smile.

That smile made my heart thump oddly. I swallowed. Looked away, afraid of what my face might reveal. The mention of his father's lands made me realise how little I knew about him. I knew he had brothers, but what about sisters? What had it been like growing up in Faery? I guessed it'd been a happy time, or he wouldn't be so lighthearted about everything.

At that moment, I could've devoted my life to learning all there was to know about him.

Yep. Massive, *massive* crush.

I'd never been one of those girls at college whose lives obsessively revolved around who they were dating or who they fancied. I always thought they were kind of dumb.

Congratulations, Bree.

You just turned into one of them.

***

The Portune were up with the dawn, preparing to leave. Before they went, Guest loped a little way off into the forest, Aodhan at his side. They spoke earnestly in low tones for a while before rejoining us.

Guest gave me a serious look. Shaggy brows lowered over blazing eyes.

*They're burning Celidon. I have to leave you now - to retrieve my master. If I leave it any longer the way may be impassable. I'm sorry to do this to you, little Bree. But I **must** get to my master. And bring him safely home.*

'I understand.' I was saddened, tears prickling the edges of my eyes. 'I wish you were coming with us. But I understand.'

Fin came to stand beside me and placed his arm round my shoulders. My stomach fluttered.

'I'll keep her safe. I promise.'

I'm sure you will. The Hound sounded amused. *There'll be a reckoning if you don't.*

As they were about to leave, I bent to hug Aodhan. He squeezed me with a surprising amount of strength for such a little creature. Those small arms were like iron bars.

'Remember, Lady Bree,' he said. 'You call on the Portune for help and we'll come. We'll always come.'

Brave as I was trying to be, I was a bit lost without Guest.

He'd been there all the way through my strange sojourn in Faery. I missed him. He was my friend, comforter and guide. Being alone with Fin was simultaneously exhilarating and terrifying.

We talked and laughed endlessly on that long walk.

I learned a bit about his childhood, which sounded happy. He told me about his brothers, Bevin and Peredur. Fin was the youngest, and had taken his fair share of teasing, I gathered.

I was surprised - and a little bit impressed - to discover Rhiannon was his cousin. There *was* a family resemblance, when I thought about it. Something around the eyes and chin.

He gave me his hand to help me over tangled roots and my skin tingled at his touch. More than once, I caught him looking at me as though he was on the verge of speech.

But every time he'd make a joke.

Or look away.

His bow was a permanent presence in his hand. He *said* he

was keeping an eye out for dinner. I suspected he was staying alert because of what the Portune reported. Was trying not to frighten me by letting on. I was even more suspicious when he insisted on giving me his long dagger, and fixed it to my belt. I stood there hardly daring to breathe as he refastened it at my waist. Sending those thrilling shocks through me.

'You can't rely on there always being a handy branch about to hit things with,' he said, referring to my encounter with the Spriggan.

Aodhan and Guest had told the story. I was still embarrassed how brave they'd made me sound.

'I can't believe how funny you find that. What was I supposed to do? Let them *eat* him?'

'A lot of Fae would.' He reached around my waist as he settled my belt so the enamelled hilt was in easy reach.

'I'm not Fae.'

I wanted him to leave his arms around me. To pull me closer. For a long moment I thought he was going to. He paused, an unreadable expression on his face. Green eyes met mine, dark as the forest and glowing like Christmas tree lights.

We froze.

The longest, stillest moment.

'No, you're not, are you? It's very easy to forget that sometimes.'

He stepped back and I nearly growled with frustration. Turning to retrieve our packs, we continued on our way.

Helen Sutton

***

The forest ended and we made our way over rolling moorland. Scrub heather and mosses, green and purple, dotted the landscape. Raw, jagged stone tore free of the vegetation to stand proud against grey sky. It was wild and barren - leaving me feeling tiny and insignificant against its immensity.

Fin assured me we were close to the Seer's home.

It was late, the sun having long since sagged beneath the horizon. Our fire was tiny but dazzling in the drizzling darkness. I couldn't for the *life* of me figure out how he was keeping it lit.

He fed it steadily, and it danced happily for him.

We sat shoulder to shoulder in a small hollow, sheltering us from the howling wind. He'd been in a strange mood all day, brooding and distant. Thoughtful. So unlike himself I was unsure how to treat him. I cast around for something to break the silence, squirmily uneasy.

'Is there anything I should know before we get there?' I asked. 'Now would be the time to fill me in on things I'll shout at you for *not* telling me, later.'

He gave a brief smile. 'Just that if you're claustrophobic, you won't enjoy going through the caves very much. Actually, I've never been down there. So we'll have to learn together.'

'Right.'

We sat in silence for several more minutes. Scent of woodsmoke and wet heather. Fin stared into the fire, lost in thought. I rooted around in my pack, pretending to look for something. Trying to hide my discomfort.

Eventually, I could stand it no longer.

I raised my head. Fixed him with a level look. 'Fin, are you ok? You've been in a really funny mood all day.'

He turned to me, shoulder brushing against mine. Green eyes intently scanning my face as he drew a long breath. Warring with some internal decision, judging by the way his shoulders tensed and the odd look he wore.

I was suddenly afraid of whatever he was going to say.

'I don't *know* if I'm ok,' he said. 'I don't think I can talk about it. It's a little strange.'

I nudged his shoulder with mine, his warmth radiating through our cloaks.

'Come on. Talk to me. Isn't that what friends are *for*?'

He frowned, a serious expression on his perfect face. 'I don't want to be your friend, Bree.'

'You don't?' My voice sounded terribly small.

'No.'

My heart stopped.

He tentatively cupped my face in his hands and I caught a waft of the wonderful sunshine spice smell that was him. The look in his eyes made the breath catch in my throat, my stomach somersault.

Slowly, as though asking permission, he lowered his lips to mine.

And kissed me.

Gently at first, then more firmly. His mouth moving against mine, warm and soft. Fireworks burst behind my eyes as he put his arms around me, pulled me closer. I kissed him back hungrily, wanting to savour his lips.

It lasted for about a hundred years.

When we broke apart I was breathless. And utterly speechless for the first time since I'd met him. He grinned, warm and incandescent.

'I think I've finally found a way of shutting you up.'

'Please will you shut me up again?' I asked, pulse racing madly.

He did.

And then he shut me up a few more times for good measure.

I'd never *been* so wildly happy.

◀Chapter Ten▶

There was a narrow fissure in the rock at the base of a small escarpment. Fin eased himself through, holding out a hand for the packs and helping me follow. It was a tight squeeze and I swore as I scraped my elbow. He grinned at me, holding aloft a small cage containing a couple of light sprites.

'Not far now,' he said. 'You ok?'

'Mmm.'

I didn't trust myself to say more without betraying my state of blind panic.

My throat was dry. The narrow cleft falling away into the darkness ahead was a tight squeeze. I'd imagined the caves as being something like Leiloken's spacious cavern. This was basically pot-holing. Dreadful thoughts of being trapped miles beneath the ground.

It was hard going.

The panic expanded in my throat - an iron bubble of pressure - until it was all I could do not to scream. Finally the way widened, and we eased or way round one last craggy outcrop and into an open space. The small circle of illumination provided by the sprites offered safety in the surrounding darkness. I stepped past Fin, peering into the inkiness beyond it.

The ground fell away from my feet. I teetered on the edge of a slope, only Fin's rapid reflexes as he caught my arm preventing me from falling. Heard the stones I'd loosened bouncing away.

They fell for a *long* time.

He swung the cage closer and I saw we stood at the top of a steep slope dropping away into the echoing nothing. I shuddered. Trying not to imagine my broken body in a heap at the bottom.

A warm arm snaked round my waist, pulling me close. My head sank against Fin's chest for a moment and he gave a shaky laugh.

'Don't they tell human children about looking before they leap?'

'Yeah. Clearly I should've been listening.' I pulled a wry face.

Our voices were loud in the hushed air. All that stone oppressive over our heads. Fin looked around, using his bow to feel for safe footing.

'We're going to have to climb,' he said, releasing me and

dropping easily to his haunches. He held the cage low before him, examining the rocky slope. 'It won't be easy - but it *can* be done.'

'Hooray,' I said weakly, giving him a double thumbs up. He smiled, all warmth and sunlight.

'I'll go first and help you over the awkward bits,' he promised. 'You'll be fine.'

He attached the cage to his belt and swung himself down the first few feet. I held onto his hand and followed.

It was a nightmarish climb.

Not being able to see beyond a couple of feet made the descent unbearable. We edged sideways more than once to find a passable bit - and several times Fin had to steady me as I lost my purchase on the almost vertical slope.

The agile Fae may've had catlike grace - but I *didn't*. And not knowing how far there was to fall terrified me. I hoped there was another way out, because I'd never be able to climb back up.

Even if I'd wanted to.

Which I categorically did *not*.

Finally it was over. We found ourselves standing on a sandy spur at the edge of a lake whose edges were lost in darkness. The water was black and still. I folded my trembling legs beneath me and sank to the ground.

Fin moved to the water's edge, crouching to clean the grit from his hands.

'That's cold.' He winced, voice echoing oddly.

The surface of the lake *erupted*.

A tall plume of water fountained into the air with a loud splash. Two immensely long, sinewy arms took hold of Fin.

He yelled in surprise.

Struggled to haul himself upright as he was pulled towards the surface of the water. Purple-nailed claws sheared through leather, biting fiercely into flesh. He managed to get hold of his knife. But the arms allowed him little room to move. It fell from his grip.

He was being dragged further in.

I *screamed*.

An icy anger wrapped itself around me. Uncoiled from somewhere behind my eyes and raged through every limb, urgent and determined.

Leaping to my feet, I fumbled Fin's dagger free of my belt. Threw myself at the arms, slashing wildly.

'Don't stab *me*.' He was in past his knees now.

A head broke the surface, noseless face dripping green slime as it turned towards us. Shark-like rows of teeth oozed black spittle as it snarled. I managed to get sink the dagger into the withered flesh of one forearm.

Hissing, the creature focussed its attention on me.

And stopped.

'Why are you hurting me, Water Lady? It's Peg. You weren't so cruel to river hags before.' The gurgling voice sounded puzzled.

Fated

She thought I was Morgen.

'Peg Powler,' said Fin. 'You were banished *centuries* ago. I've heard of you.'

'Should have listened to your mother then, Seelie boy, and stayed away from the water. There'll be sweet eating tonight. Tender Fae flesh to fill our bellies.'

She licked her blackened lips.

'Leave him alone. *Please*. Let him go.' I hoped Peg couldn't hear the desperation in my voice.

My mind ticked over rapidly, wondering if my resemblance to Morgen might actually help.

For once.

She looked enquiringly at me. 'What will you give in return if I do? I'm hungry - and travellers are few.'

'I'll bring you something else to eat. After we get out of here. I'll find something for you.'

'Take your shiny knife out of my arm and we'll talk, Lady.'

'Let go of Fin and we'll talk, Peg.'

We stared at each other in stalemate for a long moment. Peg's multi-knuckled hands unwrapped themselves from Fin. I jerked my dagger free of her arm and staggered back a few paces. Felt Fin's hand on the small of my back, steadying and warming me.

'Seems he's important to you, Lady. I think *he* might cost you more than a meal.'

'What do you want?'

'A meal eaten in *freedom*.' She hissed, striking at the surface with the flat of her hand and sending up a shower of glimmering droplets. 'We want to leave this nasty place you left us in. Surely we've been punished long enough? And for such a slight transgression?'

We kept edging our way up the spur.

'I'm not her. I'm not who you think I am. I don't *have* power like that.'

Peg's eyes narrowed, calculating.

'If you're not her, then you've her blood. I *know* Morgen. Know her face and feel. You *can* free the river hags. My sisters are starving, and we've been rotting down here for too long. Spill some of that precious blood of yours near water and call me three times. I'll eat whatever's closest - so don't let it be you.' Her tone was matter of fact. 'It has to be alive, nothing smaller than a sheep.'

'That sounds easy enough.'

'Bree...' began Fin warningly.

'No.' I didn't look at him. 'Carry on, Peg.'

'Don't be thinking you can double cross me either, Morgen girl. If you haven't kept your word in six weeks, I'll be free anyway under the terms of the binding. And then I'm coming after *you*. With Morgen's blood in your veins, you'll taste *amazing*.' She smirked at me.

'If I do this, you can't come after me. Or Fin. Is that a deal?'

'*Bree*.' Finian again, a little more urgent.

Fated

The river hag pursed her lips at me.

'We've a deal,' she said.

She drew her long arms in and sank below the surface again. When we were sure she was really gone, we stood with our arms wrapped around one another for a couple of minutes. Fin dropped a kiss on top of my head.

'Wait here. I'm going to see if there's another way out.'

He clambered up a way, easing himself along the slope. The glow from the light sprites faded into the dark. It seemed an eternity before he reappeared and dropped lightly to his feet beside me.

'There's a kind of beach a bit further along and - even better for us - there's a boat.'

He shouldered his pack again and helped me haul myself up the first few sheer feet before taking the lead. The beach was a little bigger than the rocky spur had been. And there was indeed a small wooden boat.

Of sorts.

'Will it actually float?' I asked, eyeing it sceptically as Fin threw our packs in.

'Only one way to find out.' He pushed the rickety craft out onto the water, holding the side. 'Seems sturdy enough. Come and get in.'

Once I was aboard he swung himself in after me and took the oars. I held the cage up to light the way. It was a long eerie journey into the darkness, with the steady oars beating a hypnotic rhythm - and the thought of what might be below us preying on my mind.

We spoke in low tones, our voices echoing. Something occurred to me.

'Fin, when I was ill at Tir na n'Og. Did you kiss me?'

He coloured. 'I did warn you I was only flesh and blood the night I met you.'

'Why did you do it?'

'Don't you know? You're beautiful, Bree.' His smile warmed me as much as the heated glow in those emerald eyes. 'You must have *some* idea how I feel about you, by now.'

'Do you know how I feel about *you*?'

'I got the impression you were quite fond of me last night.'

'You could say that,' I smiled, vowing internally that as soon as I got chance I was going to kiss him over and over.

Until he had *much* more than an impression.

Both feeling awkward, we dropped the subject.

***

The lake became a river, ending in another cavern. The whole thing was a huge sinkhole, open to the elements. Daylight sparked off immense stalactites, illuminating an island in the centre of the lake. On it stood a tiny cottage in a grove of apple trees. A plump cow grazed on the lush grass between them and, as I marvelled at this unexpected sight, we bumped against the shore.

Fin helped me out, laughing tiredly as I slipped on the slick surface of the lake bed and landed with a bump on my rear end.

Now I was wringing wet as well as embarrassed.

Perfect.

He heaved the craft up past the water line and hefted our packs onto the shore. The wounds Peg had inflicted were bleeding freely. Fin'd gone unnaturally pale. I caught his arm, worry gnawing at my ribs.

'You're hurt. Fin, we need to get those looked at.'

'I'll be fine. Let's just do what we came here for, and *then* we can worry about everything else.' He tilted my face towards his and softly kissed me behind a sleek curtain of blood copper hair.

I'd have happily encouraged him to do that all day - but the sound of a steady *creak creak* intruded on the moment.

A woman sat at a spinning wheel by the cottage door.

Her foot on the treadle was the source of the sound and she continued to work as we approached. She looked up and I gasped. Her teeth were long and square, extending well beyond her mouth. The foot on the treadle was big and flat, the other small as a child's. With her wrinkled face, straggly white hair and long nose - complete with wart - she was the wicked witch from every fairy tale I'd ever read.

'You're welcome here.' Her voice was as old and creaky as her spinning wheel. 'Come inside and I'll see to your comfort. It's been a long time since any of the Fae visited me.'

'We'll accept your hospitality gratefully, mother.' Fin's

courtly half bow was less fluid than usual.

He looked exhausted. Shaky.

Inside, the cottage was neat and homely. A fire glowed in the hearth and we crowded it, shivering in our wet clothes. The old woman bustled about setting the table and disappearing into another room. She returned with dry clothing.

'Put these on for now,' she said. 'No doubt whatever's in your packs'll be wet, too. You can dry them off on the line over the fire. I'm guessing you'll be here till morning so there's plenty of time.' She flapped impatient hands at us. 'Well, go *on*, then.'

Fin made me go first and I scurried into the back room clutching the loose gown. Blissful to be dry and warm. To smell baking and a hint of apples. When Fin had changed in turn, we were presented with a table laden with food. I hastened to fill my growling stomach with bread, cheese, and scones dripping with butter and honey.

Delicious.

I almost *cheered* when she produced a still-warm apple pie.

The smell alone was almost enough to make me swoon.

Fin filled the old woman in on the doings of the Seelie Court. She seemed to find it amusing, rocking with laughter more than once.

Eventually, he brought her up to speed on our mission.

She frowned, looking at me thoughtfully. Withered fingertips tapped together.

'It won't be easy, girl. Are you *certain* this is what you want? There may be – *repercussions*. For others. And for you.'

I lifted my chin. Replied firmly.

'I'm sure. Can you help me?'

'I can and I will. What does your young man think of all this?' She raised a sparse eyebrow at Fin.

'I'm behind Bree every step of the way.' He was as firm as I'd been. 'I won't let anything happen to her.'

She chuckled. 'May the goddess preserve us from star-crossed lovers! That's sweet, young Lughan. Useless - but sweet. You can't go where she's going. It'd kill you faster than a hungry river hag.'

How'd she know about *that*?

I bit my lip uneasily. 'Where am I going? What do I have to do?'

'*You've* no idea? Really? You come to Mother Holle – to a *Seer* - for advice, but you've spent time with the best of us. Didn't *he* tell you anything? Hard to imagine he wouldn't. To *you*.'

'*Leiloken*?' I was startled.

'Leiloken.' She rolled it around her mouth, foot tapping absently. 'Is *that* what they're calling him now? Not that they've much choice, poor boy, with Morgen cursing even his name. The name *she* gave him, at that. Can't be spoken in Faery. Bit of a bitch, sometimes, your ancestor.'

'*That's not true.*' Fin stood angrily, swaying on his feet.

I reached to steady him but his eyes rolled back into his head, and he dropped to the floor.

A broken marionette, face grey.

I fell to my knees beside him in panic, looking at Mother Holle. 'Help him. *Please* help him. He's hurt. Peg Powler...'

'I *know*, girl.' She bent to lift him and I helped her half-carry, half-drag Fin to the bed in the back room.

She unlaced his top and we removed it.

My heart sank at the sight.

Peg's claws had gone deep and the wounds were inflamed and angry. Tiny red lines radiated out from them, crawling across his arms and shoulders.

I swallowed hard against the knot in my throat. 'They're infected.'

'Yes. The river hags have very nasty venom in their claws. They don't let people go so easily. What did you promise them?'

'A meal later on. Can you help him?' I thought of the healer at Tir na n'Og.

Hoped the old woman had similar skills.

'I can, but it'll take time. You're on your own from here, Morgen girl. Are you still determined to do this?'

I hesitated, looking at Fin's clammy face. Wanted to stay with him till he was well.

As he'd done for me.

'Faery needs her prophets *and* her warriors, Briana. And

soon.' She spoke softly. Gently. 'You'll gain us both. We're as doomed without your *Leiloken*, as he is without you and this young lordling here. Finian Medyr has an important part to play in what lies ahead. I'll keep him safe and well till you're back.'

She busied herself tending Fin's wounds and I wandered outside, thoughts whirling. Aimlessly, I wandered among the apple trees, picking up the fallen fruit and making a pile near the cottage door. The repetitive exercise cleared my mind.

I went to Mother Holle, jerking my chin challengingly at her.

'I'm going. I *have* to. Tell me what to do. Please?'

She smiled. A grandmother's smile, full of affection and approval. 'There's a cave deep in a far-off land, where three springs flow from the rock. One'll kill you instantly if you drink from it. The earth won't accept the bodies of those who die that way. The second will curse you with an unbearable hunger that never ends, no matter what you eat. And the third, *well*...

'The third spring is the reason you're going. It cures all ailments and grants long life. Not to mention a rather useful immunity from natural illnesses. Your Leiloken needs the water of *that* one. If it's *you* that gives it to him, he'll be cured.'

'He said something about three springs when I was with him.'

'Yes, I suspect he's known about this for a long time. Which must've been hard. But it needs Morgen's blood to do it. Your blood. You. What did the queen give you? I couldn't see it clearly.'

I showed her and she beamed with pleasure. 'Very generous of Rhiannon, under the circumstances. Keep it close, child, and keep it *yours*. That's important. Not just for now - for *this* - but for your darkest hours to come. For now, you'll need it to carry the water. Listen, you'll need to find a way to dry up the cursed springs. You'll not be able to take water away from the third till you do.'

'How?'

'That I *don't* know - if your madman couldn't tell you. You'll have to work it out yourself. I'll tell you this, though. You'd have been better off doing this *before* they called your Fae blood. That cave's saturated with iron. None of the fae can get in.

'I hope you're human enough to survive it.'

I hoped so, too.

◀Chapter Eleven▶

I spent the night watching Fin anxiously as he tossed and muttered feverishly. Mother Holle told me he wouldn't wake again until the wounds were free of infection. My heart constricted at the thought of leaving him without saying goodbye. What if he woke and thought I hadn't cared enough to stay? I tried to sleep but it came fitfully. Morning arrived too soon.

'I'm coming back,' I promised, bending to kiss him. To stroke his hair back. To savour that lemons and lightning aroma. 'You just *watch*. I'm coming back.'

Mother Holle insisted I stuff my clenched and reluctant stomach with a hearty breakfast.

I'd have enjoyed it, if Fin'd been sitting next to me.

Hoisting my pack onto my shoulders, my leaden heart almost failed me as Mother Holle led me to a round doorway set in a mound at the rear of the cottage.

'I'll open a door through the Elsewhere and get you as close as I can,' she said. 'It's not a precise art, at best. Not for *most* of us, though there was *one* who could do it almost anywhere. And it needs to be a place where the veil through the Elsewhere is thin enough I won't tear it. I don't know how long I'll be able to hold it open, but I won't shut it until I have to. Your young lordling will be safe with me.'

'You can just do that? Open doorways, I mean?'

'Oh yes, all Seers can. This particular door's rather special, though.'

'Will you send me home one day? When this is all over?'

'When this is all over, I won't need to. Your Leiloken'll do it. But remember time flows differently in Faery. When you do go home, you may not find what you're expecting. If going back is what you really want? Do you *know* what it is you want, yet?' She looked at me quizzically.

I cleared my throat and put my hand on the doorknob.

A nagging thought made me turn back.

'How will I know which spring's which?'

'You won't. No-one does. You'll find a way to work it out.' She kissed my cheek. 'Now go. You aren't the only one who needs me, you know.'

I nodded, my thoughts with the Fae I was leaving.

Taking a deep breath, I stepped through the door.

***

Fated

Into glowing white fog. A wrenching feeling disoriented me when I stepped through and I stumbled. I hadn't noticed it when I was running from Leiloken.

Guess I was too scared.

This time I *did* notice - and it was nice when it stopped.

My breath hung misty in the air. I was alone for the first time since Guest found me in Celidon. With a heavy head, and stomach a knotted mass of tension, I walked through the trees around me.

And gaped in astonishment.

I was in a children's park. In the human realm.

Swings, slide, *everything*. An actual park with actual human children. In a daze - half afraid the old woman had tricked me - I slowly walked along the path through the green space.

Someone was selling hot dogs. The scent of frying onions wasn't helping my stomach one bit.

No-one looked twice at my weird clothes, which seemed kind of odd - until I looked down and saw myself dressed in my default sweater and jeans. Mother Holle must've glamoured me, I thought. When I touched my clothes, my hands met the pants and jerkin I'd been wearing. My fingers felt for the pouch at my belt, for the hilt of Fin's knife.

Still there.

Good.

Other girls wandered hand in hand with their boyfriends,

and I felt a sharp pang of longing for Fin. Had to close my eyes and breathe deeply. In my miserable state, it took a second or so for a comment made by a man on his mobile to sink in.

I ran after him.

'Excuse me. Sorry. Did you say it was Halloween *tomorrow*?'

'Yes.' He looked at me strangely. Continued walking.

I thought about that.

Took a few paces after him, and grabbed the sleeve of his jacket.

'What year?'

'Sorry?' He shook me off.

'What year is it?'

He told me, leaving me gaping after him as he muttered into his phone about stupid kids. I'd been warned time flowed differently in Faery.

I just hadn't realised how differently.

It was the day before I met Leiloken.

I'd never left.

Ignoring the dull thrumming pulsing darkly through my head, I thought quickly. I was still out there somewhere, planning to go to Jack's party with Chloe. Not knowing I was being hunted. I could warn myself.

Yeah, right.

Like I'd listen.

Even if I stopped myself going through the gorge, I'd already been Marked by the Wild Hunt. They'd come for me no matter *where* I went. And what would happen without Guest and his master to save me?

I'd die.

I could ring Mum; let her know I was ok. But how? And what reason could I give? I was still there. Hadn't left yet. Besides, I concluded with a reluctant sigh, if I hadn't gone into Faery I wouldn't be here now to call her. But I was.

So clearly I didn't.

Paradox *sucks*.

The thrumming was louder. A sudden, bone-aching tiredness seized me. In the hilly slope a cave mouth gaped, snarling out the noise. This must be the place, the feeling the iron. The closer I got, the stronger it was - and the more drained I felt.

My mouth was choked with grit. Breathing difficult.

I forced my legs to keep moving. As I approached, a small boy sat for a second on seemingly insubstantial air, tying a shoelace. It took a few seconds to understand that for him the cave mouth simply wasn't there. When he stood, I took another pace forward.

And *screamed* - as a whiplash of burning pain tore through my shoulder.

An arrow had gone right through it.

I sank to the ground, dizzy.

The kid gave me a scared look and ran off. I looked round to see a vaguely familiar Fae glaring at me, arrow nocked to fire. Spiky silver hair like a manga character, full of leaves and twigs. Clothing a weird mish-mash of fur and feathers, leaves and leather.

'We haven't forgotten you, girlie. You were *ours* before the Barghest and the loony took you. Every time *you* set foot in this realm,' He grinned, and I saw the sharp and bloody teeth I'd glimpsed that day on the bridge. '*We* hunt.'

'Please,' I said uselessly, twisting round to look up at him.

He snickered. 'We *like* it when you beg. Try and remember to do that when we finally kill you. It'll cheer us all right up. Being Morgen's whelp won't do you any good out *here*. What made you stupid enough to come back, anyway? Didn't they *tell* you we'd be waiting?'

I felt the utter despair of failure.

'I was going to cure the Barghest's master.'

If I was about to die, I may as well tell the truth.

The bow dropped to his side and he tilted his head, birdlike. '*Well* now, sweetheart. We might just want to talk about that. I thought the Seelie were all so knicker-wettingly afraid of him they'd rather *die* than see him cured?'

'I got that impression, yeah.'

'And you're going in there?' He gestured thoughtfully towards the cave mouth.

I nodded.

Fated

'You've got a bloody death wish. Can't you *feel* the iron?' He paused for a moment. Rolled glittering black eyes.'Oh, *alright*. That was your last warning shot, sweetheart. Next time we find you in this realm we'll hunt you. Go. Cure the fruit-loop. I hope it brings the Seelie *years* of suffering.' He grinned like a switchblade. 'Tell him to give them hell from me.'

I clambered to my feet, shoulder burning. The strange thrumming split my head. It was all I could do to stagger to the entrance.

Looking back, I saw the Fae boy watching me. He waved sarcastically.

I stepped into the grotto.

***

The sound of iron was louder in here. Once inside I was overcome with dizziness, slumping to the floor. The venom of the elf-shot almost killed me the first time - and I was stuck here *without* Leiloken to heal me.

Better find that healing spring fast, Bree.

As the old woman said, three springs trickled from fissures in the cave wall. I'd no idea how to work out which was which. I hauled myself along to the closest. Figured I was dying anyway - so it hardly mattered if I got it wrong.

I splashed a little of the icy water into my mouth.

And waited.

My stomach roared, hunger ravening my insides. Food obsessed me.

I yanked my pack from my back and *tore* through the provisions Mother Holle'd packed. Whole loaves of bread and an entire salted ham were crammed into my mouth as I swallowed, almost without chewing.

The obscene hunger didn't ease.

Wrong spring, Bree. Still two to choose from.

I crawled to the entrance and poked my head out, ignoring the insistent gnawing in my stomach. The strange Fae was still there.

'Shall I get you a drink of water, Sonic?' I asked sweetly.

He flashed that sharp grin and turned to leave. Glanced back over his angular shoulder.

'Nice try. I wasn't born *yesterday*, sweetheart.'

Vanished in seconds.

I looked at the other springs. The hunger and the pain were making it hard to think. How would I know which to choose? I plucked up my courage and decided on the lower of the two. The water looked cleaner, which *had* to be good. Right?

Something dropped to the floor nearby.

'Use the bloody bird.' A voice from outside.

The Fae boy.

A starling with a broken wing was flapping wildly, trying to get away. If I was right, this spring would cure it. I made a grab for it with my good arm. Captured it after a brief struggle. Holding it gently, I dribbled a few drops of spring water into its beak and watched anxiously, my stomach burning with hunger.

The bird cheeped wildly for a second then stiffened.

Dead.

Damn.

I hadn't wanted that to happen.

Lunging at the remaining spring, I dipped my hand. And drank.

Pain first, but brief. A feeling of immense well-being ran through me and I watched the arrow force its way from my flesh to fall to the floor. Unnerving clatter as it landed. The wound slowly closed before my eyes, dreadful hunger dying away. The thrumming weakness of the iron was bearable now.

I could finally think. Clearly.

Leiloken *had* spoken of the springs. His words teased the edges of my memory. I stood there, breath hanging white in the cold.

Trying to remember.

'... it won't be the same till you breathe on the springs. I've seen it ... tell them the three springs will wash away what was given, tell them ...'

I looked at the clouds of my breath.

Breathe on the springs, madman?

You got it.

Leaning towards the hunger spring, I puffed my misty breath at the water before doing the same to the one which killed the bird. With a mighty *craaacck* the cave wall sealed itself shut.

Stopping their flow.

Maybe *not* so mad, after all.

I took out the orb and held it towards the trickling water.

The flow increased suddenly as the fissure from which it sprang cracked wider. The water began to lift away from the wall and rose until it was a ribbon whirling through the air around my head. A glittering, glimmering whirl of dancing diamonds and sparkling rainbow droplets. It circled me faster and faster before diving at the orb and being absorbed by the glowing ball.

The wall healed itself with another crack, the ground tremoring underfoot as bits of stone began to fall.

The grotto was shaking apart.

I grabbed my fallen pack and threw myself through the entrance. Not a moment too soon. It collapsed in a roaring cloud of dust.

Firm hands grabbed me by the shoulders and hauled me to my feet.

'*Run*,' said the Huntsman. 'Get out of here before the others come to see what's happening. They're still here - looking for you.'

I must have looked confused again, because he added. 'One last chance, remember? Go and screw the Seelie over for me. *Cure* him. *Go.*'

I went.

Ran back the way I'd come, listening for the horn call that'd tell me I'd been spotted.

It came. Brassy and eerie.

I sprinted with all I had in me, weaving between the trees and into the bank of mist, heart pounding. Legs screaming with exertion. I felt that strange wrench again and fell, hitting the ground hard. Panting, I rolled over and looked up.

Into the smiling eyes of Finian.

'Well, *finally*,' he said.

◀Chapter Twelve▶

Time flows differently in Faery.

I knew that. But was still startled to hear that for Fin and Mother Holle it'd been over a fortnight. It'd taken all her powers of persuasion to stop him from following me into the Elsewhere.

Only the dire threat he'd cause me to fail if he *did* finally convinced him.

He was completely recovered now, and we wasted no time asking Mother Holle to send us to Tir Na n'Og. She opened a door in a cracked apple tree. Put us down a little over a day from the city.

We arrived late, but were shown straight to Rhiannon's private rooms. They were as golden and glittering as she was. Deep window embrasures and gilt edging every surface. She paced towards us, hands half extended in welcome. Blue eyes glowing brightly.

'Did you get it?' she asked eagerly.

'Yes, your majesty.'

Her smile was brilliant, eyes filling with a moist sheen. 'Waste no time in giving it to him, then. He's been - difficult - since he and the Barghest got here. We've had to post guards outside his rooms.'

'Where would I find them?'

She sent a Queensguard to show us the way. Guest met us at the door, slipping around it to speak to us outside. I threw my arms around his shaggy neck and kissed his nose. Familiar canine smell of my friend and a lingering hint of the spicy outdoorsiness that was his master.

I wanted to cry.

'I've missed you so *much*,' I said.

He nuzzled my hand and dropped something cold into it. My iPod. I wiped the slobber off, and tried the on switch. It flickered tinnily into life before cutting out.

I looked at the Cu Sidhe. Confused.

*We've brought the possessions you left with us, little Bree. My master saved them for you. Insisted we carry **them** in favour of useful things. Try to remember that when you see him. He's - unwell. Trying too hard to stay present. Won't allow me to take care of him in any way. He won't eat. Won't sleep.*

*I think he's waiting for **you**.*

I nodded. 'What do I do now, Guest?'

Did you get the water?

'Oh, yes.'

Then follow me.

Fin hovered protectively beside me as we went in. The room was a turret chamber similar to mine. Themed black and gold, not blue and silver. Gold silhouette of a striking hawk against the jetty hangings.

Leiloken sat with his back to the wall, hands clasped round his knees and head lowered. Hidden behind that tangled mane of sooty elf locks.

Master?

There was no response.

*Master, she's **here**. She has the water.*

Leiloken raised his head, strain showing under the dirt on his pale face. His eyes met mine, eerie and golden.

He flinched.

I crouched in front of him. Held out the orb, surprised when the pouch of acorns dropped into my hand.

'Leiloken? It's me, Bree. I've got the water like you said. Do you know what to do with it?'

He nodded once, eyes never leaving my face.

Juggling the iPod and the pouch, I placed the orb in his hands. The motion must've jolted the batteries into life. I was faintly aware of The Clash's 'London Calling' hissing from my earphones, before cutting out again.

Leiloken looked at the silver ball.

'Spill your blood on it.' He sounded hoarse. Shaky.

I wondered if he'd been on one of his ranting fits.

'What?'

'Spill your blood on the orb.'

I looked at Fin and he shrugged.

Removing the dagger from my belt, I cut my hand and let the blood drip onto the silver ball. It glowed with a blinding white light. I had to look away. When the light faded, Leiloken was holding a chalice decorated around the rim with amethysts.

He stared at it for a moment, then looked back at Fin and I.

'You need to leave now.' His expression was grave.

I was taken aback and it must have shown, because the madman placed a gentle hand over mine. Smiled faintly. Oddly.

'*Please*, Bree.' Softly. Honeyed velvet again. 'I don't want *you* to see this.'

We left.

I heard later that in his part of the castle no-one could sleep that night.

Because of the screaming.

***

The next day the king and queen summoned us to the audience chamber.

'Formal gown please, my lady,' said Dechtira sternly, when

I emerged from the bathing pool. Pink brows furrowed as she eyed me critically. 'It's a big deal, is this. Their majesties will need you to formally report your success before - *he* - can be welcomed back to court.'

It felt horribly restrictive after the pants and jerkin, and I was still grumbling when I went back into the main room. Fin and Guest were making themselves comfortable.

Eating *my* lunch.

'Help yourselves,' I said sarcastically, giving Fin a kiss and joining them.

*We **did**.* Guest lolled his tongue at me. *It's **done**, little Bree. My master is well.*

There was a fierce happiness in his voice and my heart swelled to hear it. I felt a bit choked, actually.

'That's brilliant, mutt. I'm pleased for you.'

*For **me**?* Guest sounded amused. *How little you understand. But do you realise you fulfilled the prophecy perfectly? 'She'll carry the forest of Celidon in her right hand and in her left, the buttressed forts of London' I'll admit - I'd wondered how you were going achieve it.*

Fin was laughing, wiping crumbs from his top. 'Sorry, Bree. Stop glaring. I know prophecies are vague for a reason - but that was a real stretch.'

I sniggered myself at the thought of the Clash representing the buttressed forts of London. Weird in this setting.

Guest put his huge head on my knee and I let my fingers tangle through his fur. Breathed in his familiar, doggy smell.

It's time. Are you ready for this?

'Sure. I don't have to do much, do I?'

Not as such, no.

I looked at Fin.

He smiled and it warmed me. 'I'll do the talking, if you like. I know how - er - *tactful* you can be.'

I accepted gratefully, nervous in ways I didn't understand.

***

The walk through the audience chamber was intimidating. The place was more crowded than I'd seen it before - and some of the fae glared openly at us as we walked toward the thrones.

We made our genuflections to the dais and Fin spoke.

'Your majesties, Lady Briana was successful. She sought and found the healing water. She cured the Barghest's master of his madness.' He grinned, a bright flash. 'He's *back*.'

That excited muttering again from the assembled fae. More glares. Hadn't they anything better to do? The honeysuckle and rose perfumed air seemed cloying suddenly, thick on my tongue. The king inclined his golden head gravely to me and the queen beamed, auburn curls dancing around her as she leaned forward slightly.

'You've done well, Lady Briana. The court recognises your efforts,' Rhiannon said.

I curtsied again, not knowing what to say.

'Please, both of you stand by us while we welcome him home. I'm sure he'll want to acknowledge your part in this.'

'With pleasure, my queen.' Fin took my arm and led me to one side of the dais.

An expectant hush filled the hall. All eyes turned towards the doors.

I was tense, not knowing what to expect from this new Leiloken.

The doors swung open.

For a few moments I didn't recognise the tall, impressive Fae stalking through them, huge Cu Sidhe at his side.

No more dirt or tangles.

Black hair waved in a long, loose curtain around a savagely beautiful white face. His eyes glowed before, but now they *burned*. Noted every expression. Every reaction. He wore the black and gold proudly, striking hawk emblazoned on his chest.

Not going for humble, were we?

To my surprise, many of the fae bowed as he passed them. Reached out to him. Others turned away or stood staring. I could hear murmurs.

'Prince Emrys.'

'Welcome home, my prince.'

There were several variations on the theme. I caught Efnyssen's eye and he glared coldly. Face still and set in rigid, angry lines.

Nope. Definitely not a fan.

Halfway down the hall, Leiloken's eyes came to rest on my face. He stilled for an instant. Looked at me, eyes intent, before striding rapidly to where I waited. Raised my hand to his lips.

'Hello, bright flame,' he said in that honey rich voice. 'I've missed you. You made your choice, then?'

'I hope I didn't disappoint.'

'I'm not sure you could.' He brushed the hair from my shoulder. Leaned down, lips grazing my ear. Whispered. '*Thank you.*'

I blinked at him, startled.

He winked one golden eye at me. Turned to face the king and queen. Fin stiffened and glared at him. Squeezed my hand briefly.

I stifled a giggle. Guest's tongue lolled in amusement.

'The court recognises you, Prince Emrys,' said Custenin.

Rhiannon held out her hand for Guest's master to kiss. He obliged, stepping back to my side.

'It's been a long time since anyone called me that. I don't especially care for it. I think Hawk will do - for now. It's hardly the first time I've gone by the name.' He glanced at Fin and I. 'I'm acknowledging the debt I owe Finian Medyr and Briana Cadman.'

'Accepted,' said Fin, a little too quickly.

'Rubbish,' I said rudely, tilting my head to look up at the former madman. 'You saved my life. You don't owe me *anything*. If you get right down to it, I owe *you* more. For patching me up.'

Hawk flashed me a swift, fierce grin. It lit his face like lightning. 'As you wish. I'll accept no debt from *you* either, in that case.'

'Fine.'

I grinned back, amused.

He turned back to the king and queen. 'We need to talk. Urgently. There are things happening you should be aware of. We're all in grave danger. Tir na n'Og will fall unless we act. Now.'

Custenin's expression was unreadable as he replied. 'We should talk this evening. I've an Unseelie delegation arriving tomorrow.'

'They're not where the danger lies, Custenin.'

Rhiannon smiled. 'You'll have your chance to explain later, hawk lord. For now, welcome home. I'm sure there's much you'll want to catch up on - before we speak.'

Hawk nodded sharply, turned, and strode from the hall as rapidly as he'd entered.

Fin, Guest and I wasted no time following.

***

Very late that evening, Guest brought his master to my chambers. Fin and I'd enjoyed a late supper and were sitting at the table, talking. Hawk simmered with barely contained anger. He threw himself into a fireside chair and glared at us.

'You ok?' I asked, mildly sarcastic.

*I think it's fair to say that **didn't** go well,* Guest growled.

Hawk fixed his attention on Fin. 'Have the Lughan declined so badly that Rhiannon was the best you could do for queen? There *must've* been other options.'

'She's handfasted to Custenin and we wanted *him*,' replied Fin calmly. 'We needed someone who'd bring us stability after all the wars. We're at peace with the Unseelie now. Have been their whole reign. He's a good king.'

'At least that gives us chance to get the Unseelie on side. Though I'm never *entirely* sure how far that queen of theirs will listen to me. I'll talk her round in the end. Something terrible's coming. I haven't seen it clearly - not *enough* - but I know the city will fall unless something's done. They just sit there, your rulers. Talking about readjustment periods and how to receive the Unseelie. I don't *need* to readjust. I'm perfectly fine.'

He frowned fiercely, sitting rapidly forwards. 'I was trying to save their people - and their city - and all they wanted to talk about was the welcoming feast for Mab. They dismissed the enemy as nursery stories. *Stupid*. I've spoken to Aodhan of the Portune and he's had much the same problem. They won't listen, too cocooned in their bubble of safety.'

Fin sat straight, very serious. He looked every inch the Fae lordling he was.

Fair and alien.

'What have you seen, Prince Emrys?'

The other Fae gave him a level look. 'Too much, lord Finian. And I told you I didn't like that name. Do you want me to describe the burning and dying? Do you want to know who you'll lose?' He glanced at me. 'Do you want to know what you'll face?'

I shuddered as a sudden breeze crept across my shoulders.

'Absolutely *not*. And *will* you guys stop with all the formal titles, please? You sound bloody ridiculous.'

Fin laughed - and was himself again. He took a sip from his cup, eyes sparkling into mine over the rim.

'Anyway,' I continued, frowning at Hawk. 'Rather than sit here talking about what's going to happen - shouldn't we be trying to stop it? What can we do?'

'We?' He looked slightly startled. 'Bree, it's war. You need to be far away from here.'

'Can you send her home?' Fin asked.

'I can. We'll need to travel to a place where the veil to the Elsewhere's thin and I'll open a door.' Swift smile in my direction. 'You'll admit I owe you that much, at least?'

I crossed my arms and shook my head. 'Not happening, boys. If you send me home I'll be killed anyway. Still have the Wild Hunt on my case, remember?'

'Lady's name!' Fin sprang to his feet, pacing. 'I need you safe, Bree. How can I think about battle if I'm worrying about you?'

He slammed a frustrated fist into the wall. I went to him and wrapped my arms around him. Breathed in his sunshine citrus scent.

'I'll be ok. I've survived so far, haven't I?'

Hawk leaned back in his chair, crossing his legs at the ankle. He'd a strange expression on his face as he watched us.

Blank and unfathomable.

'There *may* be a way, at that,' he said, eventually. 'If we bring one of these creatures here, I'd imagine *that* would prove my point nicely. They'll more or less have to protect the city, then. Bree should be safe here in the castle. Finian, are you prepared to come with me and find out how far this has gone?'

'Gladly. We saw the Portune and heard what happened to the Dryads. It *has* to be stopped.' Fin's voice was firm. 'Bree's got the last of the nursery acorns from Celidon. We need to get them to my father's lands so they can be fostered. Can we do that, too?'

Hawk smiled slightly. 'Easily enough if we're travelling through the Elsewhere. We'll need Aodhan with us to talk to the trees, so we'll make it the first stop.'

'I'm coming, too,' I said.

'*No.*' They both spoke at once.

'You're safest here,' said Hawk. 'If you were a trained warrior - as the Fae are - I still wouldn't take you. You'd be a distraction.'

'That's just rude,' I said huffily.

What *really* cheesed me off was how fast Fin agreed with him.

My strongly worded objections got me nowhere. They were leaving the next day.

Without me.

Fin would be facing terrible things. The thought of him injured or dead made my blood run cold. Couldn't bear the idea of him hurt, of losing him. I clung to him, scared I'd never see him again.

Perfectly normal reaction, that.

What confused me was that I felt exactly the same fear for Hawk.

◀Chapter Thirteen▶

To put it bluntly, I sulked.

I sulked when they left in the cold light of morning and I was still sulking when the Unseelie arrived with the dusk. Dechtira insisted we go down to the courtyard and watch. It was lined with fae jostling for a better view.

'*Watch* it!' I snapped at a goat-legged boy as he bumped my shoulder. He gave me a reproachful look and moved away.

'Will you calm down please, my lady?' asked Dechtira. 'You've been like a Spriggan with a sore arse all - Ooh, *look*. They're here.' Her wings quivered with excitement.

The ground shuddered as two giants came through the gates. They must've topped ten feet, with chains garlanding their bodies and withered heads dangling from thick belts. They stepped to either side, massive and imposing.

Six black horses bearing silver haired Fae followed. Livery black and silver. Raising silver horns, they blew a fanfare. In their wake came foot troops similarly clad, marching in effortless step.

'That's unusual.' Dechtira pursed her lips thoughtfully. 'Mab usually only sends a couple of delegates. I wonder who she's sent *this* year.'

As if in answer, an ornate black coach - frost glinting along its sides - rolled to a stop before the steps to the great hall. Dechtira gasped loudly and I glanced at her, puzzled.

She waved my attention back to the arriving fae.

Behind the coach came a throng of various Unseelie. Redcaps - only knee high, but hats dripping fresh blood - mingled with Spriggan, grey skinned Trow, and gnarly faced Duergar dwarves. Dechtira named them all for me; shuddering as she lay eyes on a group of women so ugly I felt sick looking at them.

'Gwyllion.' Venom in that silvery voice. 'They ate my brother.'

'I didn't think they were allowed?'

'It was a long time ago, my lady. There wasn't *always* a treaty.' Her voice held echoes of old sadness. 'It's why it was safer to take a post here.'

I dropped it, unwilling to pry.

The last to enter were more riders, markedly different to the first. They were made up of fae of all kinds - even what appeared to be a few humans. Their clothing a hodgepodge of fur, feathers, leather, and withered leaves.

One silver haired Fae winked a jaunty black eye at me as they rode past. I stared for a second, before realising this was who'd helped me in the mortal realm. Gave him a surreptitious wave, earning myself a glare from the Pixie.

'*What?*' I asked. 'I know him.'

'You don't *want* to know him,' she said firmly. 'He's a Huntsman.'

'Yeah, I got that when he shot me.'

Dechtira looked as though she wanted to say more, but two of the liveried soldiers stepped forward and swung open the carriage door.

They handed down a stunning Fae woman with elaborately plaited silvery hair and a form fitting black gown. She looked disdainfully around before allowing herself to be escorted inside, the noble Fae among her entourage following.

The courtyard erupted noisily and Dechtira dragged me back to the audience hall as fast as she could. Her small face was even greener than usual. If she'd been human, I'd have said she looked scared.

I pulled my arm from her grasp and made her face me.

'What's wrong? Why are we running?'

She swallowed. 'That's Queen Mab herself, my lady. She *never* normally comes here. Hasn't for centuries.' She shot me a critical glance. 'I suppose you'll do. Though I'd have done something different with your hair if I'd known it was a state visit.'

She took my arm again and tugged me into the rear of the hall. Mab and her liveried guards were advancing down the aisle and the startled king sprang from his seat to meet her halfway.

'Custenin.' Her voice was an icy tinkle.

'Queen Mab. This is an unexpected pleasure.' He took her arm and led her to the dais.

A third throne was growing, twisting up from the floor as I watched. It put out leaves and roses bloomed. Mab took her seat and petals fell as the leaves withered. The living wood blackened and aged, becoming brittle twigs. A fine layer of frost edged its way across the throne as Rhiannon leaned across to Mab with a pleasant smile.

'So good of you to visit in person, Queen Mab.'

Mab snorted. 'Let's cut the crap, Rhiannon. You aren't pleased to see me, and I don't want to be here. Are the rumours true?'

'Rumours, Mab?' questioned Rhiannon sweetly.

'Don't play the innocent. It's embarrassing in a queen. Is it true? Is he here? And don't give me *that* look. You know perfectly well who I'm talking about.'

'He should be here somewhere,' Custenin cast his eyes around the room. 'He may be with the Lughan boy.'

'With Morgen's whelp, you mean.' She wagged a finger in the king's face. '*Really*, Custenin. Do you think I'd have turned up if I hadn't heard what's been happening? Where is she? I want to see her.'

I shot a poisonous glance at the Huntsman, leaning against

a nearby pillar. He smirked and turned back to the thrones, cleaning his nails with his dagger.

The king hesitated, but Rhiannon's bell-like voice chimed out.

'Where's Lady Briana?'

Dechtira scowled and gave me a little shove. Taking a swift, deep breath; I stepped forward into the aisle.

'Here I am, your majesty.'

Mab beckoned to me with one pale, elegant finger.

'Well, come closer, girl. I won't eat you. Today, at any rate.'

I tried to swallow but my throat was dry. My legs shook as I approached her, making walking hard. Regal and cold, she was the embodiment of everything that Fin and Guest had been trying to warn me about from the beginning.

I wanted them with me so much I could barely breathe.

My curtsey was wobbly but she didn't seem to care. Glittering black eyes slowly ran over me from head to toe. After a few nervous seconds she burst into cawing laughter. Gave a slow hand clap.

'Oh, *very* nice,' she said. 'Fae enough to play with and human enough to eat. I can see why my Hunt's so annoyed you escaped. Still, I suppose you *were* necessary.' Her eyes snapped to my face. 'Where *is* Emrys? I haven't seen him for such a long time. I'd hate to think he'd forgotten me.'

I gulped. 'He's not here, your majesty.'

'Not here? Has he been forced to leave already? That's fast work - even for him.' She shot Custenin a wryly questioning look.

'I wasn't aware of this,' said Custenin slowly, 'Perhaps you could enlighten us, Lady Briana?'

'Um, he had to go and do some stuff,' I said. 'Him and Fin.'

I toed uncomfortably at the marble floor. Little sweeping movements, back and forth.

Rhiannon's eyebrows were almost in her hairline. 'What 'stuff'?'

'They've gone to see what's going on. What's attacking us, I mean,' I mumbled, staring at my feet. 'Hawk doesn't think you're taking him seriously enough.'

Custenin bristled and Mab cawed again. 'That's just too precious,' she said. 'I think I'm going to want to talk to you later, girl. It seems our hawk lord's taken you into his confidence. And that *does* intrigue me - even if you don't.' She turned back to the Seelie rulers. 'Well, are we going to sit here all day? Or are we going to go and talk? It seems we've a lot to catch up on.'

Dismissing me with a wave, she rose and took the king's arm. Rhiannon followed alone, face set. Both courts bowed as the monarchs left.

The noise level *exploded*.

Seelie and Unseelie alike chattered - and argued - amongst themselves. I felt a touch on my elbow. It was the Huntsman.

'Care for a walk, sweetheart?' he asked.

'With you? Not especially.'

'Aw, come on. I helped you.' He sighed at my expression. 'Look, we're here under treaty. I told you we can't touch you in Faery. Breaks all the rules, does that.'

Grudgingly, I took his proffered elbow and allowed him to guide me between groups of fae and out of the hall. I baulked when he tried to pull me down a side corridor I'd never visited.

'Where are you taking me? What do you want?' I yanked my arm away.

'I need to check on my horse, sweetheart. Can't trust anyone else to do it right.'

I glared at him suspiciously.

He filled his cheeks with air and puffed it out slowly, raking a hand through his manga-spiky hair. Dislodging a shower of twigs and dry leaves which clattered to the floor.

'I've already told you I won't hurt you.'

'You're Unseelie.'

'And *you're* not fae at all. So - don't go getting on *your* high horse about which court *I* belong to. You don't know half enough. Look, let's start again. I'm Cael.' He held out a hand.

After a few seconds I slowly shook it.

'I'm Bree.'

'I know. We *all* bloody know. Now.' He smiled.

I winced at the sight of those teeth as he took my arm. Began to walk again.

'Was it you who told her? The queen, I mean. About what I was doing?'

'Of course it was. She'd have skinned me alive for letting you go, if I hadn't. And believe me, sweetheart, in Caer Dubh that's *not* just a figure of speech.'

'I'm sorry you got in trouble 'cause of me.'

'Don't worry about it. I'm always in bloody trouble.' He grinned, black eyes dancing. 'The trick *is* to get out of it again.'

We reached the stables, entering through a door in the back. I looked at the frantic activity and shook my head.

'I think I'll leave you to it.'

'Aw, come on. That's my fine chap over there.' He pointed to a large bay stallion.

Trying to kick holes in the wall.

'Say,' he added enthusiastically. 'We could go for a ride later. It's going to be a gorgeous night. Crisp, cold, clear. All the 'C's. Perfect for a canter out.'

'Not happening.' I shook my head. 'I can't ride.'

Cael started in surprise. 'How in Faery have you been getting around then? Not *walking*?'

He seemed horrified. Silver brows nearly meeting his hairline.

'I've been riding with Fin.'

'Well, that's just *embarrassing*.' He snickered darkly. 'Best run along then - before anyone realises what a rubbish human I picked.'

I was only too pleased to oblige.

***

Dechtira locked us both in my rooms that night. I protested in vain.

'You're staying in here, my lady,' she said firmly. 'And I'm not going back to the servants' wing with the Unseelie here. You don't know what they're like.' Her wings rippled as she shuddered. 'Not unless you *order* me to go, at least.'

We both knew how unlikely that was.

The sun had barely crested the castle walls the next morning, when a muffled pounding shook the door.

'Come on. Open up,' A familiar voice.

'Who is it?' Dechtira sounded suspicious.

'Cael. Look, your mistress knows me. Let me in.'

I sighed, annoyed. 'Oh, let him in, for heaven's sake. He'll have the door down if you don't.'

She raised a pink eyebrow at me but complied. Cael half danced round the door, eyes shining.

'Get yourself changed, Bree. You were wearing quite sensible stuff when I saw you in the mortal realm.' He rolled his eyes at me when I didn't move. 'Come on, I'm teaching you to ride. I'll be the laughing stock of the Hunt if the others find out how useless you are. Well, don't just *stand* there.'

It wasn't a bad idea, actually.

I did feel a bit lame not being able to ride without someone behind me. It was sure to impress Fin, too. Grinning despite myself, I scurried into the bathing chamber to change. Dechtira silently helped me out of the gown, lips pressed together in a firm line.

I ignored her disapproval and followed Cael to the stables.

***

It wasn't too bad at first. Cael helped me onto his horse, and led it into the nearby woods until we reached a clearing. I must have fallen six or seven times in the following couple of hours as Cael corrected my posture and took me through the basics.

Howling with laughter each time I fell.

It was fun, despite my bruises. He was good company. And a surprisingly patient teacher. The horse kept swinging its head to glare at me balefully. Obviously unimpressed to have a rookie in the saddle.

When I was too stiff to keep going, the Unseelie lifted me back up and settled himself behind me.

'I'm not walking back if I don't have to,' he said in response to my startled look.

I leaned forward as far as I dared, squirming with the weirdness of it not being Fin behind me. A pang of loss rocked me, almost causing me to fall, as I tried not to picture him hurt. Or worse. Tears welled in my throat and I swallowed them down, ignoring the stone in my chest.

*Please, **please** let him come home safely. Hawk, too.*

I'm not sure who I was praying to, but I did it as hard as I could.

Cael stiffened and hissed, startling me from my reverie.

'What?' I asked.

'Stay quiet, sweetheart.'

He turned our mount away into the thicker undergrowth. Pulled me down from the saddle after him. I could hear other riders approaching through the trees. We peered through the dense thicket.

A staggeringly beautiful girl with long curling blonde hair came first, her mount an adorable looking grey.

What came after was *not* so pretty.

Gigantic and humanoid in shape, they were black with cruelly twisted limbs. Some kind of ichor leaked from the cracks in their leathery skin and their distorted faces were hideous. Each carried cruel looking curved blades and hook tipped knives in their deformed hands.

Silently, they formed a circle around the girl.

Nobody moved for several minutes. I almost forgot to breathe. Cael was silent beside me.

Another blonde rider followed and I started in recognition.

Efnyssen dismounted gracefully and kissed the girl's hand. She smiled at him warmly as they began to talk. I was too far away to hear what they were saying, but there was no mistaking the besotted look on her face. Chloe's looked at boys that way more often than I can remember.

Efnyssen placed a small cloth-wrapped bundle in her

hands, murmured a few more words, and left. The girl and her loathsome guardians wasted no time in doing likewise.

Cael let out a long breath, puffing out his cheeks.

'Well, wasn't *that* interesting?' he asked. 'Correct me if I'm wrong, sweetheart - but would those be what the hawk lord thinks are attacking Seelie lands?'

I nodded mutely, mind racing.

What was Efnyssen's girlfriend doing with them?

'Not good. Not good at *all*. If they're what I think they are....' He shook his head. 'They're just stories to frighten kids. I never thought they were *real*.'

'What are they?'

'*Formori*.' He spat it.

'What are Formori? Why are they here?'

'You don't want to know. You'll never sleep again.' The Huntsman wore a grim expression.

Both safely remounted, we set out for the city at a steady walk.

'We have to tell someone.' I fidgeted with the hem of my cloak.

'Who'll believe us?' He shrugged behind me. 'Not that precious Seelie pair. They're too far up their own arses to see daylight. Besides, if they won't listen to your Prince Emrys - what can *we* do? In case you'd forgotten, *I'm* Unseelie and *you're* human. No hope.'

'He's not *my* Prince Emrys,' I said stiffly. 'And he prefers

Hawk, actually. What's stopping you telling Queen Mab? I thought you *liked* grassing people up to her.'

His chuckle was mirthless. 'Not on your life, sweetheart. She's a habit of shooting the messenger. And I'm not exactly in her good books right now. She's no more likely to believe *me* than the golden moron and his idiot queen are.

'We'll need to stay quiet for now. Your,' he paused. 'Sorry - *not your* – hawk lord shouldn't find it too hard to get *some* proof they're here. Especially if they're venturing this close to the city. I just hope he makes it back.' He sounded genuinely worried.

I hoped so too. My heart became a boulder in my chest.

What had I allowed them to walk into?

◀Chapter Fourteen▶

I didn't find out for almost a week. The monarchs decided to make the most of being together, and were busily dealing with issues that affected both courts. As well as ratifying mind-numbingly dull new clauses to the treaty. This needed to be done in public and I yawned for the third time that afternoon. Dechtira's elbow made swift contact with my ribs. She frowned and I grinned at her cross little face. Cael snickered behind us.

The double doors crashed open.

Commotion.

Standing on tiptoe, I could just see two Fae heads - black and blood copper - above the massed ranks of the courts, as they came down the aisle.

Fin and Hawk.

Home safely.

I pushed my way forward, elbowing fae of both courts recklessly aside in my haste to get to them. Angry mutters and jeers followed me as - toes and gowns crushed in my wake - I arrived breathlessly at the front of the crowd.

And stopped. Horrified.

A dark smear of blood was forming along the green marble.

Hawk dragged a *very* dead creature - like the ones Cael and I had seen - behind him, Finian at his side. The corpse was hideous, but *that* wasn't what flash-froze my blood and squeezed my chest till I saw sparkles.

It was Fin and Hawk.

They were battered and bloody. Hawk limped slightly and Fin's arm was in a sling; one eye swollen almost shut from a livid cut that ran beside it. I ran to him, heart contracting painfully between my ribs. Threw my arms around his waist. He stopped. Winced for the merest second.

And pulled me to his side, smiling warmly.

'Easy, Bree. I'm ok. We'll talk later,' he murmured, pulling me forward with him.

Custenin was on his feet, golden hair dappled with the colours shining through the glass above. 'What's the meaning of this?'

'We're under attack, Custenin. As I warned you.' Hawk's level voice was pitched to carry.

'Nonsense. Mab's been here all week, and...'

'*Not* the Unseelie. As I also warned you.'

Something threatening in that too-calm voice. Little tendrils of fear danced across my skin. A forcible reminder of the otherness of the creatures surrounding me.

Hawk halted a short distance from the thrones.

Swung the body forward so it skidded to a gruesome halt at the foot of the dais. Sick-sweet smell of blood on green marble.

The hall was still. My heart thundered in my ears.

'*There's* your enemy.' He locked glares with Custenin.

Icy blue met hot gold.

The king looked away first.

Hawk continued. 'They're coming. Your people are dying. Your lands are being ravaged. Tir Na n'Og will fall. Will you *act* now?'

Loud clapping from a single pair of hands. I jumped.

'Oh *bravo*, Emrys. You always *did* know how to make an entrance.' Mab's pale, pointed face was positively gleeful.

He half turned, a smile twitching the edges of his mouth. 'Hello, Mab. I'm glad you're here. We need to talk.'

'Mmm. So I gather. Tell me. Were you sane for a *full* five minutes before you charged off causing trouble again? Or didn't you like to wait?' An arch smile. 'You are *quite* sure you're sane - aren't you?'

He ignored that, turning back to the king.

'What are you going to do, Custenin?' he asked softly.

'Finian Medyr, what do you have to say? Has he dragged

you into this folly as well?' The Seelie king frowned, hands clenched at his sides.

'No folly, my king. He's telling the truth,' said Fin. 'They've burned out most of the settlements within a ten league radius. They're trying to starve us out. We'll be next.'

'*Lies*, my king!' Efnyssen was shouldering his way forward. 'This is the same madman who killed four generations in one war. In one *battle*. Have you forgotten?Will you let him do it *again*? Can't you see this is a trick of some kind?'

He scowled at Hawk, who glared back.

If looks could kill...

'Be calm, Lord Efnyssen,' said Rhiannon. 'I'm sure we can settle this.'

I drew a deep breath and looked at the queen. 'Your majesty, Efnyssen's the one trying to trick you. We saw him with his girlfriend. And she had these *things* guarding her.'

Fin's arm tightened around my waist and I leaned into him.

'She's an innocent. An *angel*. These creatures aren't a threat,' Efnyssen was spluttering with rage. 'You don't *know* her. She ...'

Turning his back on him with magnificent disdain, Hawk raised an eyebrow at me.

'We? Who else saw this?'

I pointed at the Huntsman. 'Cael did. He was teaching me to ride.'

Mab stood. 'Cael?' she asked. 'Is this true?'

She didn't sound pleased.

'Yes, my queen.' The Huntsman shot me a filthy look as he came to stand with us.

'Well, Mab?' asked Hawk. 'You've known me since we were children. Since the dragons in the lake. Do *you* believe me?'

Mab gave that cawing laugh again. 'My dear Emrys, of *course* I believe you. I'm not blind. *I* know what those things are. Even if no-one else is prepared to admit it.

'Formori.

'The old enemy. One does *rather* hope the Lughan didn't get rid of that useful spear of theirs. Rhiannon, this is just advice, you understand. But if I were you I'd lock up that traitor *there*,' She pointed to Efnyssen. 'And peel away his skin inch by inch until he tells you everything he knows.'

The Seelie Queen looked at her in horror. Blue eyes wide.

Custenin nodded. 'We'll take the first part of your advice, at least. I think a *talk* with Lord Efnyssen is in order. We need to understand what's happening here.'

He motioned to the guards, who took the struggling Efnyssen by his arms and dragged him from the hall.

I fought a terrible urge to poke my tongue out at him.

'Queen Mab, lord husband - we've much to discuss.' Rhiannon had regained her composure. 'May I suggest we convene in the council chamber in an hour?'

Mab agreed at once. 'Emrys and the fire lordling must attend. They know things, and we need that knowledge.

Cael, you'll be there too. *After* you've seen me privately. You can wait in my quarters.'

Cael looked at me glumly and trudged away, bony shoulders drooping.

I hoped she wouldn't do anything too terrible to him. It was the second time I'd gotten him in trouble, and a surge of guilt made me chew my lip. I looked up at Fin. He winked at me.

'Agreed,' said Custenin.

***

We walked in slow silence, my mind racing. As soon as we reached my chambers, I whirled on them. Furious.

'Where's Guest?' I demanded.

'He's fine. Relax.' Fin said soothingly, reaching out to catch my hand.

I snatched it away.

'Relax? You want me to *relax*?' I snarled. 'I didn't know whether you were alive or dead. Either of you. And then you just - I didn't even know you were *back*. And you - *you*...'

I was choking on the hard knot of rage and fear lodged in my throat. 'And dragging that *thing* in and –and - *look at you both*!' The last words a howl as the knot tore in half and the tears came.

Fin put his good arm around me and rubbed my shoulder as I soaked his clothing. He shot Hawk a mock-reproachful look.

'You've scared her half to death,' he said. 'Bree, I did *suggest* going with a more subtle approach. But I got outvoted. By him and the Hound.'

Hawk grinned fiercely, eyes alight with laughter. 'That *was* the subtle approach.'

'Do you think you're *funny*?'

I sniffed huffily and dried my eyes. Allowed Fin to gently lead me to my deep chair beside the fireplace. 'And - seriously - where *is* Guest?'

Hawk folded himself into the companion chair opposite me, suddenly serious. He raked a hand wearily through his hair.

'He's gone to raise his people. We're going to need them. We're going to need everyone.'

Fin pulled another chair close to mine, wincing as he settled himself. His fingers laced through mine. Even the affectionate smile he gave me looked painful. I reached out and gently touched his face near the cut. He hissed slightly. Moved back.

I turned to glare at Hawk.

'And *you* couldn't have patched him up better?'

He shrugged, but it was Fin who answered.

'Even he,' jerking his thumb at the other Fae. 'Can't do much when you don't have time to stop. We haven't slept more than an hour for the best part of a week. Just kept moving to the next place and the next. It's a nightmare out there. Even my father's having trouble.'

'I tried to get us both to a Brownie I know, a talented healer.' Hawk's eyes fixed on the dancing flames in the hearth. 'But her home's destroyed and we couldn't find word of her. It's happening everywhere...'

The door opened to admit Dechtira bearing a tray of food. A cloth wrapped bundle swung from her wrist.

'Is that a jug of wine I see?' asked Fin, perking up.

'Yes, my lord.'

She poured him a full goblet and he sighed happily. 'Pixie, I think I love you.'

Sniffing, she handed the bundle to Hawk. 'Clean bandages and suchlike, my lord. You *both* look like you could do with them.'

He grinned, raising an eyebrow as he unwrapped it and examined the contents. 'If you get tired of working for Bree, *my* door's always open. This is perfect. And very thoughtful. I'm grateful.'

She poured more wine, serving Hawk and I. It smelled as dark and rich as it looked. He accepted a brimming goblet and leaned contentedly back in his chair, stretching his legs out. I frowned at him and moved my feet to one side.

Sodding tall Fae.

'You've torn it again.' Fin indicated Hawks leg, where blood was blooming through the bandage he wore around his thigh.

'I know. I'll tend it when I've time.'

'You'll tend to it *now*,' I flared. '*And* you'll sort Fin out, as well.'

Hawk's eyes glowed with amusement again. 'I'll get your boyfriend treated, but my injuries are going to have to wait. Unless you want me undressing in your room?'

I felt heat flood my face until my ears burned.

'Oh. Right.'

Fin's snigger did nothing to help.

'I'm going to bathe, Dechtira. Help *him* with Fin and then you can come and keep me company. I'm sure Hawk'll appreciate the privacy.' Snarky sarcasm.

Dechtira's blue eyes lit with mischief. 'Are you sure, my lady? I *have* seen naked men before, you know.'

'Don't *you* start!'

Face flaming, I fled for the bathing chamber.

***

I lay in the soothing water, trying not to imagine what'd happened to them. The idea of anyone harming Fin made me shudder - despite the warmth of the pool. What had they *been* through?

I knew I'd find out soon enough.

It was the thought of the fighting to come that twisted my stomach. Both of them would be in the thick of it. They could be killed. I could *lose* them. Lose Fin. My whole body chilled, heart stopping for a beat or two.

I *loved* Fin.

It hit me like a burst of lightning.

I loved him. And I didn't think I could face losing him without going as crazy as Hawk had been. My heart raced. Wasn't that partly what had drove him mad to start with? The loss of Morgen?

I was seized by a grim understanding of the heartbreaking sobs I'd heard in Leiloken's cavern.

What could I do? How could I keep Fin safe? Hawk was right - I was no warrior. My understanding of the kinds of weaponry I'd seen in Faery extended no further than 'Hit them with the pointy end'. I wondered if there was someone I could ask to teach me the basics.

But *who*?

Fin was injured - and Hawk's intensity scared me a little. I wasn't sure I wanted *him* coming at me with a sword in his hands. Heat pinched my ears again at the thought of him.

Bloody wind up merchant.

I think I liked you better mad.

I scrubbed viciously at my skin. Leiloken had been so gentle and soothing while he was healing me. *That* was the personality I'd expected to encounter once he was cured. *That* was the Fae I'd so nearly allowed to kiss me when he threw me into Faery. Not *this* overwhelming and driven creature. All fire and fury.

He was too angry, too alien, too fiercely beautiful, too unpredictable, too *much*...

A little shock shivered through me. Made me pause mid-mental-rant. What was all *that* about? I barely knew Hawk. I was in love with *Fin*. With the gorgeous Fae lord who'd held me and kept me safe as Diern undid what Hawk'd done to me. So why did I feel this *drawn* to Hawk?

I slid beneath the water, trying to hide from myself.

It was Morgen.

Had to be.

Fin told me she'd placed her own soul in her bloodline for safekeeping. I might be all about Fin - but it looked very much as though my eventual grandmother still had the major hots for Hawk.

And she was hiding out in *my* body.

I surfaced. 'Oh, *hell*.'

'Are you well, my lady?' Dechtira was holding out a fluffy blanket to dry me. I hadn't even noticed her come in. Too wrapped up in my emotional turmoil.

I felt myself flush again. Hoped she'd put it down to the steamy water.

'I'm fine. Just a bit nervous about what they'll decide in this meeting.'

'I think the hawk lord and your lord Finian feel the same. They're both on edge.'

I quite liked her calling him *my* lord Finian. A smile pulled at the corners of my mouth and she gave me a knowing look. Flustered, I allowed her to dry and dress me. One thing was certain. No-one could *ever* know about my conflicted feelings.

Not even entirely mine, at that.

Returning to the main chamber, I found them well stuck into the food Dechtira'd brought. Accepting the thick slice of ham Fin offered on the point of his knife, I sat beside him.

As far away from Hawk as I could get.

Fin's face looked much better, and his upper arm was tightly bandaged but no longer strapped to his chest. I ran my fingers over his swelling-free face, kissing him gently on the half-healed cut. He pulled me closer for a real kiss.

It was *wonderful.*

'He's much better. You're pretty good.' I said to Hawk, who lounged comfortably in my favourite chair.

He looked at me, expressionless. 'He'll have less of a scar than you do. Don't worry, Bree. Your boyfriend will still be pretty.'

I stiffened angrily. Ready to roast him.

No-one calls *me* shallow.

Fin laughed lightly and kissed me again. 'Don't listen to the old curmudgeon. He's just jealous I'm so much better looking than he is. *And* because I'm lucky enough to have someone as beautiful as you.' His eyes glowed with warmth as he looked at me and I melted into him.

Hawk set his goblet down with a brisk click.

'They'll be waiting for us,' he said coldly. 'We should go.'

He stood abruptly and walked through the door, not looking back.

'Cheery old thing, isn't he?' Fin drained his own cup. 'He's right, though. I should get going.'

He left, too.

I stared at the still closing door, a queer little pang squeezing my heart.

◀Chapter Fifteen▶

Tir na n'Og was in chaos. Twenty hour hours transformed it from a peaceful citadel into a place of scurry and bustle and grim expressions.

Fin, Hawk and Cael were closeted in the meeting with the monarchs for several hours. Aodhan and some of the other refugees got called in to talk.

I waited outside.

Pacing impatiently.

They looked tired but grimly satisfied, when they came out. Fin caught me by the waist and spun me in a circle.

'*Well*?' I asked, a little breathless.

Fin beamed at me. 'They've agreed to take defensive measures. The Formori are only days away. We're preparing for attack.'

'What does that mean?'

A fierce expression blazed across Hawk's face. 'It means they're going to let me raise the warbands.'

'As *if*,' snorted Cael. 'That didn't exactly go too well for you last time, did it? Not trying to be offensive, hawk lord - but you're the *last* person they're going to put in charge of an army.'

'He's right, you know.' Fin grinned at Hawk.

A funny little smile. 'We'll see. Either way, we won't be caught unaware. Mab's asked me to get her back to Caer Dubh so I can lead the garrison here - while *she* raises the Dark Host.

'It's a full day's travel to a spot where the veil's thin enough to open a door. But I can still have the first here within a week. I'll bring the Cu Sidhe as well. They know where to meet me.' He grinned at me, oddly playful. 'Guest's very taken with you, you know. You're subverting my Hound.'

'I love that mutt,' I said. 'You'd better bring him back in one piece, mister. Or there'll be hitting. *Lots* of hitting.'

He gave a mocking half bow. 'As you command.'

Cael just shook his head, cleaning his nails with his knife. 'I'm glad you're all so excited. Personally, I think it's going to be bloody *awful*. Bree, scrap the riding lessons. I'm teaching you to fight. You might actually survive this if you know which end of a sword to hit them with. No guarantees, mind.'

I stuck my tongue out at him and snuggled into Fin. That

lovely sunshine smell exploded in my nose and I closed my eyes for a second. Happy.

***

The guard went to work moving the people of Tir na n'Og into the castle itself. As the most defensive structure, dominating the city, it was the logical place for civilians like me.

Every day streams of fae flooded in from the surrounding countryside. Some so injured as to be near death, others with only the clothes they stood up in. The supplies began to dwindle, portions becoming smaller with each new influx of people.

I was in the practice yard near the main gate with Cael - about to have my first lesson - when I saw a familiar face among the ones coming through the gate.

Moving wearily - and with a burn puckering one cheek - Luydla still smiled when she saw me. She wove her way through the sparring fae, ducking now and then to escape a wild swing. Seemed *everyone* was sharpening their skills.

Preparing for what was coming.

I hugged the little woman, pleased she'd escaped the devastation of Celidon.

'Yes, that's *much* better.' Her brown eyes gleamed with warm approval as she examined me. 'You've adapted to our realm, now. Not so human any more, are you?'

'I suppose not.' I thought about it for a second. Fingered the tilted tips of my ears. 'Or rather, I'm still human. I'm still *me* - just a bit more Fae than I was.'

She chuckled. 'As you say, mortal Fae girl. If Morgen's still in there, tell her hello from me. I liked her.'

The absurdity amused me. 'I'll do that.'

Luydla hugged me again and walked wearily into the hall, small head held high; shoulders unbowed. It'd take a damn sight more than this to break these people. I felt a warm glow of pride that I was one of them.

Even in a small, human way.

Mab and her silver haired guard cantered through the yard on massive black horses, accompanied by Hawk. He reined in when he saw me, waiting for the others to pass through the other gate before dismounting.

'Walk with me for a moment?' he asked, smiling.

'Sure. Back in a minute, Cael.'

I grinned. Pleased to put off the lesson a little longer.

Cael gave an ironic salute and leaned against the wall, watching the Seelie Queen sparring fiercely with the Kingsguard captain. She moved like a panther, sleek and lethal. Jealousy made me pout.

I'd be lucky not to stab myself on the first swing.

Hawk followed my eyes and laughed. 'Stop fretting, bright flame. It's not about how good Rhiannon is. It's about being good enough to stay alive. You'll be fine. Morgen was an expert.'

'Maybe she can let Cael beat *her* black and blue in the name of self defence instead, then. Are you going to Caer Dubh now?'

'Yes, I'm off to walk her Unseelie majesty home.' We ambled across the yard, his horse's hooves muffled thumps in the chaos. 'I thought I'd stop and assure you I won't bring anyone back injured, if I can prevent it. You get quite fierce when I do, I've noticed.'

I punched his arm. 'Idiot. You just get that Hound here safely for me. *And* yourself. I care about you guys. It *kills* me to see you hurt.'

He stopped in the shadows of the gate, laughing softly as he turned me to face him.

'Careful, Bree. You're getting fond of me.'

I don't know what he saw in my expression, but the smile died on his lips. A stillness took him as his eyes searched my face. Golden and intense, I could barely meet his gaze.

What I saw there scared me.

A weird chill ran through my veins, stirring up from some buried place. Some awareness.

'You *are* fond of me.' The merest breath.

I didn't answer.

We stood for a long second, frozen. He stepped a little closer, never once looking away. The air was brittle, ready to disintegrate in a heartbeat. I didn't dare breathe. The atmosphere was too thick.

Something inside me prepared to shatter.

'I wonder...' He raised a hand to cup the side of my face. 'Morgen...'

I stepped back. Fast. Breaking the spell. Looking away,

then back at that still, white face.

At the anguish lingering in the back of those brilliant eyes.

'I'm not her,' I said.

And walked away.

***

Cael and Rhiannon both watched me walk back. I didn't turn to look at Hawk once. Rhiannon wore a peculiar - almost calculating - expression. She nodded to me abruptly and left the yard.

'What bit *her*?' I asked.

Cael frowned, unusually serious. 'Be careful, Bree. Rhiannon wanted to marry Hawk when she was younger. She *called* it a dynastic alliance. His family had the throne back then - and she wanted to rule *very* badly. Though, I don't think politics had much to do with it, if you want the truth.

'I reckon she's still carrying a dirty great torch for him - and she's *not* keen on the idea of *you* putting it out for her.' He handed me a sword. Gave my shoulder a quick squeeze. 'Just ask yourself who your hawk lord's really seeing when he looks at you.'

'He's not *my* hawk lord,' I said awkwardly. 'I told you that before.'

'Whatever.' He shrugged. 'Just wondering whether *he* knows that. Or Finian.'

I raised my weapon.

'Just *show* me which end of this to hit you with...'

He spun his practice sword in a complex movement. 'Easy, sweetheart. Basic blocks first. Raise your arm and bring your sword level with your eyes. Good. Now that's your first block...'

The lesson continued. It surprised me how quickly I got to grips with the moves. Even the Huntsman was impressed. Raising his eyebrows, he moved faster.

So did I.

It was more like remembering than learning.

My arm – my body - seemed to move without my volition, reflexes unfamiliar. Cael narrowed his eyes at me for a calculating second and swung into a wild flurry of attacking moves.

I watched - almost detached from myself - as my blade swung fluidly to meet each one with a metallic clang. My feet moved with an instinct I hadn't known I had, holding my weight on my back foot. Springing forward with every opening Cael presented me. Alive and joyful and fierce.

Eventually he raised his hands, laughing.

'Ok, Bree. *Ok.* That's enough for today.'

A snarl I hadn't realised was there fled my face. I felt my muscles relax, under my control again.

'What the hell was *that*?' I stared at my arm as though it belonged to a stranger.

Unclenched my fingers and let the sword fall. It landed in the dust with a thud, filling my nose with dirt smell.

'I'm wondering if your hawk lord knows a little more than

he's telling.' Cael was thoughtful. 'That's not you. *No-one* learns that fast. No-one moves like *that* without years of practice. They called your Fae blood - and all that comes with it. Morgen bound herself to your bloodline. She's still in there, somewhere. Looks to *me* like she's trying to protect you.'

'That's insane.'

'Hmm. Maybe - and maybe not. Look, just don't let either of those Seelie boys you're so enamoured of know. I don't think *either* of them're entirely rational, when it comes to Morgen.

' I caught Finian Medyr mooning over her portrait when we were kids. Frankly, we all had a good laugh about it.' He caught my look, rolled his eyes. 'Well, of *course* I told people. *Please*. As for the hawk lord, well...

'There's a lot of history there. Best to stay clear until you know how much of you's *her.*'

I chewed my lip, chagrined. 'You might be right. I dunno. I'll think about it, Cael.'

'Well, don't take too long, sweetheart,' He gave a gleeful smile. 'We'll probably all be dead in a few weeks - so it doesn't really matter, does it?'

'Not when you put it like that,' I said gloomily.

A pair of warm hands dropped onto my shoulders, making me jump. Fin laughed at my surprise.

'Thought I'd come and see how you were doing,' he said. 'Also I could do with getting a little practice in, myself. My bow thinks I've forgotten how to use her.'

Cael smirked, black eyes bright with challenge. 'The archery butts are just over there, pretty boy. Wanna play?'

'By all means,' Fin gave an ironic little bow. 'I *should* warn you that you'll lose, though.'

'Oh *please,* I'm a Huntsman. It's what I do.'

'I've won every archery contest in Tir na n'Og for a hundred and fifty years,' said Fin calmly. 'Let's do this.'

A hundred and fifty years?

How old *was* Fin?

I knew some girls went for older guys, but this was *ridiculous*. My stomach lurched with the realisation that he was a creature different from me. Alien to all I'd known. I loved Fin - but there was so much I didn't know. Would never understand.

I chewed my lip in confusion.

We made our way to the butts - archery targets. Bright circles a vivid slash of colour against the grey day.

Cael halted an impossible distance away. I was hardly able to make out the rings on the butts. He smirked again and raised an eyebrow at Fin.

'From here?' he asked.

'No.'

Fin's tone was flat and Cael hooted triumphantly.

'Too difficult for you, Seelie boy?'

'Too *easy*, Unseelie.' Fin turned and strode back some distance, bow held lightly in his hand. 'From here.'

We joined him.

The targets were impossibly small.

'No *way*,' I said sceptically. 'Stop showing off. The pair of you.'

Cael threw me a contemptuous look. '*Please*, sweetheart. Have a little faith. You deserve to see how good I am before I kill you.'

'You won't *touch* her.' I'd never heard Fin sound like that.

He simmered with anger, heat irradiating his tone. Tall and blazing, he was every inch the Fae lord.

'You'll die. If you ever harm her - I'll kill you, Cael. And I'll *enjoy* it.'

'She's safe while she's in Faery. You know that. But I didn't *make* the rules. I Marked her. I have first shot. And, Bree,' He looked at me earnestly 'It'd be a clean shot. I wouldn't let you suffer. That's the best I can do. Unless you want to challenge me to combat. Or join the Unseelie court. Not much in the way of options.'

'Is that what it's going to be in the end? You or me?'

A heaviness crept through me. The birdsong from the city seemed incongruous at such a moment.

Cael looked sad, bony shoulders sagging a little.

'I think so. Probably. Yeah.'

'It's moot,' snapped Fin. 'Bree's staying in Faery. With me. Where she's safe.'

He glared at the Huntsman. Who grimaced back.

I stepped between them.

'Are you actually going to show me some shooting? Or all you both all mouth?' I asked sweetly.

Cael raised his bow. A shimmer of movement - *thud thud thud* - as his arrows hit the straw stuffed targets.

Dead centre.

He winked at me. 'Impressed?'

'A bit,' I said grudgingly.

Fin pulled me to him and whispered in my ear, lips warm against the skin. I shivered.

'Count to three,' he said.

I did.

Finian uncoiled in a graceful economy of movement. He was a blur as he span and fired, barely looking at the targets. The arrows rained into them, splitting Cael's - and shredding the central butt almost to pieces. It looked like a teddy with the stuffing hanging out.

I hadn't even got to three.

Had to grin. Broadly.

Fin looked from Cael to me. Face absolutely still but a wicked gleam lighting his eyes.

'Well?' he asked.

Cael gave a shrug.

'Not bad for a Seelie boy, I suppose.' He stuck out a hand and Fin grasped his elbow in that weird handclasp thing guys do. 'Truce?'

'For now. I meant it though, Cael.'

'I know.'

I sidled up to the gorgeous Fae lordling, snaking an arm round his waist. He ruffled my hair.

'Impressed now?'

'Actually, that *was* kind of sexy.' I raised my eyebrows at him.

He laughed. 'I'll have to remember that.'

'*Damn*, you Seelie do weird things to impress chicks.' Cael made vomiting gestures as Fin kissed me lightly on the lips. 'And this is all *way* too much of the PDA's for me. I'll remember what you said, Seelie boy. As long as my girl Bree here remembers what *I* said. Think about it, sweetheart. And let me know when you've worked it out.'

He shouldered his bow, ready to trudge back to his duties for Mab. I gave him a serious nod. 'I'll remember, Cael.'

He gave a little salute and left. Fin looked at me curiously.

'What was that all about?' he asked.

'PDA means public display of affection,' I held my face up, wanting more sunshine kisses.

'I mean - what is it he wants you to think about?'

'Just training stuff,' I replied.

But all the while he was kissing me I was wondering whether he saw me - or Morgen.

◀Chapter Sixteen▶

My turmoil lasted into the night, leaving me sleepless. I tossed and turned, my blankets uncomfortably hot. The air prickling and cold.

Who *was* I?

Was I still myself? Still the Bree who stacked shelves and did homework? Still the Bree who'd stumbled unaware into this world? I *knew* I'd changed. Was less afraid for myself now - but terribly afraid for the people I loved.

For my friends.

For Fin.

And that was the issue, wasn't it?

If I was becoming someone else - becoming Morgen - where did that leave me and Fin? He'd fancied her as a young man. Would he still want *me* or would he be happy to see me change? Was it *her* he wanted all along? The girl who stepped out of the portrait and threw herself into his arms on sight?

And what about *Hawk*?

I was certain he saw only Morgen when he looked at me. His pain had been so vivid - so *raw* - in the practice yard. I felt for him.

I really did.

Way more strongly than I was comfortable with.

But I was in love with Fin. With my laughing, graceful, casually deadly, Fae lordling. Even the memory of his hands on my skin made me tingle.

So why was there a part of me that felt *Hawk* belonged to me, too?

All too much.

I dressed in my training clothes, the easiest thing to put on without Dechtira's help. Fastening my belt around me, I touched the hilt of Fin's dagger.

Wished he was there to adjust it for me.

The cold night air was slap in the face as I climbed to the roof of the turret. Looked out over the city and surrounding area. The gates were locked behind the last wave of refugees and I could see the campfires of the Formori host on the hill.

They lay like a dark blanket - a taint - on the beautiful face of Faery. I hadn't realised there'd be so many. Had been so involved in the preparations at the castle, I'd not realised they were this close.

Hawk and Guest had to pass them to get back.

A heavy little stone fractured my stomach, weighing me down.

Fear on fear on fear.

I turned my eyes from the enemy and went down the stairs.

Wandered idly through the castle grounds, alone with my terrified thoughts. There were campfires and tents in every available bit of space. Refugees from the town and goodness knows where else. It seemed as though the whole of Faery was gathered in the castle at Tir na n'Og.

Waiting. Hoping to survive.

I refused to meet the eyes of those fae still awake. Didn't want to talk to anyone.

The scent of woodsmoke grew cloying and I turned my feet towards the well near the small gate. Water would help my dry throat. It was dark - unlit - in this area of the castle. Wished I'd taken some light sprites with me. Felt my way forward cautiously and bumped into a cloaked figure.

It grabbed me, pinning me with my back towards it. Heavy hand over my mouth.

I bit down. *Hard.*

Muffled swearing emanated from beneath the hood. I caught a glimpse of the pale face beneath.

'Efnyssen!' A cold shock ran through me. 'I thought you

were safely under lock and key.'

'I told you I was influential. They couldn't keep me locked up forever. Especially when I was so *badly* deceived by the Lady Ethelynn. I believed her to be all truth and goodness. I made a mistake.'

He glared at me challengingly.

'I don't believe *that* for a second.'

'It doesn't matter what you believe, you stupid girl. Tir na n'Og's done. Finished. You can scurry all you want - gather as many fae as you like - but it's too late. A few minutes ago, Formori agents came through that gate and are opening all the others. I'll give you this chance to run. I'm not ungenerous.'

'The gate's locked. You're full of crap.'

A smile slithered across his bony face. 'I gave them the key some time ago. By this time tomorrow Tir Na n'Og will have fallen. Then Caer Dubh. Lady Ethelynn and I will rule together. I'm sure we could find a position for you in our court. I haven't had a human – *pet* - for years.'

I shook my head. Shifted my weight, preparing to run. To tell someone.

Before I'd chance to move he was there, panther fast. Blade to my throat. I reached for my dagger and a swift pain crossed my hand as his sword flickered, cutting my arm deeply.

Knocking it away from my only weapon.

I looked down at my hand, dripping blood. Onto the rough wood of the well cover. A thought occurred. I heaved the cover aside. Efnyssen sneered, never taking his eyes off me.

'How touching. She wants a last drink of water before I kill her. It's almost poetic.' His sarcasm was acidic as he waved the tip of his sword contemptuously. 'Go ahead. It's the least I can do. Throw yourself in, if you like. I'm not choosy about *how* you die.'

I swayed, a little dizzy. Watched dark blood drip into darker water below.

'I'm not thirsty,' I said, calm descending in an icy veil. 'And I don't intend to drown. *Peg Powler.*'

'What?' The Fae looked confused, stepped even closer to me. Looming. His blade levelled at my throat.

'I'm sorry. I *have* to do this. *Peg Powler.*'

He scoffed. 'You don't have the power to summon the river hags. Don't be stupid.'

'You're wrong.' I could feel the cold smile curling the edges of my lips, hardly myself at all. 'This is for Tir na n'Og, asshole.'

He frowned. Tensed to lunge at me.

'*Peg Powler.*'

I backed a few steps further from the well.

Water boiled and exploded in a spume of spray. Stinking of carrion and damp underground spaces.

Peg's long arms rose first, her ghastly face full of glee.

'A fitting meal,' she crowed. Her arms wrapped tightly

around Efnyssen and I saw him struggle. 'You keep your word, Water Lady. It's *good* to have you back.'

Efnyssen screamed as those claws tore through his flesh, dragging him inexorably into the well.

'Peg,' I said. 'Make sure he suffers.'

The ice had frozen in my veins and everything was crystal bright.

The river hag bowed her head. 'As you say, Lady Morgen.'

She disappeared in a spray of black water, taking her victim with her. His screams lingered longer than he did.

I looked at the calming surface of the water, suddenly scared at what I'd done.

What I'd *enjoyed* doing.

'I'm not her,' I said.

But I wasn't sure.

***

I ran, pushing my way past people. Stepping over sleeping fae. And was still too late. By the time I'd reached the audience hall the sounds of screeching metal and cries of horror were loud behind me. I ran into Custenin first.

'They're here,' I said breathlessly. 'Efnyssen let them in. We have to fight.'

'I know.' The king laid a hand on my shoulder. 'Go to Finian and tell him to raise the archers. South wall. Now.'

I found Fin in the council chamber deep in discussion with the queen. Passed on the King's message. Rhiannon pushed Fin towards the door.

'Go, cousin,' she said. 'Tir na n'Og needs you.'

Fin gave me a lingering kiss and darted through the doorway. Gone in moments. Rhiannon looked at me seriously.

'Try to stay clear of the fighting. Get yourself a proper sword, and stay out of the way. You're human. This isn't your fight.' She was weirdly stern and warlike in a set of fighting leathers.

'Your majesty, this *is* my fight,' I lifted my chin. Challenged her with my eyes. 'I've Fae blood. You're my people. Do you think I'd leave the people I love to face *this* - and stay out of the way?'

I shook my head. 'Give me a weapon and I'll fight.'

'The *people* you love?' She raised a perfect eyebrow. 'You mean my cousin?'

'Among others. But, yes. Mainly him.'

A strange smile crossed her face. She hesitated for a moment. 'Yes. You're right.'

She opened a cupboard built cunningly into the wall. Bright metal gleamed in savage array. Turning, she handed me a sword of exquisite beauty. Hilt bound in blue leather and silver. Sapphires winked from the pommel. I pulled it from its scabbard.

The blade shimmered as light reflected off the slender, perfect length of it.

I *drooled*.

'This was Morgen's,' she said. 'You intend to be in the thick of the fighting. As she would. Go and do it.'

I took the sword - bizarrely light in my hand - and ran from the room. Aiming for the south wall. For Fin. A chilling sound stopped me in my tracks.

A compound wail of brassy horns and eerie howling.

It was as though the wind and night joined forces to create that single primal noise, calibrated to stop humans in their tracks.

Rhiannon wasn't far behind me.

'Come *on*,' she said eagerly, pulling me up a flight of stairs. 'It's *him*. At the last minute, as usual. Come and see.'

We stood on top of the city wall, sheltered in the shadow of the doorway and crenellations.

'There.' The queen stretched out a slender hand, pointing.

The eerie sound broke the air again.

From the woods beyond the city, I saw it. A pack of Hounds, beasts of all shapes and sizes. Black, grey, even white with red ears. Flowing across the landscape. And at the front ran Guest, snarling. Feral. His red eyes blazed as he led his people towards the beleaguered city.

Behind them came mounted Fae - maybe two hundred of them - all dressed in the black and silver of Mab's court.

I *tried* not to look for Hawk.

He also rode at the front - a madman with a sword. The Fae and Hounds sliced a vicious path through the invaders. Hawk's sword was a bright and lethal blur, Guest a mass of claw and sinew.

Our reinforcements, but far too few.

Maybe a third of them fell as they fought their way through the enemy to the castle. I gagged, queasy and faint. I'd seen violence in films and on television. Thought nothing of it. I wouldn't have called myself squeamish. But the blades flashing and shrilling - turning living flesh to meat - made my stomach heave.

I looked at Rhiannon.

She stood perfectly still, a lovely - somehow tragic - statue. Her eyes never left Hawk as he brought his men through the gate.

'He'll be ok,' I said, touching her arm lightly.

Hoping like hell I was right.

She smiled at me sadly. 'Life never quite turns out the way you expect, does it? I'll tell you this, little human. When Fae love, it's passionately and forever. An unbreakable bond. We sometimes die of it. Lady knows, Morgen did. *He'll* never be free of her - and *I'll* never be free of him. Ridiculous, isn't it? Hang on to my cousin. Fin loves you. Don't leave him.'

'Never.' I promised, pulling her into an awkward hug. 'Let's do this.'

We bypassed the courtyard where the fighting was thickest.

I was glad Rhiannon - beautiful and deadly - was with me. Several times I'd to duck behind her as she fought off Formori. In the end, my sword stayed in my hand and I found myself quite adept at deflecting stray blades that came too close. Every jolt of my sword arm tore the cut Efnyssen made a little wider. Every blow I parried echoed up my arm in a symphony of pain.

But I kept going.

The queen nodded in approval.

Guest was the first one we found. In the audience chamber, a mound of slain Formori at his feet. Another attacked him fiercely. His teeth sank in and hamstrung it. Finishing it off by swiftly ripping out its throat, he grinned at me.

Little Bree! I've a message for you.

I couldn't look at the dead things on the floor. At the casual violence with which Guest acted. He wasn't some cute puppy. He was the *Barghest*.

But I loved him, so I put my arms around his neck - and kissed his bloodied nose.

'What's the message, mutt?'

*My master says to tell you I'm in one piece - so there's to be no hitting. Does that make any sense to **you**?*

I laughed, amazed at my own amusement - under the circumstances.

'Perfect sense,' I replied. 'Where is he?'

*In the courtyard. He's coordinating the Unseelie. We lost some. He's taking it personally. He always **does**.* The Hound shrugged massive shoulders. *You're safest in here. Wait it out. My master and Fin wouldn't want you in* *danger.*

'Stuff'em,' I said cheerfully. 'I'm sick to death of being told to stay out of things and stay safe. I'm going out there. You coming?'

Rhiannon was through the door almost before I could blink. Guest and I followed.

The courtyard was a nightmarish scene. Surreal to see the lovely castle in this state. Bodies lay where they fell. Fae with missing limbs - with fatal wounds - groaned for mercy or help. None came. The ring of steel and grunts of men and women engaged in combat choked the air.

Rhiannon moved like a tiger - fierce and swift - cutting her way to where the thickest of the fighting seemed to be. Formori fell around her as she almost casually sliced through their ranks.

Trying to get to Hawk.

He was at the top of a small flight of steps, moving with fatal precision. Sword an extension of his arm as he dodged this way and that. Spinning, cutting. Destroying the vile Formori like some kind of whirlwind.

Thoroughly enjoying himself, going by the feral grin on his face.

It was *weird* to see him like that.

To see the deadly creature *I'd* unleashed on Faery. My gentle healer. My honey-voiced physician. A whirlwind of cold fury as he danced with his opponents, making killing look easy.

Taking a deep breath, I raised my sword.

Plunged into the melee.

Now's the time, Morgen, I thought. If you're there. *Now's the time to help me.*

My blade danced in response, body moving without thought or effort. Knew I'd care about the violence - about the slaughter - later. For now only icy anger mattered.

I snarled with joy at each creature that fell beneath my sword. My arm no longer hurt. This was beauty - and pleasure - and joy. *This.* I know I took a few blows that should've knocked me over. A dodge that wasn't quite fast enough saw my stomach cut deeply, sliced by the edge of a Formori weapon. It didn't hurt.

That amused me.

I sliced the creature in half, laughing at the shrivelled things which fell out as it hit the ground. Guest kept me company every step of the way. He was a snarling mass of rage. The nightmare dog all children fear. The thing in the dark with red eyes. He ripped and tore, helping me clear a path.

I reached the steps a few beats behind Rhiannon. She looked surprised to see me behind her and I felt my face stretch in a savage grin.

'This is *fun*,' I said gleefully.

Hawk turned towards me, expression momentarily frozen. I thought I understood what he saw, as I stood there with Morgen's sword in my hand and the light of battle in my eyes.

It wasn't comfortable. I looked away.

'Get her somewhere safe - and *keep* her there,' he snarled at Rhiannon. 'She shouldn't *be* here.'

'I can fight,' I said. Doing just that.

'You don't *understand*. I see things. The future. Rhiannon, please...'

The queen glanced at him, not breaking off her deadly dance with the twisted things besieging us.

'She's handling herself well.'

Pulling me behind him - one armed - Hawk gestured to the door we were defending. 'Guest, get Finian. I don't care if he *is* in charge up there. They all know what to do.'

'He's on the south wall,' I supplied helpfully.

'Rhiannon, take Bree to the council chamber. And keep her there. It's defensible. Only two doors. Guest, get Fin to meet them there. But by the Lady, you *will* keep her safe. *Do you understand?*' His intent eyes met the crimson gaze of the Cu Sidhe.

***Yes**, Master.*

Guest leapt back into the middle of the fighting. I realised we were one of very few pockets of remaining resistance. No matter how many we killed, more came. Like the ocean, wave followed wave.

We waited to drown.

'Come on,' The queen bundled me towards the door. 'He'll be unbearable, otherwise.'

Hawk turned briefly as we went through.

'Be safe' he said. And touched my face. That icy cold tingle again.

And then we were inside and running for our lives.

◀Chapter Seventeen▶

It seemed too quiet in the small council chamber as Rhiannon locked the door behind us. Heavy tapestries muffled the sounds of carnage, but the dim light from the tiny high windows did nothing to soothe.

'We'll not worry too much about the other door for now,' she said, dropping the heavy bar into place across the doorframe. 'Very few people know where the passage is, anyway. Just my family and the hawk lord's.'

'Why only them?' I was curious.

'We're the only two families to rule since the city was built.' She shrugged. 'We can defend that door if we need to. It's you I feel sorry for.'

'*Me*? Why?'

'Because the Formori will get in and kill you before anyone else arrives.' She paced towards me on silent feet. 'I've tried, Briana. I've tried to befriend you. I quite like you, for what it's worth.'

'What are you talking about?'

Every nerve in my body jangled as I moved around the long central table. Tried to keep it between us. The scent of the wax used to polish it hung like a vapour in the air.

'Emrys.'

There was a very peculiar look on Rhiannon's face. Half pity and half something else entirely.

Something predatory.

'*Hawk*? What about Hawk?' The back of my neck prickled

'He's always going to see Morgen when he looks at you. We all will. And you're not her. But ...' She sighed. 'He'll never see *me* at all - while you're here. I'm so sorry.'

She sprang, leaping up onto the table. Padded towards me. I backed away, sword raised defensively.

Metal clashed as the dance began.

Rhiannon was fast. Too fast. That ice cold force within me kept pace with her. Parrying, blocking. I dodged and felt the wind of her blade pass my throat.

Made a mistake.

I stumbled. The half second it took me to right myself was all it needed. She was there, standing over me. Blade resting against my leaden heart. Tiny smile on her lips.

I was going to die.

A thrumming noise distracted me, the air seeming to buzz

for a second.

And Rhiannon fell.

She hit the floor, all her beautiful hair spreading around her like a halo. Wide blue eyes sightless and staring, as if shocked by the arrow that had grown from her throat.

It was gorgeous and grotesque.

I looked round. Guest and Fin had entered by the other door, I realised. Guest's huge shoulder held the tapestry aside. Fin's bow was in his hands. His face was white and set - but his eyes burned like green lanterns.

He didn't say a word.

He'd just killed his cousin - his *queen* - And he didn't say a word.

Guest tugged the arrow from Rhiannon's neck. *As far as anyone's concerned the queen fell defending Bree.*

Finian nodded and turned away.

'We have to go. We're evacuating the city,' he said tonelessly.

***

The carnage was dreadful. Every room and passage bore the marks of savage fighting. The smell of burning from various parts of the beleaguered city was a heavy pall in the air.

Fae and foe alike lay where they fell.

We found Dechtira near the north gate in among a peculiar assortment of fae. Seelie and Unseelie together, they fought their way towards freedom. We joined them. The Pixie paused long enough to hug me, one armed.

'Time to go, my lady.'

'This is the last useful exit, Bree. Bugger off while you can.' Cael sounded entirely too cheerful for someone wearing so much gore. I tried not to notice that his teeth were freshly stained as he appeared beside me.

'We go together. All of us.' I said, squeezing through the jammed gate.

Shoulder to shoulder with the Huntsman.

My master's staying here. I'll see you safe and return for him. He intends to hold our rear with Custenin and the remains of the Host.

Fear bloomed through me. Spread like ink in water.

'Hawk's *what?* Get him out! Go *now*. Don't wait for *me*, you idiot dog. *Go!*'

***Yes**, little Mistress.*

Guest was gone. Just that fast.

And then something unthinkable happened.

I'd turned towards Fin. Dechtira - on his other side - grinned at me. The grin died as a bright length of metal bloomed from her chest. There was a sound, a kind of slick gurgle.

The Formori kicked her from the end of his blade and Fin smoothly ran him through.

My friend lay in the dirt, one glimmering wing crushed

beneath her. I was paralysed. Couldn't breathe for the longest second. Everything was diamond bright. I opened my mouth to scream.

And Fin pushed me into Cael's arms.

'I'm trusting you, Huntsman. You know where we'll meet?' There was something horribly lifeless about his voice.

Cael raised his sword in salute. Fin kissed me once. Hard. Lemons and sunshine and smoke and blood.

And turned and fought his way back toward the castle.

'*Fin!*'

He was leaving me.

He was actually *leaving* me.

Cael gripped my arm tight, dragging me along as the crowd carried us down and out of the city.

'Let go, *asshole*.' I fought him. Wanted to go back for Fin and Hawk. 'Let me *go*.'

'Not a chance, sweetheart.' He pulled me into a shadowed alley as more Formori thundered past, slaughtering evacuees as they went. Dark, blurred blades and crimson blood. 'If you go back now, you'll kill Finian. He needs you safe so he can concentrate. They *both* do. Sod it, all three of 'em if you count the Hound. Trust them. They'll be there to meet us - I *swear* - but you need to move now.'

He patted my shoulder awkwardly. Pushed me firmly towards the street. I managed a weak and watery smile.

The dance began again.

Cutting, slicing, ducking, running. Not feeling. Not that. Just reacting. My heart a chip of diamond, ice hard. None of which explained the tears that blurred my sight and ran down my face without a sob to announce their passage.

The city was a nightmare.

Worse, because I wasn't going to wake up.

Some things emblazon themselves on your mind so strongly you'll see them forever when you close your eyes. A series of vignettes, simple and stark.

Fae bodies mangled and torn, lying almost lip to lip with the Formori who'd killed them. Who'd been cut down in turn.

The brassy clear note of the horn.

'The last stand of Tir na n'Og,' said Cael. 'Remember this.'

And I knew somewhere behind me my friends - the creatures I *loved* - could be dead or dying.

No time to think of that. Time to keep moving. To be hauled to my feet by the exasperated Huntsman when I tripped over the bodies of the slain.

Cael standing over me once when that happened. Holding off three Formori. When they were dead, I took his hand and we ran again.

The scent of smoke, bitter and choking. The heat from the burning woods. The sound of screaming. The sight of the wounded and dying. Those would always be with me.

Tir na n'Og fell.

***

True dawn found us miles from the city. A dirty, exhausted column of people. No-one stopped except to pick up those who could no longer move unaided. I'd never been this way out of Tir na n'Og before and the unfamiliarity added to the dreamlike feeling. It's strange how far you can walk and still smell burning. Still see thick plumes of smoke rising from what was once a city.

A place of beauty.

I sank to the side of the road, beyond the end of my strength. Cael was having none of it.

'Get up,' he said savagely, scrawny hand extended to haul me to my feet. 'Get up - or I'll tell those two Seelie idiots you're so fond of you lay down and *quit.'*

I got up.

He was half carrying me by the time we stopped.

Beyond the crest of the valley was a wooded vale. Burned in places, but whole enough that the trees provided shelter. We melted into them gratefully. It was a rag-tag bunch who spread themselves among the trees. No-one really spoke. Just fidgeted or stared into the distance, shocked and despairing. There was nothing to choose between noble Fae and lesser. No difference between Seelie and Unseelie. We were all just fae that day.

We mourned.

The ice thawed around my heart and with every drip - every fresh crack - the pain grew until I could stand it no longer. I dropped my head on my knees and cried thick, choking tears. They were black with smoke, and so was the mucus staining my pants. I'd a taste in my mouth like I'd been eating charcoal.

A nudge at my elbow. Cael handed me a waterskin, rolling his eyes at the spluttering noises I was making. 'Go easy. We'll not be able to refill for a while.'

'Thanks,' I said absently.

'Good thing I spend a lot of time in your realm, sweetheart. Or you'd just've offended me for *life*.'

'Sorry, Cael. It's just...' I trailed off, seeing Dechtira's smile.

Seeing Dechtira's death.

'I know.' He looked serious. 'We'd best give them till midday - then we're out of here. I hope Rhiannon and Custenin got them into some semblance of order at the end. Come to that, I hope your hawk lord's as good as he thinks he is.'

'He's not...' I began.

'Yeah, I know.' Cael plucked listlessly at the moss we sat on. 'We've got to head for Caer Dubh. It's more defensible than Tir na n'Og. Then they'll come there.' He flicked a clump at the branches above us. 'And what then?'

'We'll fight. We have to.'

'Well, of *course* we'll fight. The question is...'

I never got to find out what it was. Hooves beat loudly at the earth, branches breaking. Cael was on his feet in a heartbeat.

'Wait here.' He darted between the trees. Those of us who could still stand were on our feet.

Ready.

He returned with a smile. 'It's ok. It's them. The rearguard. They don't look so good, but they're here. Some of them.'

'Fin?' My stomach was in my mouth.

Pleasepleaseplease.

He nodded. 'He's safe. Hawk and the dog, too. I *told* you they'd be here to meet you.'

I let out a shaky breath. 'Oh, thank god.'

Fin found us first. He looked tired and his clothes were stained with soot and blood. I gasped in horror, hand flying up to my mouth.

'It's ok, Bree. It's mostly other people's.' He peered down at himself with a rueful grin.

My hands dug into the sweetly rotten leaf mulch as I thrust myself to my feet. *Threw* myself into his arms. Dirty and smelly as we both were, it was the sweetest kiss I'd ever tasted.

There wasn't time to enjoy it.

Hawk and Guest chivvied us all along, erupting through the glade like a tornado. We weren't safe staying this close to the city, and the king - though badly hurt - was organising a mass exodus in the direction of the Unseelie Court.

One foot fell wearily in front of another the rest of that day.

We stopped only once to refill our waterskins. The respite from walking was all too brief. The sun was well below the horizon before we stopped for the night. Some enterprising souls strung up blankets between trees as makeshift tents, others just rolled themselves up in their cloaks.

I was in a strange world far from my own. Involved in a war I should never have known about. Tir na n'Og was lost. And yet as I looked at Fin's face and felt his arms around me, I'd never felt more at home.

◀Chapter Eighteen▶

We'd made camp around the edges of a small lake in a rocky wooded valley. The ground had been climbing steadily as we entered the foothills of the mountain range that stood grey and forbidding ahead of us. The reflected glow of the campfires rippled as a breeze skimmed across the water, and muted sounds of speech choked the air as thickly as the woodsmoke.

I sat between Fin and Guest, staring into the flames. Cael was rolled up in his cloak, apparently asleep. No-one spoke. The silence felt fragile. Each lost in thoughts it wouldn't be wise to share.

Hawk dropped to the grass on the other side of the fire, slinging a pack down beside him. He stretched wearily.

'Where did *you* disappear to?' I asked, only half interested.

'Seeing to as many of the wounded as I could. Thank the

goddess Luydla and some of the other Brownies got out alive. I couldn't begin to treat a tenth part of these people on my own.' He raked a hand tiredly through his hair. 'Is that a wineskin, Finian?'

'Surely is.' I snagged it from Fin. Reached across to hand it to Hawk, wincing sharply at the tugging pain across my abdomen.

He took it. Gave me a sharp look. 'You're hurt?'

'Yeah. Managed to get my stomach cut when me and Rhiannon...' I faltered on the name. Drew a swift breath. 'When we were fighting through to you in the courtyard.'

You should let my master look at that for you. Guest settled himself more comfortably, resting his blood-smeared head on his paws. *For myself, I think some sleep's in order.*

He yawned, red tongue impossibly long in the firelight.

'You're ok, mutt. I'm sure it'll keep for another time.' I caught his yawn, shaking my head. 'Anyway, Hawk's done his bit for tonight.'

'I don't mind.' Hawk reached for the pack he'd thrown down.

'Seriously. I'll be fine.'

'You're being silly,' said Fin, squeezing my shoulder. 'Let him patch you up, then we can *all* get some rest.'

'I can't.'

'Why not?'

'I don't want to undo my top in front of everyone.' I

sounded as sheepish as I felt.

Cael snickered loudly beneath his cloak. That helped *lots*.

Hawk rose suddenly.

'Come on,' he said. 'We'll find somewhere no-one can see you. Not that I'd imagine anyone would be looking.'

'*I'd* be looking,' teased a muffled voice.

'Get bent, Cael.'

I stood and aimed a kick at his prone form. He snorted with amusement.

Even Fin was grinning.

Traitor.

***

Hawk managed to find a secluded thicket back beyond the treeline. A couple of light sprites followed us, dancing around his head and calling weird highlights from his hair. Their piping song seemed sadder and slower than usual, as if they'd caught the mood from the dispossessed fae.

'They like you,' I said.

He batted one gently aside and smiled. 'They're air elementals. My family are air fae. We all command one type of glamour more easily than the others. Different fae call different elements. Finian's family are fire fae. Cael's Wild Hunt, so he's earth.'

'What about Morgen?'

'Water. Surprised?'

He set his pack down and indicated I should take a seat on a rotten stump. It smelled sweet and earthy as I settled myself.

'Not really.' I thought guiltily of Peg Powler.

Unlacing the front of my jerkin, I raised my shirt just enough to expose the cut. The night air was cold and stinging.

Hawk sat on his haunches in front of me, examining the injury. He shook his head.

'You were lucky. Another inch and that would've been nasty.'

'Glad I dodged.' I hissed a fast breath as he began to clean it. 'Did you have to use *cold* water?'

'You wouldn't let me do this near the fire,' he pointed out reasonably.

I scowled and picked at the stump, sending woodlice scuttling for cover.

When he applied a thick grey salve I couldn't help jerking back at the initial sting. Hawk caught my arm and held me still as he finished plastering it on, deftly bandaging my stomach.

'You *must* tell me when you get hurt, bright flame.' Hawk began to replace items in his pack as I rearranged my clothing. 'You're not truly Fae. You can't take the punishment we can. Infections are deadlier for humans here. Be sensible.'

'Oh, *that's* rich! Coming from the guy who threw me into Faery Fae-struck! You didn't even warn me about the place. I could've been killed or eaten in *hours*. You weren't so bothered *then*.'

It sounded as snarky as I felt.

Good.

'Yes, I was. It's why I sent the Hound after you.'

I gaped.

'*What* did you just say?'

'I woke Guest and sent him after you. To avoid the possibility of your being killed or eaten in hours.'

He was still crouching, fussing with his pack. I stared at the top of his black head for a moment, icy shock trickling along my spine. I'd always assumed it'd been a symptom of Leiloken's madness that he'd done that. Never really held *Hawk* responsible.

But now it seemed...

'You knew what you were doing.'

My voice emerged a croak and I cleared my throat. Gripped the side of the stump tightly to steady myself.

Hawk didn't even glance up. Just kept his head down. Inky waves shrouding his face.

'Yes, I knew.' Very quiet.

The anger boiled out from the little hot place behind my eyes and danced along every nerve. I stood and backed away a few steps.

'Then you did it on *purpose*. You dumped me here on purpose. I gave up my chance to go *home* for you, and I'd never even have *been* here if you hadn't thrown me out without so much as a by-your-leave.'

I advanced on him, one trembling finger pointed accusingly.

He looked at me then, face serious.

'I did what I had to. I knew what was coming - what Faery was facing. You were my best hope. Of being here. Doing what I've to do. Once I realised you were of Morgen's line...'

'So I'm just collateral damage, am I?' I interrupted. 'A sacrifice to save the many? Well, Bree might die - but it doesn't matter as long as *I* get to go home. No need to keep *her* safe.'

'*No.*' He darted to his feet, imposingly tall. Warm edge of anger in his voice. 'You were *never* a sacrifice. *Never.* I'd tear Faery *apart* to keep you safe, if I had to.'

A rising gust of wind made me shiver. Danced across my face and neck.

Hawk grabbed my shoulders, looking intently into my eyes.

'Tell me you believe me.'

'I believe you.'

The words were out before I meant to say them.

He drew a controlled breath. Closed his eyes for a second before releasing it slowly. 'I'm sorry. More sorry than you know. I wasn't precisely - myself - at the time. Not entirely in control. Enough to know what I was doing, though. Enough to understand the danger I was placing you in. I couldn't hold my grip on myself long enough to explain. Not to *you*. You were hard to look at, bright flame. Do you understand?'

'Yes. Morgen.' I thought for a moment. 'So is that why - I mean - I thought...'

My voice trailed off and I looked away.

On second thoughts, this was a conversation I'd rather *not* have.

'You thought what?' Hawk's voice was very level.

The light sprites trilled in the air above us as I tapped my hands nervously against my leg.

'It's silly, really.' I kept my eyes fastened on the floor. 'When you threw me out there were a few seconds I thought you were going to - *well* - kiss me.' A fast embarrassed laugh.

Hawk stilled.

Motionless and blank faced.

Cool hands on my shoulders. Long, silent seconds while my cheeks and ears took flame.

Then a quiet question.

'Would you have let me?'

My turn to go still. I slowly turned my face up to his. He looked calm; Fae unreadable. The golden colour of his eyes glittered strangely in the green light cast by the sprites. Backlit with that weird Fae glow.

'What?'

'Would you have let me kiss you?'

'Hawk, I was Fae-struck. That's not fair!'

A flicker of amusement tugged the edges of his lips. 'Yes, you were Fae-struck. Even so, you were still yourself. Still knew what you were doing. Or are you telling me that you and Fin got up to a lot more on that journey than Guest was aware of?'

'No. Fin was a perfect gentleman, actually. And it's kind of hard to think my way clearly through all *that* now. I didn't even realise what I felt for Fin was *more* than being Fae-struck till after I was cured.'

'But you *are* cured. And I need an answer. It's important.' His fingers were tighter on my shoulders now. His expression fiercer. 'I *need* to know how much of her's still there, Bree. How much of Morgen survives - somewhere in you. There's a reason. So I'm asking again.'

He took a quicksilver step forward, closing the little distance between us. Leant down to look me in the eye. Blazing gold bathing my skin. His face so close to mine, I felt his breath cool on my lips.

'Would you have let me?'

My heightened pulse battered through the palms of my too warm hands and neck, but something icy was uncurling from around my ribs. Pacing urgently through my veins. Urging me to close the narrow gap between his mouth and mine.

'Yes,' I said.

He swallowed, stepping back rapidly. For just a second

something dark flitted across his face. The blank mask dropped back into place. Stooping for his pack, he turned and walked wordlessly back the way we'd come.

I stood, my hand clasped over my mouth.

Wishing I could recall every word I'd said.

A rustle of movement off to the side. A darker shadow outlined against the darkness.

'Wasn't that touching?'

I stared at Fin in shock. His normally bronzed skin looked ashy pale in the faint light. Unfamiliarly blank, he was the Fae lord again. Alien and untouchable. I swallowed hard.

'How long have you been there?'

'Long enough. Aren't you going after him?' Fin spoke coolly, politely.

'Why would I go after him? Where did *that* come from?'

'Oh, I don't know. Maybe from hearing you say you wanted to kiss him.'

'Not what I said, Finian. I said I'd have let *him* kiss *me*. While I was Fae-struck. Before I met *you*.'

'Not how it looked.'

Only now did I notice the tic jumping in the corner of his jaw.

'Fin...'

'Would you have let him if he'd tried just now?'

I opened my mouth and hesitated. For a moment.

For too long.

'I see.' He gave a short, bitter laugh.

'No. You don't. Not at all. I've no interest in Hawk that way. *None*, Fin.' I looked at him miserably. 'It's just - Morgen *does*. She's in my blood. Alive, somehow. I don't know what you want me to do about that.'

'So.' He leaned back against a tree, a long silhouette. 'The blood wants him and I want you - and where does that leave us?'

'It's not like that. I - can't help being a little confused, sometimes.'

I was horribly cold. Scared. Tried hard to summon words that'd make him see.

That'd make him understand.

They didn't come.

I watched his head and shoulders slump forward for a moment. He pushed himself up straight.

'I don't think I can live with your confusion, Bree.' He moved towards the edge of the thicket, turning as he drew level with the stump I'd sat on. 'Let me know if you ever work it out.'

Then he was gone.

And my heart shattered into sharply splintered fragments.

Cutting me to the bone.

◀Chapter Nineteen▶

I sat on the rotten stump, numb with shock. Until I could bear to sit no longer. My legs were leaden as I stumbled back to the fire to find Cael alone. He was swigging heftily from the wineskin and chewing on something I didn't want to look at too closely.

'I've got to hand it to you,' he said, without looking up. 'I've heard *I* can be pretty annoying - but you must be *really* good. Those two Seelie boys have *both* gone off with faces like slapped arses. Bit of a problem 'cause apparently the golden moron's summoned them. I bet you were shouting at them. Again. Did you shout?'

He offered me the wineskin, grinning up at me.

'No.' Flatly.

I took a long swallow, wincing at the coppery taste left by Cael's bloodied mouth.

'Oh.' His eyes widened, then narrowed speculatively. '*Oh*. Well, then. I suppose the question is - which one are you going after?'

'Hawk. I need to talk to Hawk.'

He could speak to Fin for me. He could explain.

The Huntsman raised his eyebrows. 'You do surprise me,' he said, taking back the wineskin. He pointed off around the shadowed edge of the lake. 'He went thattaway.'

With a nod, I walked slowly in the direction he'd indicated, passing sleeping fae. Those who couldn't sleep barely glanced up at my passage. Eyes filled with shadows. I was maybe a third of the way round when Guest spoke to me.

Over here, little Mistress.

I turned. The great Hound sat beside a smaller version of Luydla's mound. It almost pulsed with energy. My confusion must have been written on my face.

The Dryads made this for the king. My master and the Brownies are with him now. He was sorely wounded in the retreat.

'He'll be ok, won't he? Hawk's good. I mean, he healed me.'

The fight left Custenin when Rhiannon's body was found. The Brownie woman is good, yes – and my master's the best healer in Faery. But they're not gods. They can do only what they can. Guest shook his shaggy head mournfully.

'Aren't we philosophical tonight, mutt?' I hesitated, unsure what to do. 'I wanted to talk to Hawk. But I guess it can wait.'

It won't have to wait too long, I think. The king's also sent for the Lughan boy. He'll not want my master there when he talks to him.

The Hound was right. It couldn't have been more than an hour before I saw Fin walking towards us, stony-faced and unfamiliar. He didn't even glance at me. Just spoke to Guest.

'Tell your master I'm here to see my king, Cu Sidhe,' he said levelly.

Guest closed his eyes. Moments later the door bloomed in the hillside. Hawk stepped out, a slight slump to his shoulders.

'Custenin wants to talk to you. Listen to what he has to say. There's not much time.' Sombre words and sorrowful honeyed velvet.

Without a reply, Fin shouldered his way past the taller Fae and entered the mound. The entrance closed behind him. I shuddered at the look on his face.

'What's happening?' I asked.

Hawk looked sharply at me, opened his mouth to reply, and closed it again.

'Walk with me for a moment,' he said. 'And I'll tell you what I can.'

We wandered a little distance away and I realised it was so we wouldn't be overheard by the concerned Seelie who stood in knots near the mound where their king was dying.

Hawk leaned against a tree, ankles crossed. Reminding me with a sharp pang of Fin's stance earlier. He tipped his head back against the trunk and closed his eyes.

'Custenin's dying,' he said. 'There's nothing I - or anyone else - can do. It's a matter of time. A short time. He wants Fin to go and fetch his father.'

'Because the Lughan hold the throne,' I guessed, and he nodded wearily.

Opened his eyes again to seek my face.

'And because they also hold the spear of their founder. Which may be the thing that wins this for us.'

'Mab mentioned that.'

Dropping to sit on the cool grass, I plucked aimlessly at random strands.

'She's always been a clever girl.' I could hear the smile in his voice. 'The Aspara and some of the other winged fae arrived tonight. They've been watching the Formori, covering our rear. The Formori are preparing to move out again, Bree. They won't be content with Tir na n'Og. They'll get bored with destruction - and they'll follow us.'

'Then we need to get to Caer Dubh. As fast as possible. That's what Cael said.' I tugged out a whole handful of grass. Dangled it from my fingers, surrounded by the wholesome smell of earthy roots.

'He's not stupid, either.' Hawk sighed, sliding down the tree to sit beside me. 'I'll...' He paused. 'I've told the king I'll open a doorway through the Elsewhere and evacuate everyone to Caer Dubh in stages.'

I smiled, feeling slightly cheered. 'But that's good, isn't it? We can all get away, regroup. We might win this thing,

Hawk. You were *always* going to make sure we won, weren't you? You don't strike me as the losing type, somehow.'

He gave a low laugh, warm and smooth as chocolate. 'I'm touched by your faith. It's more people than I've ever moved before. The size of the doorway I'll need to create and sustain...

'I'll need to be able to see where I'm putting people down as clearly when the hundredth - the *eight* hundredth - passes through, as when the first does. I'll need to hold the picture of our destination firmly in my mind throughout. It's the sustained mental effort that makes it hard.'

'But not impossible?'

'Oh, far from impossible.' He sounded brighter, but it was strained. 'I told Custenin we'd have to take it in stages. Not too great a distance at a time. I just need some sleep first. I'm exhausted. I can't *remember* the last time I got any real sleep. Don't look so alarmed, bright flame. I'll be able to do this easily enough with some rest. I just need to see your Fin again, first.'

I wanted to tell him that Fin wasn't mine any more - that he needed to talk to him - but that would've been petty and selfish under the circumstances.

Instead, I sat with him and waited for Finian to emerge.

When the doorway opened at last, I didn't see it. Lost in my own miserable thoughts. It wasn't until Fin spoke - voice sharp - that I realised he'd come to stand over us. That boy could move like a cat.

'You wanted to talk to me, hawk lord?'

'You know what the king wants you to do?' Hawk stood again, voice sympathetic.

'I do.' Fin was all mask, all cool courtesy.

'And you're willing?'

'I'm at my king's command.'

'So destiny begins to catch up with you, Finian Medyr.' Hawk spoke softly. 'When shall I open the doorway for you?'

'As soon as possible. *Now* for preference. I want...' Fin glanced at me. 'I want to get away from here. As soon as I can.'

'Fin, *please*...' I began.

He ignored me. Just continued to talk to the other Fae in that calm, hateful tone.

'How will we find you? Will you come for us?'

'No,' Hawk was equally calm. Relaxed. All signs of weariness and worry buried under another of those disturbingly impenetrable blank Fae faces. 'I'll reopen the door in one week. Exactly. Be there.'

'We will.' Fin half turned to look back at the mound and I realised his pack and bow were already on his shoulders. An ungainly silhouette. He seemed to sigh silently, his head drooping for a fraction of a second. He turned back.

'Shall we get going?'

Hawk nodded. 'As you wish.'

He led us a few paces aside. Stopped before a tree trunk, wide and ancient. A great crack split it, forming a cavernous hole as tall as I was. He laid a hand on the trunk, eyes spookily unfocussed for several seconds. Like he was staring into some other reality.

A white fog - glowing and eerie - began to crawl and eddy around the tree, filling the crack completely.

'Travel safely,' he said to Finian. 'No unnecessary risks. And remember, one week. That's all I can promise. Any longer may well be too late.'

Fin took a deep breath and finally looked at me. *Really* looked at me. Face pale and lips almost bloodless. His eyes glittered like emeralds, glowingly hot and painful.

'Be safe,' he told me.

And stepped into the Elsewhere.

After a couple of minutes Hawk lifted his hand from the trunk and the mist faded away.

'I need to sleep,' he muttered, rubbing a hand across his face. 'You should rest too, bright flame. Find Cael and stay with him. He's probably the best person you can have with you while we evacuate.'

'What about you? Will you be ok?'

'I'll get the Barghest to sit with me. He can be a bit fierce about people disturbing my sleep.' He smiled, half yawning.

Smiling in return, I did as he'd suggested and returned to our fire.

Cael was deeply asleep, spiky silver hair poking from the end of his cloak. It wasn't long before I was too, my cloak rolled equally firmly around me.

***

I flinched awake, squeaking at the feel of the Cu Sidhe's cold nose against my neck. He whined softly.

Come quickly, little Mistress. I'm worried.

I sat up, shivering and rubbing my stinging eyes. 'Worried about what?'

Cael stirred at the sound of my voice, muffled though it was by the early morning mist. He rolled onto one elbow and looked enquiringly at me. I shrugged.

'Spill, mutt,' I commanded. 'What's up?'

Look at the other bank of the lake. You see the doorway they've formed?

I peered through the mist, grateful for the sharpness of vision that'd come with my Fae blood. Several tall trees on the far side of the lake bent towards one another, branches tightly interlaced. Forming a huge arch. It loomed over the lake, not too high, but vastly wide.

*It's too **big**.*

'Chill, Guest. Hawk told me about this last night. He knew what it needed to be like. He said it'd be fine.'

I stretched, feeling my shoulders pop.

It felt good.

*And maybe it **would** have been, if he'd gotten any rest. If* *he hadn't...* Guest whined again.

'Hadn't what?' I spoke sharply, catching a little of his worry and feeling it thrill along my neck.

*Hadn't seen what he saw. He had another vision last night. It's left him drained. I think what he saw was - unpleasant. He didn't react well at **all**.*

'I thought he was cured.'

Cael sniggered. 'You can't cure someone of being a Seer, you dozy git,' he informed me loftily. 'Don't you know *anything?* You cured the madness, not the talent. Guest, am I right in thinking you want my girl Bree here to nag him into sleeping? To delay our departure before he kills himself - or the rest of us?'

Guest gave a growl, eyes fixed on the other bank.

*It **was** my thought, yes - but it's too late. He's committed now.*

I looked back at the arch. Already filling with that glowing white mist.

'We've got to *stop* him,' I said.

'The Hound's right. It's too late, sweetheart.' Cael looked worried.

Not a comforting sight.

I must go to him.

'I'm coming with you.' I followed the Hound as he loped towards the great arch, Cael at my rear.

We'd to push our way through ranks of fae waiting to

evacuate. They allowed us through with ill grace. Unwilling to lose their place in the queue, but equally unwilling to halt Guest's momentum.

His master sat with his back against a tree making up part of the vast doorway.

The frame was almost full of the swirling mist, the assembled fae murmuring eagerly among themselves.

After several long minutes Hawk opened his eyes and nodded to a Fae I recognised as a captain of the Kingsguard. People began to hustle through. We stopped beside him. Waited for him to look at us. His eyes were huge and blue shadowed against his pallor.

He smiled oddly at us and lowered his head, hands clasped around his knees.

'Now what?' I asked.

*Now we wait. **No**, little mistress,* said Guest as I stepped closer to Hawk. *Don't disturb him.*

'I wasn't going to.'

But I was afraid for him.

It took all day and into the night before everyone was through. Hawk slumped lower and lower as time went on. Guest kept making little whimpering sounds. Eventually, I lowered myself to the ground beside Hawk. Slipped my hand into his.

A strange tug, almost a lessening of myself. Dancing waves and ripples of loss.

Of something.

'Nearly there,' I whispered. Doubted he heard me until I felt a slight squeeze of the fingers. Minimal pressure.

I didn't realise I'd nodded off till Cael shook me awake.

'Come on, sweetheart,' he said, pulling me to my feet. 'The Hound says we've to make tracks. We're the last few.'

'The king?' I asked.

Cael shook his head.

I sighed and looked at the great black Hound sitting guard over his master.

'You'll bring Hawk through safely, won't you? Make sure he's ok?'

Guest's tongue lolled. *Of course. What else should I do?*

Shouldering my pack, I nodded and sent one last, worried look in Hawk's direction before following the Huntsman through the cool fog. The wrench of disorientation was worse this time. Harsher. Fog eddied strangely as we emerged onto a broad plain, edged by snow capped peaks.

It was *much* colder here, and I shivered helplessly.

'Unseelie lands,' said Cael. 'Home at last. Shall we get you to a fire, sweetheart? Pathetic how humans can't take a bit of cold.'

'No,' I said through chattering teeth. 'I want to wait for the others.'

It was a slow forever before they came through the fog. Just silhouettes at first, gradually gaining clarity as they approached. Hawk was leaning fairly heavily on Guest, but he grinned triumphantly.

'Hawk? Are you ok?' I was anxious.

He looked all wrong, I realised, as they came closer. Brilliant eyes dull, movements weirdly jerky.

'No-one's ever done that before,' he said.

And dropped like a stone to lie motionless and pallid at my feet.

The Cu Sidhe *howled*.

◀Chapter Twenty▶

I called in my favours.

The Portune were easily persuaded to raise a mound from the earth as the Dryads had from tree roots. Hawk lay inside, tended by Luydla and her people - happy to help - while the Hound and I waited anxiously. I bit my fingernails until they bled.

The Seelie mourned their king around us. No state funeral for Custenin. No long ceremonies to send him to his rest.

He'd sleep forever in the dryad mound by the lake.

I was surprised how sad his loss made me.

Cael lit a fire close by the Brownies' mound and left us to it. Went to seek news of his Hunt, while we sat in tense vigil. It was almost another full day before Luydla emerged, swaying on her feet. Guest jerked upright. I knotted my hands tightly together. Icy fingers of fear tracing my spine.

'He lives,' she said. 'He lives but won't wake.'

'But he *will*?' I peered up at her. Begged with my eyes.

'Maybe. Maybe not.' The little woman's voice was shaded with sadness. 'We wait now.'

So we waited.

***

The next day dawned and I sought Cael out, unable to sit there any longer.

I'd lost Dechtira. Lost Fin in a wholly other way. Did I have to lose *Hawk*, too?

Not an option.

Unthinkable thought, knotting my stomach and sending waves of terrified nausea crashing through me.

Eventually, the silence and the brooding grew too much. I needed to find something to do other than scare myself half to death with 'what-if's.

So.

I demanded Cael train with me

We found an out of the way spot - and sparred furiously.

I threw myself into the fight. All my rage and pain and loss and frustration channelled into the sport. Cael nicked me for the fifth time in an hour, shaking his head ruefully.

'You're letting emotion get the better of you,' he noted. 'You can't afford to lose focus like that.'

I picked up the sword he'd sent spinning from my hand and gestured helplessly with it.

'I know. I'm *rubbish*. Morgen usually takes over.'

'Maybe Morgen's letting emotion get the better of her, too. He's *her* hawk lord, isn't he?' Cael executed several Fae-fast passes with his own weapon. 'Maybe you *both* need to focus.'

So we continued.

For two days - aching in every muscle - I trained as often as I could with the Unseelie Huntsman.

I wish it'd helped.

Nothing did.

On the third day I called out for Luydla and she opened the doorway to let me into the mound. It was a small, bare, earthen room. A ledge protruded along one side, holding what I recognised as fae medical supplies. A broader platform, deep with soft moss, jutted from the other side.

There lay Hawk, cloak drawn up to his chin.

Looking all *wrong*.

I took a few steps towards him, barely aware of Luydla ushering her two Brownie companions out of the mound. He was greyish, ashen. Chest barely rising and falling with his breath.

For a moment I thought I was too late. Felt my pulse falter.

Couldn't *breathe*.

I must've made a noise, because Luydla said. 'He lives,

mortal Fae girl. *He's* not so easy to kill as all that.'

I tried to smile. Failed.

'How long till he wakes up?' Shaky words.

'I can't say. In this state it could be weeks - even months. He's pushed himself to the limit of his strength and skill. Drained himself of glamour beyond his ability to replace it. That's not so easy to come back from. Some never do.' She gave a dispirited little shrug. 'He's gaining strength physically, but I can't speak for his glamour. Or his mind. After all he's already suffered in *that* department...'

'I see.' I touched his pinched face, horrified at how cold he felt. 'He's *freezing*, Luydla. We need to get Mother Holle. *Now.*'

'Mother Holle is a talented healer, yes. But I'm better. Trust me. I'm doing all I can for him.'

'Mother Holle can open doors through the Elsewhere,' I said crisply. 'Fin's expecting to be coming back here in three days with our reinforcements. Hawk said it'd be too late if we left it any longer. If *he's* not here to organise it, *I'll* have to. We need her. I'm going to try and get her here.'

'And how are you planning to manage that?' she asked. 'Mother Holle lives as far beyond Tir na n'Og as we've already come. There's no time to summon her. Only the Seers can travel that fast. We'll do what we can. I promise no more.'

'I hear you.'

I brushed Hawk's hair back from his face, soft and silken waves under my fingers. Looked into Luydla's warm brown eyes.

A steely resolve made me lift my chin at her.

'But I think I know someone else who *can* travel that fast. I'm going to try something. Pray it works.'

***

Stepping out of the mound, I caught the arm of the nearest fae - a winged blue girl. Her wings shimmered in a way that made my stomach twist, remembering Dechtira.

'Where's the nearest water?' I asked.

She pointed.

I walked until I reached a wide stream, almost a river, flooding down from the mountains at our back. It cut a shallow ravine through the landscape before falling away down the slope, almost turning back on itself. Hidden by a stand of trees, I looked around to make sure no-one could see what I was up to.

With a deep, steadying breath, I removed the bandage from my hand and cut the wound open again. Allowing my blood to drop into the water.

Please.

Please let this work.

'Peg Powler,' I said quickly. 'Peg Powler, Peg Powler.'

I stepped back involuntarily as the familiar explosion churned the water and flung shining droplets into the air. I smelled Peg almost before I saw her. Green seaweed and rotten meat. Two equally hideous faces rose behind her.

Her sisters, I assumed.

'What do you want, Water Lady?' Her gurgling voice wasn't unfriendly. More curious than anything else.

I forced a smile.

'I need your help, Peg. I need you to tell Mother Holle to open a door and come here.'

'Why would I want to do that?' She sounded genuinely puzzled. 'River hags are free of those caves now. We won't return. I'd have thought you'd know that.'

Her sisters snarled in agreement.

'*Please*, Peg,' I asked, aware of a pleading tone to my voice. 'You can travel fast. Faery needs her - or we *all* fall.'

'Faery needs her.' Her voice was flat, sceptical.

'The hawk lord needs her, too. I think...' I swallowed, throat dry and eyes misting. 'I think he's dying.'

She shrieked with triumphant laughter. 'Oh, then I *don't* think so. Your so-called 'hawk lord' is no friend to river hags - and neither are you. *Morgen*, I'd deal with. Maybe. For the right price. But she isn't with you right now - is she?'

'Faery will fall,' I repeated desperately.

'Much we care,' hooted one of the sisters. 'Let Faery burn. Formori taste just as good as you Fae. Plenty of meat on 'em.'

Peg smacked her lips in noisy agreement. 'No deal, water whelp. Burn. *We* won't mourn you. As a matter of fact,' she said slyly. 'We're hungry now. I can't touch her, sisters

- but *you're* welcome to feast.'

The hideous creatures behind her began to extend long, slimy arms. Reached for me, moving slowly forward. I stumbled back, feet catching on clumps of grass. The foetid stench of them grew stronger as if called by their hunger.

'We made a deal, Peg.' High and frightened. 'You promised you wouldn't harm me.'

She smiled maliciously.

'True – but I said *nothing* about my sisters, girl.'

'*Oi!* Hold it right there, ugly!' A loud command from behind me.

The River hags froze as Cael appeared at my side, cruelly hooked knives in hand. I shot him a grateful look. He frowned, serious as I'd ever seen him. Black eyes glimmered with gleeful menace.

'This woman's under Unseelie protection,' he said. 'You won't harm her on Unseelie lands.'

'Oh?' asked Peg. 'And do you *have* the authority to make that claim? Will your grandmother support you?'

'Of *course* she will. She's never been able to stay mad at me for long. The woman *adores* me.' He grinned wickedly, giving them the benefit of those disturbingly pointed teeth. 'Well, go on then. Bugger off.'

With a grumble - and a last, hungrily lingering look in my direction - the river hags disappeared beneath the surface. We stood silently, watching the ripples die away. Turned and walked back in the direction of Hawk's mound.

'Check *you* out being all badass.' I beamed at the Huntsman in relief. 'Who's your granny? The Incredible Hulk?'

'No.' He sheathing his wicked blades and winking at me. 'Mab is. That's why I joined the Wild Hunt. Not cut out for court life, see?'

My mouth dropped open in surprise.

'Am I the only person left that's not sodding noble in some way?'

'That'd be why they call us the noble Fae.' He stopped, gesturing grandly at the ground. 'Take a seat, sweetheart. I think it's time *you* learned some of the facts of fae life.'

I sat reluctantly on the springy grass and raised my eyebrows at him.

'Go on, then,' I said.

He dropped cross-legged in front of me. 'Thing is, sweetheart, you *are* noble Fae. Whether you like it or not - and it's high time you bloody acted it. Those Seelie boys of yours are so busy trying to protect you, they've never taken the time to teach you to protect yourself. I have.'

He held my gaze, pointed face serious. 'When you make a deal in Faery, the realm itself holds you to your word. Your *exact* word. That's why you need to be so bloody careful how you phrase things. You didn't do that with Peg, did you?'

'No,' I admitted. 'I think maybe Fin was trying to warn me about it. But I shut him down.'

'*And* another thing. Is it true that when your hawk lord —

no, don't interrupt. You can talk after – that when *he* came back, the pair of you stood in front of the entire court and refused to accept each other's debt? A life debt?'

'Yes, but...'

'Then you've caused yourself *another* problem. You might want to ask him what that means. What it's caused. Unless he's told you?'

'No.'

'Thought not.' He narrowed his eyes, hands toying with his dagger hilts. 'Likes to keep a bit too much to himself, doesn't he? Just out of interest - what did he say his plan was when he brought us here?'

Weird that with my Fae eyes I could see him so well, even in the dark. Could gauge his expressions so accurately.

'He said we'd take the evacuation in stages. He told Custenin that before he died.'

'Did he tell *you* what he planned? - or what he'd told the *king* he planned?'

'What difference does that make?'

'Rather a lot, actually. Do you know where we *are*, Bree? Why we're all so scared to be here?' A little savage.

'Halfway to Caer Dubh?' I guessed.

Cael shook his spiky silver head. 'Ask him that as well.'

'I'm not likely to be asking him anything, am I? He's out for the count. Or hadn't you noticed?'

I was getting a bit fed up hearing lectures on my safety

from a Fae who'd shot me.

Twice.

'And *another* point.' Cael was relentless. 'While you're having a word with yourself - have a word with Morgen, too. She'll help you fight and stuff. But where is she now, when we need her? He's *her* hawk lord - and we're all in the crap if he doesn't wake up. We *need* the rest of the Seelie forces. Where the hell is she now? Is she too *chicken* to actually help? Or do you think maybe she just doesn't *care* for him enough?'

It began behind my eyes. The familiar icy calm I'd begun to associate with Morgen's presence.

Except this time, calm *wasn't* the word.

Boiling, burning ice spread through every limb, my veins a glacial web. I watched myself become distant, thoughts riding passenger in my own mind.

Without my volition, my body stood.

Morgen was in control.

My face turned toward Cael, who'd pushed himself to his feet when I did. He hovered in front of me with a faint, expectant frown on his face.

'Out of my way, little Unseelie.' It was my mouth, my tongue.

Not my voice that emerged.

Cael paled.

'Oh, *shit*,' he said. And stood aside.

Fated

Morgen marched me rapidly towards the mound, Cael hurrying to keep up. My hand touched the earthen side and the door appeared. I felt a curious little loss - a weakening - as it did so.

Inside, Luydla busily stirred up some kind of elixir in a small pot. Not a pleasant smell, too sour and bitter. She turned, surprised brown eyes widening as she looked at my face.

'You know me?' That other voice from my mouth again.

Luydla inclined her head. 'Yes, Lady Morgen. I remember you.'

'Leave us.'

I stood stock still, unable even to twitch a finger as Morgen waited for the Brownie to leave.

We turned towards Hawk and - for the barest second - I felt what Morgen felt. A profound sense of sadness. Of dreadful, destructive guilt. Of appalling sorrow - and brightly blazing love.

Fiercer and hotter than fire.

For the man she'd cursed. The Fae she'd died to break. She shut the link down quickly.

Blocked me out.

But I saw enough to feel gut-churningly sorry for both of them.

She sat me down beside him, perched on the edge of the platform. He looked *awful*. Too still, and half unreal. Morgen used my hand to stroke his hair, caress his pale face.

'My fierce Hawk,' she whispered with my lips. 'My merlin boy. Still taking things too far. How many more times must I save you?'

The hurt in that would've made me cry.

If I'd been in control of my eyes.

Bending forward, she placed the softest of kisses on his still lips. Pulling back, she concentrated - and something which smelled like summer rain and felt like the tide, began to spill from my mouth. To enter his mouth and nostrils. That tug, that same strange feeling of loss. But stronger. Smoother and more intense.

It went on *forever*.

Hawk stirred uneasily, turning his head to the side and frowning faintly.

'Morgen,' he murmured. 'You *know* I don't like...'

He stopped.

His eyes snapped open, hand fixing Fae-fast round my wrist. Morgen gathered herself and fled, taking refuge buried in the back of my mind and bloodstream.

I snatched my hand away and leapt to my feet.

Rubbed my wrist like I'd been burned.

'She's gone,' I said.

And called for Luydla.

She exclaimed with pleasure to see him awake. I backed out of the mound and left her to examine him.

Fated

Talk about *awkward*.

◀Chapter Twenty One▶

Sitting on the side of the mound outside, I started to get angry. Why was I so furious with Hawk? So hot and unhappy and cross?

I counted off the reasons on my fingers.

One. Putting Morgen in that position, which led to...

Two. Morgen and Hawk putting me in the position of being a gooseberry in my *own body*.

Three. Keeping things from me about this debt thing.

If Cael was right.

Four. Not telling me where he intended to bring us - when everyone else seemed to know and be uneasy about it.

Again, *if* Cael was right.

Five. Pushing me to say I'd have kissed him - and losing me

Fin in the process.

Big, big reason, that.

Huge.

Six. Sending Fin through the Elsewhere to face god-knows-what, before I'd had chance to make up with him.

Seven. Almost being unable to bring Fin and the Seelie troops back.

But mainly Fin.

Eight. Almost *killing* himself, rather than be sensible and get a bit of sleep.

Nine. Generally being a smug, arrogant, infuriating *asshat*.

I was absolutely boiling with rage. Kept expecting my ears to whistle like a camping kettle when the steam came out. My hands clenched into tightly balled fists and tension crackled along my neck and jawline.

'You ok?' Cael appeared beside me, oddly hesitant. He dropped easily to sit cross-legged.

'No. I think I might kill Hawk myself.' I snapped. 'I'm giving Luydla five more minutes - *five* - then I'm going in there to give him a piece of my mind.'

The Huntsman snickered, pulling a leaf from his hair and shredding it.

'Wouldn't want to be him, then.'

I sat in glowering silence.

But only for five minutes.

I called out for Luydla as the mound wouldn't open to my touch now Morgen was gone. I'd no idea how she'd done it, and even less how to do it myself. Assuming I even could. The Brownie motioned me in.

Hawk sat on the edge of the low platform, long legs stretched out comfortably. He raised his eyebrows questioningly when he caught the look on my face.

I focussed on Luydla, ignoring him.

'Is he better?' I asked.

Her eyes twinkled at my cold tone. 'Yes, Lady Bree. He seems to be in good health.'

'And he'll be able to open doorways? To bring Fin and the others back?'

'I see no reason why not - as long as he doesn't overreach himself.' She was smiling.

'And if he was involved in a *small* skirmish before then, he'd still be able to do that, yes?'

I was biting the words off short, jaw too clenched to speak properly.

Her smile became a grin, burn scar puckering cheerfully.

'That should be *fine*, dear.'

'Good.'

I turned to the patient, watching the exchange with barely concealed amusement. Glared at my clenched right hand.

Pulling it back and twisting my body to add speed - I punched him.

Hard.

Right in the face.

My wrist immediately began to hurt. At least I split his lip for him. Would've been more impressive if I hadn't been aiming for his eye.

Raising a hand to his lip, he wiped away the blood and looked at me. Face blank. It lasted half a second - then he surprised me completely.

He threw back his head, and began to laugh.

Real, gleeful, helpless laughter, almost irresistibly contagious. It took all my self control not to join in. Luydla was laughing too. Deep chuckles.

I forced my face to remained blank and still.

'I assume,' he said, when he'd pulled himself together. Eyes still alight with humour. 'You're going to tell me – probably at length - what that was for?'

'I have a *list*.'

'Luydla, would you please be very kind and leave us for a short while?' Hawk flashed a grin at the little woman. 'I'd much rather be shouted at in private.'

She snorted humorously and left, the door disappearing behind her.

'Well?' He sat a little straighter. 'What's on the list, bright flame?'

I stood, arms folded. Glared at him. A strange look crossed his face and he dropped his head to examine his hand on his knee, hair a curtain hiding his expression.

'I have questions - and for once I want straight answers from you. About all *sorts* of things. Cael seems to think it's significant we wouldn't accept one another's debt. You can start by explaining why that is.' I frowned. 'And *don't* lie.'

'But I *can't* lie to you, Bree.' He raised his head and met my eyes, oddly wary. 'That's one effect of the debt bond. You can't lie to me, either. Try, if you like.'

I started telling him the sky was green, just for the hell of it. Was stopped by an odd reluctance. The words refused to come - and I almost growled with frustration. Hawk watched me steadily, lips quirking at the corners as I tried to lie.

And failed.

'Don't be ridiculous,' I said, instead. 'So. We can't lie. Isn't *that* wonderful? Any other little side effects I should know about?'

He nodded. 'One or two, yes. We can share glamour. Pass it between us as Morgen did for me. Anything *we* do together using glamour is more potent than any other fae working in tandem.'

'Glamour being?'

'The name for the natural magic of Faery, and hence the fae. I thought you knew that.'

He foraged through his pack, which lay beside the platform and came up holding a wineskin. Offered it to me.

'Drink?'

I shook my head. Watched with narrowed eyes as he took

a deep pull. Fiddled with the end of my plaited hair, fingers stiff with annoyance.

I'd have hit him again, if my wrist hadn't hurt.

Only *harder*.

'Much better,' he said, with a happy sigh. 'I do prefer the wine Mab gets at Caer Dubh. Pleasant after all that white Rhiannon insists on serving. Stop glaring at me, Bree — there's nothing we can do about the debt bond now, in any case. And there's only one other effect. It's a life debt we each refused. We've an increased concern for one another's safety. Debt bonded fae will go to - essentially - any length to protect one another.'

'Oh, bloody *brilliant*,' I said sarcastically. 'And I don't suppose *that* little gem occurred to you at all while you were busy knocking yourself out trying to move us? Did it *once* register that *I* might be worried? Has anyone ever told you you're an idiot?'

He said nothing, looked away.

But I was on a roll.

'And another thing. You actually had me so worried - had *Morgen* so worried - that she possessed me.'

My voice rose louder and higher. My hands actually shook with rage.

'*Possessed* me! Can you imagine how horrible that is? Not to be in control of your own *body*? Your own *mind*?'

I realised what I'd said. And stopped dead.

He met my eyes.

Golden pain.

'Yes,' he said.

And just like that I wasn't angry any more.

I slumped down on the platform, next to Hawk. Peered unhappily up at him.

'You really stitched me up,' I told him dully. 'You *knew* I couldn't lie to you when you were patching my stomach up. What you made me say, Hawk - that's not fair. And you cost me Fin doing it. He was listening. I'll not forgive *that* in a hurry.'

He turned to face me, pulling his legs in more comfortably. Expression oddly gentle.

'I'm sorry.' Tiny frown over warm gold. 'That wasn't my intention. I'd never deliberately hurt you, bright flame. If there's anything I can do to help?'

I dropped my head into my hands, tears prickling my eyes. Fingers clenched in my hair, I took a steadying breath or two and lifted my chin to meet his gaze again.

'Talk to him. Explain. Please. And you can damn well tell me what you *were* intending.'

'I'll talk to Finian, I promise.' Hawk's honeyed voice turned grave. 'But I daren't tell you too much. I needed to know if Morgen was still there. Not only for my peace of mind, though I'll admit it helps. But because there's a very slight possibility we're going to need her. She's my fallback plan.'

'She's *what?*'

I was pretty sure I wasn't going to like where this was

going.

'I've seen certain things that *have* to happen in this fight with the Formori. And I'll do all I can to make them happen. I've also seen things that I very much want to *prevent* happening. No matter what it might cost. Morgen may be able to help with that. If all else - if *I* - fail.' He sounded uncertain. Looked almost afraid.

Weird as hell.

And *very* unlike Hawk.

'Are you going to tell me?' I asked.

Did I really want to know?

'I think that would be - unwise.' He hesitated for a moment, watching me. 'Bright flame, there *will* come a day when I ask you to do something for me. Without arguing. Or questioning me. Do you think you'll be able to do that?'

I snatched the skin from him and took a sip, buying thinking time. Handed it back, and answered slowly.

'I'll make the best decision I can at the time. That's all I *can* do, if you won't give me details. You're asking me to trust you - without trusting me.'

He nodded. 'That's a fair answer. I haven't given you much reason to trust me so far, have I?'

'Nope.' I shook my head firmly.

Hawk laughed again, hair dancing round his face. 'Perhaps you'll be relieved to hear your part in this is almost played. I'm interested. Why haven't you told anyone about Peg and the traitor?'

I gaped at him. 'How did *you* know?'

That fierce, fast grin again, making his eyes glow.

'Seer,' he reminded me. Smugly. 'You did well. Efnyssen deserved everything he got.'

'Yes. He did.' I wasn't ashamed. Had seen too many of the consequences of Efnyssen's actions. Vehemently, I blurted '*And* I'd do it again, if he were here now.'

I lifted my chin and dared him to contradict me. He just smiled again, sweet and a little sad.

'So fierce now,' he said softly. 'So very Fae. Bright flame, what have I done to you?'

I played with the laces on my jerkin for a moment. Though about it.

'You've made me your conscience,' I said, smirking.

He looked at me quizzically.

'You can't lie to me, Hawk.' Now I was grinning. 'So. I'm going to follow you *everywhere* - and keep you honest. You're getting *nothing* past me again. And it's your own fault.'

He took a thoughtful swig from the wineskin, offering it to me. I accepted. It kept the cold out.

'Are you serious?' he asked.

My reply was firm. 'Deadly. If we're more powerful together, then I'm helping you bring Fin here. Every step of the way.'

'That might actually help.' His expression turned thoughtful.

I thought, for a second, he was going to say more - but the door blossomed in the side of the mound and Cael slipped through the widening opening. Spoke as he began to fiddle with one of the jars from the shelf.

'Bad news, hawk lord,' he said. 'The winged fae have been and checked on the Unseelie troops. They're still almost a week away – and they're *still* aiming for Tir na n'Og. None of these Seelie idiots will land and tell 'em where we are 'cause they think they'll get eaten. *Honestly.* Treaty's just a difficult word to some fae...'

'Where are they?' Hawk was calm, but something alert had woken behind his eyes.

Cael named a place. I don't recall the name, but Hawk knew where he meant. I tried to look as though I understood what they were talking about. I'm not sure I succeeded. They worked out that if Cael could get to Mab and her troops - and bring them over the mountain - we could have them with us in around five days. Much better odds.

'Will Mab listen to you? Are you sure you want to be the one to tell her?' Hawk asked.

Cael laughed darkly, replacing the jar and almost oversetting it. 'It's not the whole family she threatens to skin on sight. She quite likes *me*. Hawk, you're asking me to tell Mab that *you* want her to bring the Dark Host *here* - to this place. To make a last stand. Her face is going to be *brilliant*. I can't bloody wait.'

I frowned, puzzled and suspicious.

'What's so important about here?' I asked.

Cael snickered, almost dancing with glee. 'Tell her, oh mighty hawk lord. Go *on*. Tell her where we are.'

I raised my eyebrows at Hawk, who ran a hand through his hair and sighed.

'I've fought here before,' he said. 'It didn't go well. I'd imagine you've heard about it. It's certainly been mentioned to me several times since I got back.'

Understanding finally dawned.

'Oh, you've *got* to be kidding.'

'Nope,' said Cael, still smirking. 'He wants us to fight right here, where he wiped out the last army he had to play with. And most of a couple of others, to boot. Classic. Typical hawk lord, in fact.'

I stared at Hawk, who shrugged and smiled uneasily.

'Wonderful. Just perfect,' I said, with some sarcasm.

Cael laughed when I facepalmed.

◄Chapter Twenty Two►

I was as good as my word.

Once Cael had gone, still sniggering, I stuck to Hawk's side as if glued there. Watched him like the bird he was named for.

And couldn't have been happier at the irritation on his face.

On the appointed day, Hawk led me back to the place where the veil was thinnest. To my surprise, he just reached out a hand and somehow *tore* a door through what had been empty space.

I raised questioning eyebrows at the Cu Sidhe.

*He doesn't **need** a physical gap to create a door.* Guest sounded amused. *It does make it easier, but it's not necessary.*

'And he couldn't have done that back at Tir na n'Og?' I asked sourly.

No, little Bree. Only in places like this where the veil between worlds is most fragile. Were he to do this anywhere else there's the very real possibility he'd destroy the realm. He gave that doggy grin. *And he probably doesn't need any encouragement doing that. He manages it perfectly well on his own.*

'If you've both quite finished,' said Hawk, half amused and half exasperated. 'I'd rather like to concentrate. Stand with me, Bree. I may need you.'

I positioned myself beside him. Watched in fascination as the hole in the air - the doorway of glowing mist - grew. It was soon larger than a barn door.

Hawk nodded at the Hound, who darted through to collect the Seelie troops. It was only minutes before the first horses, three abreast, came through.

Finely dressed and with proud faces, the leading riders were clearly Fae of importance. Two men and one woman, they rode past us with barely a glance, heading for camp. I think the woman was the only one who so much as turned her head to smile slightly. The Fae in the middle looked strangely familiar. Stern faced, with red hair and the blazing hand and spear on his surcoat. Of course. Fin's father, Lord Lughan.

I can't say I took to him.

Something about his self-satisfied look set my teeth on edge for reasons I couldn't have named.

More came through. On and on in an endless wave. A

seriously impressive Fae warband in full battle array. There must have been a dozen or different families represented there, judging by their insignia. And that was just the noble Fae. Lesser fae poured through after them, creatures of every shape and size. Some small and fast, others large and lumbering – but all with the same look of implacable intent. Of fierce determination.

Real hope fluttered through me on silken wings. Maybe we *could* win this thing. Maybe everything would actually be alright, despite the loss of Tir na n'Og.

I tried very hard to convince myself I wasn't looking for Fin.

I was *totally* looking for Fin.

He came through at the head of the Lughan troops, a Fae who could only be his brother at his side. My beautiful lordling looked magnificent. Tall and straight in the saddle, blood copper hair shining like fire. I couldn't prevent a wistful little sigh escaping my mouth.

Look at me, Fin. *Please* look at me.

He turned his head as though he'd heard. His mouth gave a funny little twist when he saw me standing with Hawk, and he nodded formally.

It was all I could do not to scream.

To throw myself to the ground and bawl like a baby.

Once they'd ridden past, and there were only strange Fae around us, Hawk grabbed my hand. I tried to jerk it away, thinking he was trying to comfort me - and still too cross with him to allow it.

His cool-fingered grip got tighter and I looked sharply up at him.

'Oh, *hell*. Hawk?'

What little colour he ever had in that pale face was gone, and his eyes seemed a little unfocussed. He didn't look good. Morgen may have fed him our energy - or glamour - or whatever the blazes it was called, but he clearly needed more time to recuperate.

'Hound, what do I *do*?'

He needs glamour. Can Morgen show you how to help him?

Guest had spent the last couple of days grilling me, intrigued by the idea of my silent passenger. He had a point, though. Time for my ancestress to make herself useful again.

Help me, Morgen. Help me to help Hawk.

She answered.

Icy coils wove through my body and travelled down one arm, binding themselves like weeds around the hand that clasped Hawk's. Just the faintest hint of cold licked at my brain, teased a strange-familiar knowledge into life.

And I knew what to do.

I pushed the glamour down and along. Forced it past my hand and into his. Waves and ripples in peaks and troughs, like tiny oceans playing along my arm. He gained a little colour, looked less ashy. The lines of that proud face relaxed as the glamour hit him and took effect. Concentrating, I kept pushing, trying to control the flow that weakened me as I forced it away.

Gave as much as I could.

I came to myself when Hawk dropped almost threw my hand from him. He frowned as he peered down into my face.

'Enough.' Sharp and alert. Himself again. 'You'll leave yourself weak.'

I sank wearily to the grass as the last troops came through and watched that glowing doorway dwindle away into nothing. Guest sat at my side, massive head on my shoulder.

'Quit panting in my ear,' I grumbled.

He just lolled his tongue at me and licked my face.

Damn mutt.

Hawk was grinning when he pulled me to my feet. Laughter sparked in the back of those golden eyes and I narrowed mine at him.

'What are *you* so pleased about?' I brushed the grass from my pants.

'We've to go and negotiate with Finian's father. He's the head of the Lughan - and they get to choose the king. Technically, he could take command of the warhost.'

He looked immeasurably pleased with himself. I scurried to keep pace with his long strides, perplexed.

'And that's funny because ... ?'

He gave a low laugh. 'I'm the last Seelie prince. In name, at least. It's actually turning out to be useful, for once.'

'Well done. I'm pleased for you,' I said. 'But I've still no idea what that means.'

'He's going to have to sit and wait for us before he can do anything, Bree. He's waiting to see if I pull rank. I never would, but *he* doesn't know that.' Hawk's smile was vicious, almost predatory.

I began to laugh myself. 'Oh, I *see*.'

'I'll have to get him to speak first,' he said. 'Let's see what title he gives me. I'll know how to play it from there.'

'Well, *this* should be interesting.'

Interesting wasn't the word.

Intimidating would've been be closer. The ranked riders formed an ominous mass, They'd stopped close to the mound the Portune raised for Hawk, forming a rough circle.

Lord Lughan and the other two high ranking Fae sat very prominently in the centre.

Hawk and I advanced into the middle of the circle. Fin's father was clearly calling the shots, sitting stiffly straight in the saddle a pace or two ahead of the others. It was odd to see someone else wearing the green and gold that I'd come to associate purely with Fin. The other Lord was blonde. His livery was a dark burgundy.

It was the woman who interested me.

She was pale and slight — tall, like all the Fae - with waving black hair and a plain grey gown. No insignia. No fancy fae touches. She looked almost nun-like, a serene expression on her beautiful face. Her eyes widened slightly when they met mine. A startled look, gone in a heartbeat, leaving her as blank and serene as before.

We came to a stop several feet from the Fae nobles. I scanned the circle anxiously for Fin. He was just behind his father, tension evident in the way he sat. Fin was usually so relaxed in the saddle, it stuck out a mile.

I wondered what was about to happen.

Hawk stood beside me, ridiculously tall and unmistakeable in black and gold. Colours echoed perfectly in the black hair falling around his shoulders and the golden eyes glowing with mischief. He gave absolute blank face to Lord Lughan and remained silent.

I followed suit.

Hawk looked an *awful* lot more relaxed than I felt.

My eyes crept back to Fin. He looked at his father's back and then at Hawk. Turning in my direction he gave a wry grimace.

I know, I thought. I've no idea how this is going to go, either.

Daren't grimace back while his father was right in front of me, looming on his horse. There were no words to say how badly I wanted to go to Fin. To talk to him. To touch him.

Instead, I assumed my blandest face and watched his father. A faint tinge of colour was starting to creep up from the ornate collar of Lord Lughan's tunic, spreading across his neck and face. He grew even stiffer.

He's getting mad.

Play this carefully, Hawk.

If anything, Hawk seemed to take this as his cue to assume an even *more* casual stance. He stood there wearing an idly pleasant expression, the look of a man with all day to spare and nowhere pressing to be. But his eyes glittered a little too brightly.

I think he was actually *enjoying* himself.

Madman.

Lord Lughan fixed pale green eyes on me, letting them travel up my body from my feet - until he was forced to meet my gaze. I didn't so much as blink. Just stared him coolly down. He didn't appear to like what he saw, mouth twisting slightly.

For some reason this gave me an odd little surge of triumph. I still don't know whether it came from me or Morgen.

We were together on that one.

After the longest time I'd ever lived through, Finian's father wrenched his jaw open and spoke curtly to Hawk.

'Prince Emrys.' He gave the barest nod.

Yes! I wanted to punch the air.

Decided it probably wouldn't help.

Settled for a smirk.

'Lord Lughan.' Hawk was at his honey-toned best, smooth

and amiable.

Fin's father dismounted and - taking this as a signal - the Seelie warband followed suit. Began to drift away to care for their mounts and make camp. Soon there was only the sketchiest circle surrounding us. Fin stayed in position behind Lord Lughan, hands light his horse's reins. Watching closely. He looked very serious, the Fae lordling again. He also looked impossibly, heartbreakingly, gorgeous.

It was like being Fae-struck again. I just wanted to throw my arms around him.

Focus, Bree.

The wintry air stirred into a slight breeze and I fought hard not to shiver. Didn't want to be the weak human now.

'Is there somewhere we can speak privately?' asked Fin's father.

A tiny, odd, smile curled the edges of Hawk's lips.

'Of course,' he said. 'We'll use this mound, here. You understand Lady Briana's privy to all my counsels?'

The muscles around Lord Lughan's eyes tightened slightly, but he forced a smile in my direction.

'Certainly,' he said. 'As long as *you* understand the Lake Lady's a necessary part of all mine.'

The smile Hawk turned on the Fae woman was genuine. Affectionate. I don't think I'd seen him smile that way before. She returned it, grey eyes warm.

'I *insist* on it,' he said, still smiling.

He moved to help her down from her horse and said something unintelligible in a low voice. I heard a stifled feminine laugh, and the woman looked amused as we walked to the mound. Strange, how familiar that laugh was. And I couldn't place why.

She certainly seemed to know Hawk rather well.

I'd *enjoy* grilling him about her, later.

We entered the mound, which seemed horribly crowded with four of us in the confined space. The woman began to examine the medical supplies on the shelf, a little smile playing round her mouth.

Finian's father stood centrally, forcing the rest of us to arrange ourselves around him in a cramped circle. The Lake Lady, behind him, was still lifting pots and sachets to smell them. One or two made her frown, but most seemed to please her.

'It's a fine thing, to have so much that will be useful already prepared.' Her voice was soft and mellifluous.

'Luydla's a good healer,' I replied.

She smiled warmly at me, leaning against the wall of the mound, and I found myself returning it almost without realising. Standing close to Hawk, I was unsure what to expect. I'd always been left out of meetings before and I suddenly felt awkward. Gauche.

Hawk stirred slightly, drawing our attention.

'As there isn't much time, I'm going to be blunt,' he said.

'*There's* a surprise,' murmured the Fae woman, eyes full of humour.

Lord Lughan ignored her.

'What do you have to say, Prince Emrys?' he asked. 'What is there you *can* say? Here? In this place?'

'You weren't so hostile as a child.' Hawk spoke quietly, levelly.

'I still had parents and a grandfather, then,' snapped the other Fae. 'Maybe you remember them. *You* left them *here* - along with half the fae in the realm.'

'What happened here was never my intention, Barra. And I've paid the price for it all. Lost more than you will ever comprehend. Fifteen hundred years of madness, grief and shame. Will you still upbraid me now? After all this time?'

Despite myself, I reached out and took his hand, curling my fingers into his. Fifteen hundred years? Suffering as I'd seen him suffer?

I pitied him, a vice squeezing my ribs and driving out breath.

He gave me a small, sidelong smile. Eyes soft and unfathomable. Something sad in that, somehow. It almost hurt.

'Very well,' said Barra Medyr. 'I'll not say what I've wanted to since then. Not today. I'll just ask you this. Do you intend to make a claim for the throne?'

'I've never wanted it. But I *do* want one thing, if I'm going to forgo my claim.' Hawk smiled that weird smile again.

Lord Lughan stiffened suspiciously 'Which is?'

'The Seelie warhost. All of it. Under my command.'

Barra looked startled, head jerking back as if he'd been struck. Light green eyes full of glittering disbelief.

'Are you trying to kill us all? Here? *Again?* Do you think people will *follow* you?'

'Do *you* still believe in redemption? As you once did? You owe me, Barra. I'm calling it in' There was an odd note to Hawk's voice.

Still honey smooth and courteous, but somehow it wasn't the kind of voice you argued with.

Lord Lughan sighed, nodding grudgingly. 'I see. Very well, I'll pay my debt. The warhost is yours - for now. But the Lughan continue to hold the throne.'

'Agreed. I've never claimed any title for myself but Hawk, bar one - and even that's long forgotten.'

The Fae woman laughed, jetty waves dancing around her lovely face. Barra turned to look, as if he'd forgotten she was there. She advanced on Hawk and embraced him warmly. Smiled, lightning fast, and peered up at him through sooty thumbprint lashes.

'I've missed you, big brother. It's been far, far too long.'

Brother?

That was why she looked familiar. She was Hawk's sister. No wonder there was something familiar about her. They'd the same shaped eyes and smile, the same hair. I should've seen it.

He held her tightly for a moment, eyes closed, then released her.

'I've missed you too, Ganieda. We should talk. Soon.'

Lord Lughan began to laugh, half reluctantly. 'I'd forgotten you were Avallachin, Lady Ganieda. I think most of Faery has.'

I took this as my cue to pipe up.

'There *is* one other thing,' I announced.

Three faces turned curiously in my direction.

'Finian. He's to be under Hawk's personal command. At all times.'

Hawk regarded me through thoughtfully narrowed eyes for a second, then he smiled. Sharp and brilliant.

'You're right,' he said. 'I'll need Fin.'

Lord Lughan didn't look happy with the idea, but he agreed. And left. Ganieda patted her brother's cheek and paused in the doorway to give him one last, affectionate look, before following.

As soon as the door was closed, Hawk sank onto the sleeping platform. Just folded, elbows on knees and face in hands. Hidden behind that curtain of sooty, silky waves.

I folded my arms.

'What's wrong with *you*? You got what you wanted.'

'I wish I dared tell you,' he said in a muffled voice. 'Wish I *could* share this with someone. With *you*. You'll understand soon enough. Oh, bright flame...'

Another long, worryingly silent second.

Then he raised his head and met my eyes. 'For the first

time, I'm truly afraid. Terribly afraid.'

'Hawk, you're scaring me.'

This was so out of character. Disconcerting. I shifted uneasily on my feet, scraping the ground with the tip of my foot. Rapid little arcs in the earthily scented dirt.

More muffled words. 'You're right to be scared, bright flame. More right than you know.'

Oh, *really* not helping.

Fear lanced through me. 'Is it Fin? Is something going to happen to Fin?'

'What? *No.*' Hawk jerked his head up. 'He'll come close to danger, I won't deny it. But I've seen him on the field. He'll leave it alive.'

'Promise?'

I hated how small my voice sounded.

Hawk rose swiftly and placed his hands on my shoulders, smiling his weird little smile as he looked down at me.

'I promise, Briana Cadman, that I will *personally* ensure your Finian walks away from this battle whole and alive. You've my word.'

He couldn't lie.

Thank all the Gods - he couldn't lie to me. Fin would be safe.

I sagged with relief, able to breathe again.

'There's one condition,' he continued. 'I want you to give me your word you won't take the field. That you'll stay here, or somewhere well back. Away from the fighting.'

I stared at him, aghast.

'Hawk, I...'

'*Please*. It's essential you stay away.' He was actually pleading, face a mask of concern above me. Naked fear at the back of that luminous gold. 'I've seen things, Bree. Things that'll go wrong if you fight. Things you wouldn't like if they happened. Things I won't *let* happen - whatever the cost.'

I sighed. 'I can't argue with your visions. You'll be safe too, won't you? You've seen that?'

He smiled sadly then, and touched my face with gentle fingers, before gathering himself and leaving the mound. I followed. Watched him stride through the Seelie host, upright and apparently fearless again.

Oh, Hawk.

What've you seen?

◀Chapter Twenty Three▶

I jumped, preoccupied, as a warm hand touched my shoulder. Smiling up at Fin, I caught the faintest hint of his sunshine citrus smell.

Ooh, lovely. I've *missed* that.

'So,' I said. 'Your dad's interesting.'

Fin didn't smile back. Just looked tired and sad. It was all I could do not to wrap my arms around him and try to kiss it all better.

'He's a good man. He's just worried,' he replied. 'We - the Lughan - will bear the brunt of this war. We're the only ones who can use the spear. It was tied to our glamour centuries ago.'

Some of the nearer fae were watched us curiously. I took his arm and tugged him away. Pulled him around the side of the mound. We sat on the opposite slope, looking toward the mountains, almost shoulder to shoulder.

'I don't get it, Fin. What's so special about a spear?'

'It's the spear of Lugh, our ancestor. It has certain special properties, apparently. Legend says it's how we defeated the Formori last time.' He gave a little shake, a shudder. 'They're dead, twisted things we're fighting, Bree. *Undead* things. Animated by some unnatural form of glamour. Against *everything* my court stands for. Against *nature*.'

I pulled a face. 'And the spear kills 'em? Great as that is, were you expecting them to just stand there while you stab them all in turn? Because I have to tell you - that probably won't work.'

A sweet, sad smile. I couldn't bear seeing him looking this way, so defeated. He's one half of my world, and I felt helpless in the face of his unhappiness. Wanted to lean into him. To touch him. To scream at him.

I did none of them.

'We need to kill the person - potentially *group* of people - responsible for controlling them.' His eyes scanned the horizon, hands tapping against his knees.

'No pressure then.'

It's true what they say about being in love. My heart beat faster, breathing shallower.

'Peredur's got it. He's good. He'll manage.' Seeing my look of confusion, he added. 'My eldest brother. My *only* brother, now...'

'Oh, *Fin*. I'm so sorry.'

There was a brief silence. Faint voices all around, piping and rumbling. Distant song drifting past on the rising, frost scented breeze.

Fin sucked in a sharp breath and turned awkwardly to face me. 'Bree, look. There's something I need to say...'

'There you are. I've been looking for you, Finian. I'm going to need you with me.'

Hawk stood smiling down at us, relaxed and seemingly happy again.

I could've *cursed* him.

Twice.

Fin stiffened. The look he gave the other Fae wasn't friendly.

'I've heard.' He folded his arms, voice flat.

'And I've heard what happened to your brother. To your lands. I'm sorry, Finian.' Hawk sounded sympathetic.

'Yes. Only two of us left who're capable of what you're asking of us, hawk lord. The odds aren't improving for you, are they? Tell me - given where we are - do you think it'll take long to get the pair of us killed? To get *me* out of the way?'

'And I thought Barra was hostile...' Hawk shot me a humorous glance. Pulled his cloak more closely around him as the wind became colder, fiercer.

I shivered.

'Fin, please,' I said, touching his arm. 'Hawk's your friend.'

'Is he?' Fin met my eyes - distant again - and turned to glare coldly at Hawk. 'You've a strange way of showing it.'

'Bright flame, would you excuse us for a moment, please? It may be time for that little talk we discussed.'

I nodded gratefully at Hawk and stood. Patted Fin's tense shoulder.

'Be nice,' I said. '*Both* of you.'

I went.

***

Wandering through the camp, I heard it before I saw anything. The sound of raised voices. Of shrilling horns and screeching metal. Sounds I'd never be able to forget. Fae all around sprang to their feet. To their mounts.

Turning, I ran back to the others.

'They're *here*,' I panted.

They didn't have to ask who I meant.

'Find your brother,' Hawk told Fin. 'He knows what to do?'

'Yes, but you've no guarantee it'll work.'

'Still the best hope we have. Bree, with me.'

I followed Hawk to the front of the mound. Watched the door appear at his touch.

'Inside,' he said briskly.

'*What?*'

My sword was already in my hand. I was ready to fight. *Wanted* to fight.

In lieu of reply he grabbed my arm and threw me firmly inside. I span to face him.

'What the *hell*?'

He sent me a satisfied smile as the door disappeared. And I realised.

I was trapped without anyone to open it again.

'*Hawk!* Let me *out*, you smug bastard.'

I banged against the wall, the earth crumbling moistly beneath my hands.

'Open, damn you, mound. *Open*.'

Nothing happened.

Morgen, are you there? Let me out. Let me out *now*.

An icy little lick of annoyance, almost a mental slap. Then she was gone.

'Fat lot of use *you* are,' I snarled. Not caring that I was talking to myself. Kind of. 'When did you start agreeing with *him*? You're supposed to be on *my* side.'

I hurled my sword angrily across the room.

It landed with a dull thud, scuffing the ground. A roar of pure frustration erupted from my throat.

I felt like throwing myself to the floor and tantruming like a toddler.

Instead, I paced - cursing profusely. Wall to wall. Over and over. Kicking the pile of soil I'd dislodged across the floor.

Kicking the soil I'd dislodged...

That was *it*.

Going back to where the door had been, I tugged my dagger from its sheath and began to dig furiously.

Screw *you*, Hawk.

I'll tunnel my way out.

I dug like a woman possessed, great swathes of soil seeming to come away with every frenzied movement. It was a long, sweaty time before I realised the hole wasn't getting any bigger. That the pile of soil hadn't grown. Bloody glamoured mounds.

'Oh, *hell*.'

I slumped on the bed, thoroughly disgusted.

How could Hawk expect me to sit quietly in *here* - like some naughty child - when the Fae I loved were out *there* fighting? I could hear very little from outside, just faint echoes of the sound of battle.

Now louder, now softer again.

I flinched with every distant clash of metal and muted cry.

I *knew* Fin was coming back. Hawk'd promised. Didn't stop me worrying, though. Or being frightened. Maybe I'd have coped better if hadn't been so afraid for *him*, too. He'd made me no guarantees about his own safety, after all.

Fear and fear and frustration. At not being there to help him. To defend him.

Stupid bloody debt bond.

I kicked Hawk's pack viciously. The wineskin hit the floor,

making a gurgling slosh. I narrowed my eyes at it with a Cael-esque smirk. Wanted me to stay in here, did he? Well, nobody said I *couldn't* help myself to stuff while I was waiting. I uncorked the neck and took a deep draught. Maybe I could get tipsy enough to *really* rip into the pair of them.

When they came back.

If they came back.

It was a long afternoon. I spent it alternately sipping and sulking. And going through Hawk's pack on sheer principle. There was nothing interesting in there. Nothing I hadn't seen before - but the mild malice of trashing his privacy made me feel better. I wasn't even neat putting it back.

I *wanted* a fight. Wanted him to shout at me.

Wanted him to come back.

To be *able* to shout at me.

You'd think it'd be impossible to sleep in those circumstances, but the wine made me drowsy. I found myself awoken some time that evening by a smiling Fin. I stretched clumsily, muscles aching where I'd fallen asleep slumped over my own knees.

'You're ok.' I let him help me up and threw my arms around him.

Not caring about the blood on his clothing. About *anything* - other than that he was there. His arms tightened round me and he lay his face against my hair, letting out a slow breath.

'Yes, I'm ok. Were you really that worried?'

I pulled back and looked mutely at him for a second. He winced as he took in my expression. Shook his head.

'Silly question. You're Bree. Worrying about us is what you *do*, isn't it?'

Still gripping him tightly - and with no intention of ever letting go - I asked 'What about Hawk? And Guest, of course? And Cael?'

'They're fine, love. They're all unharmed, so you can stop looking so scared. Can we talk tonight? Properly?'

He called me love! Had he forgiven me?

I nodded eagerly. 'Yes, please.'

Cupping my cheek with one hand and running a thumb across my lips, he smiled again.

'My father wants to see me, but I'll be back. Soon.'

'Hurry. Please.'

He left me again. But this time it didn't hurt.

***

Outside, I climbed the side of the mound and stood at the top. All around I saw injured fae being tended by Brownies and other healers. It was a dreadful sight. We'd incurred terrible losses. The dead were being moved by friends and kin now the enemy were gone, withdrawn across the plain.

Not far enough for my liking.

I *hated* them.

Could see their fires and hear their celebrations. In our

camp, tents had been raised nearby, pennants snapping above them. This was where the injured – those who *could* be saved - were carried. So many of them. My eyes prickled painfully and I told myself it was the wind.

Were we going to *lose*?

I stood there till my legs ached too badly to stand any longer. Then I sat there instead. Watching and waiting for Fin. Saw no sign of him. Once or twice a fae with blood copper hair caught my eye and I looked away, disappointed.

In the end it was Hawk who came for me, a cloth wrapped bundle cradled awkwardly in his arms. Fatigue hidden - but there if you knew how to read him.

I was getting the hang of it.

'Get *lost*.' I hissed, pushing myself to my feet as he climbed up to me. 'I'm not talking to *you*. Not unless you want to hear exactly what I think of you right now – and I have to warn you, it's *not* flattering.'

'I need you, Bree. We've to talk to Fin. Someone saw him heading for the stream.' He looked out at the Seelie forces, frowning. 'His brother's horse was cut from under him.'

'Peredur's dead?'

That left everything on Fin's shoulders, surely?

'No, but he's lost an arm. The spear's shattered.'

I gasped in horror. 'What are we going to do? Without the spear...'

'*We* do nothing. Fin does. That's why I need *you* with me.

In case he won't listen to me. I'm not exactly his favourite person at the moment.'

I let him lead me from the mound, a cold little knot forming in my chest. The copper-sweet tang of blood rose from the grass and mingled with the muddy smell of churned earth.

I felt sick.

'How much of this did you see?' I asked.

He just shook his head, eating up the earth with those long strides. I scampered to keep up.

'We'll talk later,' he said. 'If you'll find me after you've spoken to Finian.'

'I thought *we* were speaking to Finian.'

He glanced at me sideways, an oddly affectionate expression on his face. 'And you're not going to want to talk to him in private once I've said my piece? We're finishing this one way or another tomorrow, bright flame. Make it right between you. I know *he* wants to.' His voice was gentle, nearly sad. 'It would bring *me* some peace, too.'

I grinned.

And he was forgiven.

Grabbing his arm, I pulled him towards me and hugged him. Hard. Forcing him to a halt, and almost making him drop the bundle.

He raised his eyebrows and gave a low, warm laugh, returning the embrace one-armed.

'As Fin's so fond of saying - Easy, Bree.'

We found Fin slumped beside the stream, not far from where I'd summoned Peg. He looked utterly defeated. Head in his hands and bow thrown carelessly down beside him. It made me uneasy to see him so close to the water. There was no Cael to speak for him if the river hags were lurking around.

'Fin?' I was hesitant to disturb him.

He looked up, face haggard and unreadable. Pale beneath the light tan.

'I heard. About your brother, Peredur.' Soft sympathy in my voice.

I tried to think of anything at all I could say that would make it better. Had nothing.

Hawk threw the bundle down at Fin's feet. It clattered as it landed.

'Unwrap it.' His hard tone brooked no argument.

I shot a glare at him. How dare he speak to Fin that way? Finian's mouth tightened but he carefully – wordlessly - unwrapped the bundle.

There in Hawk's cloak was what could only be the spear of the Lughan and - as Hawk had said - it was shattered. Useless. The wood was almost silver, pale as moonlight where it'd splintered beneath Peredur's horse. There were a few long slender lengths of whole wood, but most was shards.

Fin looked at it, expression strange.

'Why are you showing me this?' he asked. 'I already know we're doomed.'

'If you think *that*, you aren't looking carefully enough,' Hawk replied calmly. He stooped and picked up one of the longer lengths, offering it to Fin. 'This wood's not from this realm. I'd imagine Lugh got it from one of the Formori initially. *That's* why it worked. Because it's from their realm and glamoured against them. Never because it was a spear.'

'Why are you telling me this, hawk lord?'

'Think about it. It's your skill we need now. Your unbeatable ability.'

I was confused. Hawk held the piece of wood out to Fin again.

'One perfect arrow,' he said softly. 'One perfect shot. Destiny's calling you again, Finian Medyr. Will you answer?'

Slowly, Fin extended his hand and took it. Stared at the slender length of silvery wood.

'I think I have to.'

He still sounded unhappy. Hawk nodded to me and left. Guess that made it my turn.

I sat next to Fin. We listened in silence to the gurgle of the rushing water. He turned the piece of spear over and over in long, slim fingers. Eventually I spoke.

'You're going to survive it, you know. Hawk saw it.'

A smile. Weary, but it lit his eyes like green candles.

'Yes, he said he's had to answer some rather awkward questions lately. Did you *really* punch him?'

'Split his lip and everything.'

'Wish I'd seen that.'

'So does Cael.'

'I'll bet.' His smile widened, and he placed the piece of spear gently down beside him. 'I'm sorry, Bree. The debt bond thing just never occurred to me. We *never* let that happen anymore - and with good reason, too. It's dangerous. He's going to try and keep you off the battlefield tomorrow, you know. He asked me to help him.'

'He can *try*,' I said with some asperity.

'Actually, I want you to listen to him. I need you safe. I'm in love with you.'

Oh. My. Goddess.

'Say that again?' I whispered, rocked to the core.

'I love you, Bree.' He took my face in his hands. Those brilliant green eyes almost burned with emotion. 'Stay in the mound. For me. If you still care.'

'*Care?* Are you *kidding* me?' I wove my fingers through the hair at the back of his head. Pulled him towards me. 'I love you, too. You've no *idea*...'

I didn't make it to the end of the sentence.

He kissed me as if he were trying to draw me into himself. As if he'd never stop. I returned it hungrily. We were fire and water. Heat and cold, both burning. He tasted of sunshine and home and Fin.

It was *perfect*.

But it didn't last.

All too soon he was away to get his arrow crafted and fletched. I sat there for a while. It was entirely possible we'd lose tomorrow. Possible we'd all die in the end.

But it didn't wipe the broad smile from my face.

◄Chapter Twenty Four►

The morning was misty and bitterly cold. I awoke in the predawn half-light, yawning widely. Snuggling back into Fin's side, I could easily have slept again. A quiet voice stopped me.

'Bree, can I talk to you?'

Hawk sat at the other side of our fire, poking idly at the flames with the end of a bent sword. It occurred to me that I'd forgotten to go and seek him out the night before. Too preoccupied.

'Sure.' I stretched and sat upright, yawning. 'What's up?'

'Not here. Walk with me.' He grinned suddenly, rising in a rapid, smooth movement. 'I say that to you a lot, don't I?'

I pulled myself to my feet, settling my cloak firmly around me and buckling on my sword belt.

'Yep. You've no idea how stupidly annoying you actually are, Hawk.'

'You sound like the Huntsman. He keeps saying the same.'

'I like Cael. He's very astute.'

He laughed softly. Held out a hand. I took it and we wandered down to the stream, moving some distance along the bank - away from the few fae who were awake and filling waterskins. He stopped and dropped my hand, turning to look out towards the hushed camp.

'It'll be today,' he said. 'Everything I saw. It's going to be today.'

'Is that a bad thing?'

'Maybe. I won't know until I see how one or two of my preparations play out.'

'You're the hawk lord,' I teased, nudging him. 'Surely you're not saying you could be *wrong*?'

He took a deep breath and turned back to me.

'It's not being wrong that frightens me. I *know* I'm not wrong. I rarely am. You remember I told you the day would come when I asked you to do something for me?'

'You want me to stay off the field. I know.'

He nodded, the wind lifting the hair from his shoulders and setting it dancing around his tense face. A dark intensity in him, strange and new.

'There's - it's - more than that. I wanted to ask you - would you take my sword to my sister? After?'

The blood froze in my veins. I stared at him in terrified incomprehension.

Blurted 'Why would I need to do that?'

'I...' He stopped.

I'd never seen the confident Fae so uncertain of himself.

So at a loss for words.

It took an elastically stretched moment to understand what he was asking - what he was telling me.

Time snapped back.

The horror of it hit me hard, sudden grief almost knocking me from my feet. His face blurred as my eyes filled and tears began to spill silently down my cheeks.

'Don't die,' I whispered, shaking. 'Not you. Don't you *dare.*'

Hawk smiled gently, pulling me into his arms, so I could hear his heart beating in his chest. Bent and tilted my face up to rest his forehead against mine. Eyes closed and skin cool against my heated face.

'Please,' he said gently. 'Who else can I tell? Who else can I ask these things of, if not you? *They,*' I was aware of one arm unwrapping from around me and waving vaguely in the direction of the camp. 'Need to have faith in me. To follow me.'

'*Hawk...*' I was choking on the knot in my throat.

'Listen to me. Please.'

He pulled back a little and looked me straight in the eye. Sadness on sadness in that vivid gold. In that fierce, beautiful face.

'No, bright flame. I'm not coming back. I've known for some time, now. *Please* don't interrupt.' He deftly forestalled the words burning to escape me. 'This is hard enough as it is, without either of us saying anything to make it harder. I promise I'll keep your Finian safe. If I've to get every last fae on this field slaughtered to get him into position and keep him safe - I'll do it. For *you*. Do you understand?'

'Yes, but...'

'No. No buts. You need to know that, because you need to know why you can't take the field. I don't doubt you can fight. I don't think I've ever doubted you at *all*.'

He stopped for a moment and closed his eyes, sighing softly so it breezed over my face.

'Bree, I saw you die.'

Words like a bucket ice water to the face. I drew a sharp breath, but couldn't speak. Had no words of my own. He continued.

'If you fight today, you'll die. Saving Fin. There are other ways of achieving that. You're not doing it, bright flame. I won't *let* you.'

'Oh.' My voice was tiny.

Hawk shook his head, a smile playing around his mouth. 'That's the first time I've ever known you not to argue. I can't decide whether I'm impressed or disturbed.'

'Stop making jokes, damn you. How can you be making *jokes*?'

I couldn't stop the tears. Could barely breathe. He didn't answer this time.

Just kissed my forehead softly and held me for the longest time, before leading me back to the fire.

***

The camp stirred and prepared to meet the day. Hawk shook Fin awake and they disappeared into one of the gaily coloured tents erected by the noble Seelie. Guest sat at my side, apparently as lost in thought as I was myself. I daren't ask him if he knew about Hawk.

Didn't want to be the one to tell him.

Bree, you are a *coward*.

Suddenly the Hound sat upright. Peered out into the mist, ears pricked.

'What?' I asked, scared we'd be attacked – again - before we were ready. Before Hawk and Fin were ready.

I hear horses.

'Is it the Formori?'

He shook his shaggy head. *Follow me, little Mistress, and you'll see.*

We dashed through the camp, pausing as we registered the riders coming down from the mountains. I squinted to see, but the cheer from the fae around us made it plain enough what was happening.

The Unseelie had arrived.

They poured onto the plain in a great flood. Hundreds and

hundreds of them. I felt a nudge at my back and glanced back to see Hawk, Fin and Lord Lughan pushing their way through the gathering crowd.

Fin grabbed my hand as they passed, and tugged me along in their wake.

The first ranks of the Unseelie came to a disciplined halt. Mab rode at the front with a cheerfully waving Cael beside her. I grinned broadly at him as we approached, relieved to see them.

The Unseelie queen waited until we were well within earshot and called out.

'I'm disappointed in you, Emrys. Cael tells me you've started without us. That's not very sporting, is it?' She cawed with laughter.

Hawk was laughing too, his earlier unhappiness seemingly gone.

'We've missed you, Mab.' He strode over to her mount and grinned up at her, golden eyes alight. 'Incidentally, I need your warhost. May I have it, please?'

She allowed him to hand her down - still laughing - and patted his cheek as he set her on her feet.

'Perhaps. You never change, do you? Let's get the talking out of the way, cousin. Before the Formori get bored - and start the war without us.'

Cousin? But Hawk was Seelie. Wasn't he?

I looked at Fin in confusion. He caught my bewildered expression, and grinned.

'Later,' he murmured. 'Let's just say *he's* the reason we don't interbreed any more.'

'Pretty good reason,' I muttered back.

Felt a stab of disloyalty.

Why had I said that? Today of *all* days? Knowing what I knew?

I'm sorry, Hawk.

Fin's father snapped his name and I realised that the Seelie and Unseelie commanders were leaving, heading for the tents. I watched them go - until a punch on the arm reminded me Cael was back.

'Miss me?' he asked.

'Let me think about that.' I pretended to ponder it for a second. 'No.'

'Yeah, you did. You missed me.' He draped his arm round my shoulders and began to steer me back into camp. 'Which is absolutely why you and that mutt are about to feed me. I'm bloody *starving*, sweetheart.'

I *had* to feed him. He went on at me until I did. One of these days that boy's going to have to learn to cook his meat properly before eating it. It even smelled half-raw.

Seriously gross.

Before long everything was organised. Fin and Hawk sought us out as the combined warhost began to form ranks, preparing to move out.

'We can't stop, love.' Fin wrapped warm arms around my waist and hugged me. 'Stay well back. I'll see you tonight.'

I turned my face up for a kiss, as my stomach hit my shoes.

It was time.

It was happening *now*.

Disentangling myself from Fin, I took a couple of paces towards Hawk. He wouldn't meet my eye. Instead, he went down on one knee and fussed the Cu Sidhe, hair a dark curtain hiding his face.

'You remember what we discussed?' he asked.

Yes, Master. Guest gave the most desolate whine I've ever heard.

So he *did* know.

'You stay with your mistress now, Barghest. For as long as she needs you.'

Hawk rose and turned to Cael. 'Mab's asked me to command you to stay with Bree, Huntsman. Keep her as far away from the field as you can. *Stop* pulling faces. I know you don't like it, but it's not up for negotiation. Who better or more competent to guard her? I trust you, kinsman. Are you ready, Fin?'

Fin gave me another swift, delicious kiss - and they turned to go.

I *ran* to Hawk.

'No,' I said. '*Please*, no.'

He opened his mouth and I thought he was going to say something. To reassure me. He didn't. Just swallowed hard and held out his arms, eyes blazing gold as they met mine. An almost smile softening his face, he hugged me to him fiercely – too briefly - and gently pulled away. Cool brush of lips against my forehead.

Nononononononono.

Without another word, they mounted up and were lost among the milling ranks of fae.

Gone.

I've *never* felt such utter despair.

Not even while Fae-struck.

I dropped to the grass and began to sob. Wrenching, heartbroken sounds. Soul-rending anguish. Guest, beside me, threw back his head and howled. Just once - but it was the most unbearable thing. It felt like hours. It may have *been* hours.

By the time I'd pulled myself together, the mist had been burnt away by the wintry sun and the sounds and odours of battle were sharp on the air.

Cael hovered uncertainly, looking from Guest to me and back again, hands fluttering over his dagger hilts. Black eyes shrewd and face full of suspicious intelligence.

'What's going on? What am I missing here? *Other* than the bloody battle, obviously.'

It took several deep gulps before I could gasp anything out.

'Hawk's going to...' I couldn't say it. Wouldn't. 'He's not coming back, Cael.'

He scoffed. 'Have a little faith, sweetheart. He's maybe not *quite* as good as he thinks he is - but if anyone can walk away from this...'

No. *He's seen it. Seen this battle. My master won't return.*

'Well, *shit*.' Cael puffed out his cheeks and sat himself slowly and carefully beside me. As though I were a frightened animal. 'What happens? I mean – oh, I don't know *what* I mean. And why's it so all fired important my girl Bree here stays out of the way, Hound? She's bloody good with a blade. Surely given the bond she should be there to help him?'

She can't.

'Why?'

'I'll die too, if I go with them - if I fight today. That's what he saw.' Words as flat and lifeless as I felt. 'I'll die saving Fin.'

'But...' Cael stopped, frowning.

'It's ok. He said there're other ways of saving him.'

'*Did* he, now?' Cael toyed with a leaf, spiky head lowered. 'And did he happen to mention what those ways *were*?'

A strange foreboding seized me.

'Guest, how's Hawk going to keep Fin safe? Answer me, mutt.'

The Cu Sidhe whimpered softly.

Mistress, if you command I have to answer. ***Don't*** *do this.*

'I command it.'

I was on my feet suddenly, icier than Morgen.

There's only one way to prevent Finian's – and your - death today, Mistress. An acceptable substitute must play *the role you would've played. Must perform the actions **you** would've performed.*

It took whole seconds to catch on.

'What do you mean, an acceptable – *Oh, Hawk, no!*'

My horrified cry rang loudly in my ears. My sword was in my hand faster than I'd have believed possible. I began to stride towards the sound of battle, all savage movement and fury.

'Guest, Cael, with me.' Angrily snapped words. 'No-one's dying in *my* place today. Especially not Hawk. The *idiot*.'

On my back, little Mistress, said the Hound, strangely respectful. *You'll be safer thus till I get you into position.*

I did as he suggested. With Guest beneath me and Cael cutting a path before me, I took the field.

To die for the Fae I loved.

◀Chapter Twenty Five▶

It was the same swift and deadly dance I'd known at Tir na n'Og. We barrelled through the rearmost ranks of our warhost and were soon in the thick of it. Cael was graceful and lethal ahead of me, Guest a snarling killer beneath me. I swung, slashed, parried, ducked. Harder to fight on Guest's back. It was the Hound and the Huntsman who kept me safe. I looked around frantically, a cut above my brows sending stinging drops of sweat and blood into my eyes.

How were we supposed to find them in *this*?

It was appalling.

I'd seen a battle fought back at the city, but this was warfare on a scale I hadn't imagined. The Formori monsters towered over the fae. Twisted and hideous. They fell by the score all around - but there seemed to be no end to them. More came constantly.

Dodging a blade that almost took me - and my neck - by surprise, I saw Cael grab another Huntsman.

'The hawk lord,' he demanded. 'Where?'

The other Huntsman pointed with his blade, before turning and savagely spitting another of the enemy. 'There's a mound,' he shouted, almost unintelligible over the noise of battle.

We changed tack and cut our way through in the direction he'd indicated.

Guest almost unseated me. Leapt suddenly to one side to avoid being crushed beneath a Jack in Irons. The giant fell beneath the combined attack of at least half a dozen Formori.

One raised its head to snarl at Cael as we passed.

He responded by leaping on the creature, ripping out its throat with those pointed teeth. I barely had time to feel sickened at the bloodied grin turned in my direction - and the shouted 'Peg was wrong, Bree. Formori taste like *shit*!' - before my attention was commanded by the Formori bearing down on my other side.

My blade leapt in my hand. I slashed and ducked and *thrust*.

And the creature fell.

No time to enjoy the white hot blaze of battle, to feel the blood singing in my veins. I was all worry, all fear.

If I was too late...

If I was too late, I'd lose one of them. Not an option. No

matter which.

We continued the fierce and dizzying dance until we drew near the mound. More properly, the thing was a massive rock protruding from the plain, covered in places with earth and grass. It was ringed by the enemy and I saw no obvious way to ascend.

Swore through clenched teeth.

Guest's voice rang clearly in my head.

Hold tight, Little Mistress.

His muscles bunched beneath me as he sank into a crouch and we were airborne. I gasped, startled. We flew over the heads of the Formori to land awkwardly atop the mound. My sword had fallen from my grip - jerked from my hand during the leap - and I drew my dagger, rolling from Guest's back to stand next to Finian.

He was oblivious.

Eyes narrowed and hands a blur, his arrows cut a deadly swathe through the ranks of the enemy. Hawk was a couple of paces away, one of a knot of fae fighting furiously to keep the mound free of Formori. I realised it was all for Fin's benefit. He needed the elevation to make the shot that would end this.

Hawk glanced in my direction. And froze. Stilled for the merest moment.

He looked horrified.

Frightened.

I smiled reassuringly. Saw the expression on his face

change as his eyes fixed on something behind me. Sensed - rather than saw - him gathering himself to move. Felt a fierce blast of wind eddying around me.

Turning, I saw one of the enemy had broken through. His sword was raised and I realised that Fin, my Fin, was the target.

Lazily - almost dreamily - I stepped between Finian and the Formori.

He struck.

I was terribly cold. My mouth filled with the coppery taste of blood, and I looked down.

The familiar hilt of Morgen's beautiful sword protruded from my chest. I saw the shining steel pulse with my failing heartbeat.

Felt nothing.

A strong arm caught me as I fell. There was a terrible tearing noise, a sense of wrongness. Everything happened in slow motion as I saw the glowing white mist, and knew that Hawk had torn a hole in reality.

He threw me into it.

***

I landed on my knees, hands braced against the floor. The sword hilt barely cleared the ground. Every breath was a gasped, painful effort. It took several moments to gather myself before I could look around.

That glowing white mist surrounded me in every direction. Even the ground seemed to be made of it, though it felt solid enough beneath me.

Why wasn't I dead? What had Hawk *done*?

'Don't you know? You're in the Elsewhere. The space between one heartbeat and the next. You'll not die here - but you won't live, if I send you back'

I jumped, startled. Ahead of me the mist was thickening, coalescing into a solid, glowing form.

A woman.

'Well, I can't stay here.' I stared at her curiously.

She looked like me. Almost like me. Her face was a touch longer and there was no silver streak in her hair – but the sense of her presence was as familiar to me as my own.

'Morgen,' I said. 'You're Morgen le Fey.'

She smiled in acknowledgement. Same tiny dimple in the corner of her mouth that I'd seen in the mirror all my life.

'And you're Briana,' she replied. 'Last of my daughters and most like me of them all. As you say, you can't stay here. It's no life, merely stasis - and long exposure would end in madness. But it gives us a chance. Do you want to live?'

'Not if it means anyone else – if *Hawk* - has to die in my place.'

'That *will not happen*.' Determined sincerity sounded clearly in her voice. 'You've my word. *I* don't want him to die any more than *you* do. Let me rephrase the question. Do you want to help him *win*?'

'Yes. Oh, *yes*.' I replied fervently.

'There may be a way.' She approached me, trailing mist, and gently brushed the hair from my eyes. 'Stand up, Bree. I need to examine the wound.'

She helped me drag myself to my feet. I'd been afraid my hand would pass straight through hers, but it was as firm as my own. She laughed gently at my reluctance, touching the hilt of her sword and closing her eyes.

The slight vibration it caused was *agonising*.

'A nasty injury,' she remarked. 'Given time I can repair it - and time's not an issue here. But I'll need to repair each muscle - each artery - individually. And that will be painful and the cost will be high. For both of us. Will you pay it willingly?'

'What will it cost?'

'Your very *self*, child. My blood's in the blade of this sword and that gives me a little leeway, but in order to repair the damage, you and I must combine. There's no other way I can do it.'

'Combine?'

'Our very souls must become as one. One soul - one *person* - for all time. I'll live as you live and die when you die. We'll lose our individuality to one another, and I can't honestly say what we'll become. *Will* you do this?' Her face was intensely sad as she spoke and she caressed my cheek gently. Icy cold fingers.

'Will it help *them*? Fin and Hawk and the others. Will it help them if we do this?' I was scared.

Didn't want to die - but to become someone else was

daunting.

Would I lose myself entirely? Did it matter if I saved my friends?

'More than help. We can show them how to win this. My poor Hawk seems to have forgotten all we learned. All we discovered. But *that's* between us. For now, will you do this? Will you help me save my hawk lord - and my realm?'

It was no choice at all.

'Yes,' I said, steeling myself.

With a terrible heave, Morgen wrenched the sword from my chest.

I *screamed*.

The glowing woman dissolved, became a thick ribbon of mist. She entered the wound and began her work. I felt every second of the awful process by which she skilfully repaired the damage to my heart.

Screamed till my throat was *ragged*.

Then screamed some more.

I hope never to feel agony like that again. It lasted for days on days, it seemed. Time meant nothing here. I didn't hunger or thirst, just screamed and sobbed as my flesh slowly knit itself back together.

Morgen entered my mind - my very core - and I realised I was no longer alone. We melded and merged one into the other till there was no difference between us.

Bree was Morgen. Morgen was Bree.

We opened our eyes and stood slowly, abandoning the terrified ball we'd curled up into. The process was complete.

We were *whole*.

And we'd a job to do.

Picking up our sword, we sought the tattered edge of reality which Hawk had torn asunder and stepped through the hole, onto the battlefield.

***

Fin was no longer shooting. His pale, stricken face was turned towards Hawk and he was shouting.

'...have you *done?*'

Hawk looked equally shocked, unable to meet Fin's angry gaze. All around them fae were fighting, keeping our elevated position clear of Formori.

Cael was on top of the Formori that had struck me, wicked teeth and blades in full play as he tore it limb from limb. Tears streaked his pointed features.

Beside him, Guest was a devastating force. He snarled and tore his way through any opponent dumb enough to get close to him.

We stepped free of the rift, taking everything in with the fastest of glances. The cries and metallic shrieks of battle filled our ears. Amplifying our voice with a subtle touch of glamour, we spoke.

'Hello, boys,' we smirked. 'Did you miss us?'

Fae heads across the mound turned in my direction,

before plunging back into battle with renewed vigour.

If anything, Fin and Hawk went paler than they already were.

'Put it down, Cael,' We instructed the Huntsman. 'It's already dead.'

Cael gaped at us. Leapt to his feet, looking wary.

Fin was with us in one great stride, warm arms around us.

'*Bree*!'

We smiled.

'Easy, love,' we said. 'We're more than Bree alone, now. And we've work to do.'

We turned to Hawk and held out our arms. Watched his eyes widen as comprehension dawned.

He hugged us for a swift, fierce second and said 'Morgen. Mistress of the Elsewhere. You always *were* my fallback plan.'

'You're an idiot,' we said crisply. 'Look around you. We represent all four elements here. The wild glamour of Faery will come to our call. *How* many years is it since we worked this out? You can't be thinking clearly at all. Cael, take Hawk's hand. Fin and Hawk, take mine. Why can't you make the shot, Finian?'

'The person who's raising − controlling - all these creatures, is too far away,' said Fin grimly. 'They squat at the back of their forces, out of range of our archers.'

'Then we'd better bring them closer.' We met Hawk's eyes. Held them seriously. 'You know what to do?'

He nodded. We remembered we'd done this before.

And it was *fun*.

Glamour danced between our linked hands, all four of us enveloped in its elemental beat. Outlined in flaring power as the four elements met, merged and became *more*.

We called the rains. And the sky split as a torrential downpour lashed at the rearmost ranks of the Formori army, driving them forward.

Hawk's glamour surged beside and through us, whirls and eddies of dancing air glamour. And the sky boiled, clouds racing as the howling winds forced the enemy forward under their relentless onslaught.

Earth glamour followed - from Cael - tasting of rich, dark loam and the relentless power of mountains. The ground itself heaved and danced beneath their feet. It buckled and groaned, deftly urging them towards us.

An idea occurred. Fire to fight fire.

Drunk on the power flowing through us, we commanded the ancient armies to awake. Behind the enemy, the dead Hawk left on this plain so long ago began to climb from the earth. Not a pleasant sight. With a negligent thought, we commanded them to harry the Formori from behind.

Fin gasped. A sickened little sound.

We could see them now, the Formori who commanded these creatures. Maybe two hundred of them, horses rearing in terror beneath them. They must have lost twenty to thirty of their own as Faery itself rejected them. All looked perfectly normal - almost Fae - like Ethelynn.

One hooded figure sat stiffly on horseback, grey cloak pulled tightly around him. I could taste the power - the tainted darkness - emanating from him.

'That's him, gentlemen,' we said, nodding towards him. 'Finian, can you make the shot?'

He nodded firmly and I let my hand slide up his arm till my fingertips just touched his back at arm's length. We pulled the glamour back into our body, and the wind and rain abruptly stopped. The earth stilled. The dead dropped and lay unmoving.

'*Now*,' we said, sending it in a flaring rush up our arm and into Fin.

He nocked the arrow. Drew back the bowstring.

And burst into flames.

An incandescent figure, attention focussed intently on his target as the arrow burned fiercely.

He released it.

We watched it fly, glamour guided - and the hooded figure fell.

A perfect head-shot.

We *crowed* in triumph.

All around the field the great Formori beasts fell like broken puppets. Wheat bending before the wind, they simply dropped. From twisted, undead monsters to corpses, in the blink of an eye.

Our warband raced to surround the mounted enemy. Those few, normal Formori who were that remained of that great army. The odour of rotting flesh permeated the air, tainting every breath as the creatures began to decompose with nauseating speed.

We let go of Hawk's hand and lifted our fingertips from Finian's back. I saw Hawk release Cael almost simultaneously.

All three of them turned to look at us with accusing expressions.

Our head throbbed dully as the glamour rush drained away.

'It's over,' we said.

Satisfied.

Fin was trembling, an appalled look darkening his handsome features.

'Bree,' he said. 'What you've just *done*...'

He covered his face with his hands. Drew a ragged, steadying breath.

Cael spoke then, a queer tone of satisfied respect in his voice. 'You raised the *dead*, sweetheart. That goes against everything those morons stand for. No more Hunting you, sweetheart. You're one of us now. You're *Unseelie*.'

We trembled at the thought.

Fin moved so swiftly he took us by surprise. Held us close and kissed us violently, searchingly. Hunger and love and sadness. We knew it was the last time. That it could never be the same.

Seelie and Unseelie can't be together.

After a long forever, he pulled back. Turned away. Head bowed and face curtained in a long fall of blood copper and despair.

'I'd better go to my father,' he said tonelessly. 'The Seelie have work to do. I'll be needed.'

We stood there and watched him leave us.

Again.

◀Chapter Twenty Six▶

The Fae celebrations lasted well into the night, after the Portune raised a large mound over the dead. Immediate danger past, they withdrew into two distinct camps. Each court celebrated with their own. Flickering coloured sparks leapt above the fires, snapping like fireworks. The sound of raucous singing hammered the air.

I walked away into the dark, the Cu Sidhe at my side.

He let me mope for a while, then nudged me with his snout.

*We should go in **this** direction, little Mistress.*

'If you like.' I shrugged, uncaring.

*I **know** you've heard the Seelie are crowning Barra Medyr tonight. I saw your face when you were told. Typical of the man to elect himself. We can't enter their compound. It's warded against all but their court. But the procession will* *pass this way. You can at least **see** Finian, if nothing else.*

My interest kindled, I walked a little faster.

They came soon enough, a torchlit procession of fae. Jubilant and singing as they passed us

Fin walked at the front beside his father.

I wanted to weep at the sight of his still, set face. Met his gaze. Worlds of bewilderment and pain in those green lantern eyes. I watched him helplessly. He turned as he walked, twisting to keep me in view.

I hoped and feared my face told him everything I needed him to know. How much I loved him. How heavy my despair. How different *everything* had become. It was the longest and sharpest of moments - then his father spoke briskly to him and he faced the front again.

They were gone.

I walked blindly away in the direction they'd come.

'It's over, Guest,' I said.

***Nothing** is over. The Seelie have a kingdom to rebuild. And there are prisoners of war to deal with. There's still work to be done, little Mistress.*

'Not by me. It's over for me. I can't stay here. I'm afraid of what would happen - of who I'd become. Do you understand?'

The Hound stopped and dipped his head to me. A gesture of affectionate respect. I bobbed a little curtsy in return. He reared up on his thick hind legs and placed his huge paws on my shoulders. Lowering his head, he slowly and deliberately licked me from chin to hairline.

'*Eww,*' I said, scrubbing my face with both hands. 'Damn *mutt.*'

He laughed his huffling laugh at me and padded away into the night.

I turned resolutely away.

Walked on, drawn by something I didn't understand. A strong pull that demanded my attention. Some way past the last of the fae camps, a small, lonely fire flickered sullenly. Making towards it, I knew I'd reached the place where the veil was thinnest. Where we'd arrived with the fleeing Seelie.

A lone figure sat beside the flames, long body a hunched shape beneath his cloak. Wineskin held loosely in inattentive hands.

Hawk.

I smiled.

'What are you doing here?' I asked.

'Waiting for you to come and ask me to send you home. That *is* what you came to ask, isn't it?' He looked up. Smiled his weird little smile.

'Got it in one, oh wise Seer.'

I sat beside him, watching the sparks dance heavenward.

'About today...' he began, a strange note in that rich voice.

'I don't want to talk about today.' I cut him off. 'Let's just say I don't know whether to kiss you or *kill* you for what you attempted – what you *did* – out there. And if I were you, I wouldn't be in any hurry for me to make up my mind. Because I'm going to end up yelling at you either way. But I owe you my life. And I'm grateful.'

'I see no debt. You took to that field for me. To save my life, as well as Finian's. And you did. *I* owe *you*.'

He placed a tentative arm round me and I let him pull me into him. Laid my head on his shoulder. Smiled a slower, wider smile.

'I guess I can't see any debt there either, hawk lord. For much the same reason. And maybe that binds us to each other doubly, but we'll just have to live with it. How much of this *did* you see?'

'Bits and pieces at different times. I wasn't certain who you were until after we'd healed you of the elf shot. Until I'd seen your face. Seeing you again at Tir na n'Og confirmed it. That silver lock in your hair's quite distinctive, you know. I first saw you die the night I sent you into Faery. That's when I knew the Formori were coming. I thought if I could get back here I could deal with them - and prevent your death. Could save the realm and still save you.' He grimaced wryly. 'I may have caused more problems than I've solved.'

'No delusions of grandeur *there*.' I snagged the wineskin from his unresisting fingers. Took a long pull, breathing in his spicy, outdoorsy scent.

'Which one of you was it, bright flame? That went too far today?'

'You mean which of me raised the dead?' I shook my head,

pulling a face. 'I'll never tell. It hardly matters now, anyway. We're one. Not quite Bree and not quite Morgen. *I'm* someone new - and *that's* going to take some getting used to.'

We sat in companionable silence for a while, listening to the fire crackle and the distant sound of song.

'Was there a thin place, then?' I asked, already sure of the answer. 'Where you tore the hole?'

He gave me a sidelong glance and shook his head. 'I'm going to have to repair it as best I can and hope it holds. I've made a start. I could end up the most hated creature in Faery for a while. Again.'

I smirked at him. 'Thought you'd be used to that.'

'I *count* on it.' That fierce grin, fast and dazzling. 'Would you stay for a while? For me? If I asked you to?'

I swallowed dryly. Had to look away. 'That's one of those things I'd rather you didn't ask, Hawk. For several reasons, actually. But, no. I can't stay. Not now.'

'Well, then.' He rose quickly and held out a hand to pull me to my feet. 'Let's get you home.'

I watched as the glowing doorway formed, turning only once to look back at the fires dotting the plain. To listen to the music and smell the smoke. The blood on grass.

'I'm ready,' I said.

The slight wrench as I stepped through the Elsewhere barely bothered me. Hand cool around mine, Hawk kept me company to the tree line of Marham Woods.

Fated

We stopped, and I turned to face him.

'I've got you as close as I could, but you can't stay forever, bright flame,' he warned. 'You won't age as they do. Stop frowning, you can have many good years yet. And I'll be ready – waiting - to bring you home to Faery. For as long as it takes.'

I took a deep breath, filling my lungs with the familiar taste of Marham. Wrapping my arms around Hawk, I gave him a fierce hug. He hugged me back, whispering several soft sentences against my hair. Too low and fast even for my Fae hearing.

'Look,' he said, eventually. 'They're coming for you.'

I broke free and turned to see wavering torch beams picking down the sloping path. Looking down, I tweaked my glamour until I wore a dirtied and stained version of my Will Scarlett outfit.

'How do I look?'

'Awful. It doesn't suit you at all.'

I laughed. 'What did you say to me a moment ago?'

'Really, Bree. Just because I can't lie, doesn't mean I have to tell you.' His brilliant eyes gleamed with mischief.

Glancing back at the slowly approaching lights, I took a deep breath.

'I suppose this is goo...'

A long finger stilled my lips.

'*We* don't say that,' he said firmly, giving me a little push onto the path. 'Just go. And live.'

I did, not daring to look back.

Chloe and few of the boys met me as I ran up the gorge path. Her face was still pale with fright, and tearstains had blurred her mascara. Black clumps sat like freckles on her tiny, worried face. She threw her arms around my neck.

'Has it gone? Oh, Bree. I'm just glad you got out of there alive,' she panted breathlessly.

I looked back to see the last of the mist receding into the wood. The doorway had closed.

'Yeah,' I said. 'So am I.'

***

It was about six weeks before I decided to write all this down.

Cael's visited me twice in that time. Once he waited for me outside college - the other he blatantly knocked on my door. Mum thinks he's in my English class. It seems Mab wants him to keep an eye on me.

I suppose I'm part of her court, now.

He's been teaching me to control my glamour. And to withstand the feel of so much iron around me. Of course, I've a natural advantage there. I'm still kind of human, after all.

As far as how much of me is Bree - and how much Morgen - goes?

Honestly, I don't know.

It feels as if I've been this way forever. I know some things I didn't when I was just Bree. I'm both of us. There's a whole *raft* of issues I'm still dealing with. I've found a way of doing that, and it got put into practice a week or two ago.

There's a lot about my Morgen half that's causing me problems.

They're another of those things I don't want to talk about.

Not right now, anyway.

When I began this, I decided I was writing it for one particular person.

For *you*, Hawk.

I can't lie to you, so addressing this to you has kept me honest. Your turn to be *my* conscience, I guess.

But I want you to know this – because this much I *do* know.

When Morgen cursed you, she saved your life. The others would've killed you. A straight execution. That was the reason. You deserve to know that - to understand. I'm not going to discuss it any further, so let's leave it there.

I *might* be prepared to talk about it one day.

But I wouldn't hold your breath.

My hope is that you'll give this to Finian. To my Fin. Because I need him to know the truth. *All* of it. To remain in Faery - and not be with him - is more than I could stand. He was Bree's great love. And when Fae love it's passionately and forever.

Forever.

Even when it hurts enough to tear you in half.

Rhiannon was right about that. I truly regret her death. Any guilt *there* is for you and I to bear, hawk lord.

Not Fin.

It's not Fin's fault.

I've told it all now. All that I *can* tell. I'm going to give a copy of this to Cael next time I see him and ask him to bring it to you. The other copy can go in a box under my bed with Fin's dagger. With my sword and fae clothing. Then I'll wipe this off the computer. It's not something I'd want Mum - or anyone else - to find.

There's one thing I'd like to know, though.

I might not have been able to hear you, Hawk, but I followed the movement of your lips. Got the gist of what you said. Most of it, anyway. Know what it was you told me.

It's nice to know someone's proud of my courage and all the rest.

But which of us were you talking to?

Morgen or Bree?

I've *never* known which of us any of you were really talking to. Except the Huntsman. That's one reason I couldn't stay. I think maybe if I did, Bree would end up lost in the general Morgen-ness. In what Morgen wants.

I don't want to lose Bree.

I want to live.

Fated

So there you have it. This gets put away and I get on with my life.

My boss doesn't bully me into extra shifts any more and I never go to parties that don't interest me. I'm not scared or unsure. No dog makes my heart pound or my legs tremble. I've our wonderful Barghest to thank for that. After *him* all the others are puny. Chloe says being chased must've acted as aversion therapy and keeps teasing that she'll buy me a puppy for Christmas.

If only she could see the Hound I already *have*.

I'm printing this out now and shutting the machine down. My bath's almost run and I've to start getting ready. I've organised a night out with Chloe and a few of the girls.

It'll be fun, Hawk.

I'm going to *live*.

Briana Morgen Cadman

Marham

◀**Epilogue**▶

I'm writing this for me. For the sake of completeness. It's been a month since I finished my tale.

Just this one last extra sheet and a couple of other things to tuck in with the manuscript.

I asked Cael to give it to Hawk, and he was as good as his word. He came by a couple of hours ago and handed me a package.

'It's from the hawk lord and Fin,' he said. 'The dog didn't send anything. You know what dogs are like.'

'Are you coming in?'

He shook his spiky head. 'I don't think so. I reckon I'll leave you to it. Later, sweetheart.'

He even hugged me before he left. Awkwardly - but an actual hug.

Fated

Bless him.

I raced to my room and sat on the bed for a while looking at the package. Was half eager, half afraid to know what was in it.

I undid it. A slender, intricate silver chain slid into my hands. A charm bracelet of exquisite Fae craftsmanship. A tiny silver dog decorated one link and a small locket another. Forcing it open with my nail, I peeked inside. A coil of hair gleamed at me from either side. One inky black, the other a burning blood copper. A lump rose in my throat and I lay the pretty thing gently aside on the duvet.

Within the wrappings lay a letter - sealed with wax and imprinted with the Lughan sigil - and a smaller, tattier scrap of parchment. I unfolded the smaller one first.

As expected, it was from Hawk. It simply said

'Both of you'.

And I suppose I'm satisfied with that.

The wax on Fin's letter broke with a crisp snap. I thought for a moment I caught the scent of sunshine and lemons as I unfolded it and read.

Bree,

I understand everything. Let me say that first because I know you'll just scan down for it till you see it.

I understand.

*I love you and I'm sorry and I'm miserable and there's so much to **do**.*

Let me start again.

Yesterday the hawk lord burst unannounced into my study and slapped your manuscript down on my desk.

'Read it,' he said. 'Now.'

Well, you know how he gets. He handed me a jug of wine, took it back just long enough to pour himself a very full goblet, and planted himself in front of my fire. Where he glared at me until I began to read.

I don't remember when he left.

There is no way I can tell you everything I thought and felt as I read your words. My cousin Rhiannon was right.

I love you with all that I am.

*I know you're not wholly my Bree any more - and I'm no more certain how I feel about that than you are. But if there **is** any way for us to work it out together, I swear to you I **will** find it.*

You've my word.

Hawk's given your manuscript to the Hound, who's on his way to the Glass Isle to leave it with Ganieda and the Lake Ladies. They'll keep it sealed away, secret and safe. We can't let some of its contents become general knowledge. Hawk dashed off too, pleading urgent business elsewhere. Or should that be Elsewhere?

I killed Rhiannon, Bree. Not you. Not Hawk.

*Treason is treason, after all. And I want to live. I want **you** to live, too.*

And just so you do know in the end ...

*I always saw Bree. Only and **always** Bree.*

With all my heart

Fin

It's sitting folded next to me. I'm putting all this away in my box.

For now.

B.M.C

THE END